It Doesn't Take a
Genius

It Doesn't Take a
Genius

Olugbemisola Rhuday-Perkovich

SIXFOOT
PRESS

First Edition
Printed in Canada
This book is set in 11.5-point ITC Century Book
Library of Congress Cataloging-in-Publication Data available
upon request
Distributed throughout the world by Ingram Publisher Services
ISBN 13: 9781644420027

Visit sixfootpress.com

It Doesn't Take a

Genius

Chapter One

The last day of school is the perfect opportunity to make peace with Mac. Or at least prompt him to rethink his plan to ride his bike past my house all summer yelling, "What you got, loser?" the way he did last summer after I won the school debate trophy for the third straight year. Which, since I won that one, *loser* doesn't really make sense, but I guess yelling, "What you got, winner?" wouldn't either. I could have answered, "Well, I've got the trophies you wanted, even though you're older than me," but though I'm considered *smart* smart, and not people smart, even I know that's probably not the way to go. Mac is pretty smart himself; we're both honor roll regulars. He's also a full-fledged, first-class, Grade A GOON, even though he tries to disguise himself as an ordinary kid. One who's second-best on the school debate team. I'm just saying.

Anyway, he won this one, and let it never be said that Emmett Charles isn't a gentleman *and* a scholar (I don't think anyone's ever said that, maybe my mom.) "Congratulations, Mac," I say, holding my hand out (and up too since my body hasn't gotten wise to the fact that I'm thirteen now, and he's like NBA-size). I try not to make a face, but the locker next to Mac's is giving off a smell that could destroy a nation.

"Shut it, tardigrade," mumbles Mac, shoving my hand away. He goes back to dumping what looks like ten years' worth of papers and books (and maybe some fossilized sandwiches) from his locker into his backpack.

"Interesting name-calling, Mac. The water bear is definitely a resilient and miniscule animal, so . . . nicely done. That might be a way to describe me, even though *technically*, I didn't actually lose, so there's nothing for me to be resilient about, and . . . ahem, uh, anyway . . . I'm serious, stellar job yesterday! I thought your argument in favor of corporal punishment at school was convincing, mostly because of your enthusiasm for, um, school-sanctioned beat downs." I'm working hard not to inhale; Mac doesn't seem to notice that there might be a decomposing body tucked away right next to him. I probably should have stuck with just *nice job* because from the expression on his face and the way his fists clench, he doesn't need me to remind him that he didn't exactly beat me this year. That he's *never* beaten me at debate—and he's tried to. A lot. That's a fact. My big brother, Luke, is always reminding me that sometimes the facts matter less than I think they do.

"You really are the dumbest smart guy around, aren't you?" asks Mac, slamming his locker door. "I don't want your compliments. I don't want your attempts to be the bigger man, which"—he looks me up and down—"is *technically* impossible. I don't want your anything." He walks away.

Except maybe my three debate trophies, also my science fair award, and Spelling Bee record. And little does he (or anyone else) know, I'd managed to avoid a catastrophe yesterday.

I clear my throat. "Let's put our friendly rivalry behind us! You won! You're debate champion! Debate KING! It's all yours," I call out. I'd said I was taking a break, but only I know the real reason why I'd dropped out of the competition at the last minute. Luke had given me a funny look when I'd announced that I was opting out of competing, but luckily he was too excited about his big news to pursue it.

"Uh, excuse me, can you move?" says a voice at my back. "You're in front of my locker."

I turn to see Terry Campbell frowning at me. Mac is way down the hall. I almost want to give up and see what happens when Terry opens *his* locker, because that smell is bad enough to make me want to risk it all to find out what it could possibly be. But . . .

I run after Mac. I'm risking a lot—maybe literally my life at this point, if Mac's balled up fists are any indication—but I need to make sure that he knows that if I had competed against him, I would've won. Because that's what I'm supposed to do. And like Yoda said: Do or do not. There is no try. Or losing.

I pull up next to Mac and do a decent job of not taking two steps for his every one. The halls are pretty empty already; when that last bell rings, people clear out fast.

"What do you want now, mosquito?"

"I don't get it," I say. "Why are you still mad at me?" I try not to breathe like I'm in the middle of the annual fitness test, but Mac's pace and my end-of-the year backpack make me feel like I've been thrown into a Very Junior Iron Man competition. I'd placed squarely in the forty-second percentile for height and weight at my last checkup. For once, not a score I wanted to brag about. Luke keeps telling me that he had a big growth spurt between thirteen and fourteen, so mine should start any second now. He didn't even laugh when he caught me doing the Stretch-Grow-Let's-Go workout that I'd found online.

Mac stops walking. Thank God. "Shut up, bedbug. I can't even enjoy my win because it's all about you. *You* didn't compete. *You* would've set a new record. You, you, you. Excuse me for just wanting a *little less you* in my life. Too bad you're not the brother who's leaving."

Mac continues outside, and since I'm going the same way, I follow. But I stay a few steps behind, because, you know, it doesn't take a genius to see that he's also mad. Like, BIG mad.

I look around for my brother. He'd planned to leave during his free period so he could get the car from Mom and drive us and our locker contents home from school. I also want to catch Luke before he runs into Mac. Luke and Mac have a history. Because Mac and I have a history. And right now, it's in the present.

"Looking for big brother to save you?" Mac moves closer to me. "Better get used to him not being around. Maine isn't exactly around the corner, so next year, you won't have him to fight your battles."

"You're just jealous," I say. Luke's artwork had caught the attention of a fancy boarding school, and they offered him a scholarship for his last year of high school. I guess I shouldn't have been shocked, Luke is Luke. But even I hadn't realized how good he is.

"Nope. Sorry, bro. But maybe *you're* jealous. You got your little trophies and certificates, but Luke's getting invited to the big leagues. I guess *he's* the real genius—"

"You got a problem, Mac? Other than your usual ones?" Luke has come up out of nowhere. Like a superhero. He's even taller than Mac, wears his shirts a little small so girls can peep his muscles, and his fade is tight and gleaming. Now he'll tell Mac off and we'll speed away in the car, leaving him in literal smoke. (Mom's car is in desperate need of a tune-up.)

"No problem, except for your termite little brother. You going to come to the rescue as usual, or let him fight his own battles?"

"You're kind of pathetic, you know that, right?" Luke rolls his eyes. "Getting this shook by a twelve-year-old kid."

"Thirteen!" I say. The last school bus wheezes away. There are a few staff cars left in the parking lot, and some teachers are already at the bus stop across the street, pretending that they don't see us kids now that school has ended. Our city is too big to walk everywhere but too small for something cool like a subway system.

"Not the time, Emmett," he mutters. Which I guess means it's also not the time to remind him that he agreed to start calling me E.

Suddenly Mac laughs. "You're right," he says. "Whatever. I'm out." He starts walking away, then turns back and calls, "And congratulations to you, Luke! I'd say that I'll miss you, but I won't. Especially since I'll have your beetle brother all to myself in September." He smiles a smile that makes me feel sicker than the smell of Terry's locker. "I can't wait."

"Yeah, well, many beetle species are useful to humans, which is more than I can say about you! Let's debate *that* in September," I yell back, knowing that Luke is going to have to coach me all summer. There's no way I'll set foot on that debate stage if winning's not a sure thing. "Because I'll be back in competition mode! So get ready to be number two once again!" I turn to Luke and hold up my fist for a bump.

He hugs my shoulders instead and sighs. "You did not just say *number two*. Come on, beetle boy. The car died and Mom had to get it towed to the shop. We're walking home."

We start down the street and pretend we don't hear Mac's honk when he drives by.

"What was that about anyway?" Luke asks. "This time, I mean."

When we'd been practicing during debate meetings, Mac had . . . been better than me. I knew it, and I could tell some of our teammates knew it too. And I wasn't about to take any chances, so I dropped out. "I have no idea," I say to Luke. "I was truly trying to congratulate the guy on winning the debate tournament, which, as you know, I didn't do this year, so . . ."

"So . . ."

"So who's to know who would have won? I mean, I think that's why he's mad. Because he didn't just want to win, he wanted to beat *me*."

"And you didn't give him the opportunity," Luke says. I glance over at him, but he's staring straight ahead.

"Worked out that way" is all I say. I don't even like debate, to be honest. But I'm good at it, and I learned early on that's what matters. People love a winner. When you win, everyone sees you. And if people don't see you, maybe you're not really there.

Chapter Two

On the way home, we walk past the pet spa that used to be a laundromat and the wine shop that used to be a corner store where you could get everything from Catholic candles and paper towels to hot, fresh empanadas.

"So maybe this is a good time to talk about our summer plans," I say. "I've been thinking about some things we could do to make it extra special, since you're leaving." I can't keep the accusation out of my voice, and I hope Luke doesn't notice.

"You don't have to make it sound so dramatic," says Luke. "I'll be back for breaks and stuff. And I don't know what kind of extra special things you have in mind. We usually just come home from camp and watch movies, right? Anyway, I'm just trying to chill and get ready for my senior year."

I like watching movies. I whisper a minor-level curse, and I enjoy that, because even though it's not a real cuss word, I wouldn't dare say it in front of Mom, who threatened to wash my mouth out with soap when I said the principal sucked. "Why do you have to be such a Donnie

Downer? I was thinking we could talk Mom into getting one of those projector things and have *film screenings*. Invite our friends over and stuff. Remember we talked about doing different themes? Like a whole festival even?" Luke shrugs. As a car speeds up to make the traffic light, he holds his arm up to keep me from stepping into the street. "And I thought we could do stuff like go to GameGear—"

"They're closing down," says Luke.

"Oh."

"I haven't played video games in a while, anyway. I think it saps my creative spirit."

"That sounds like something Mom would say," I mutter. "Not the brother who had the family's highest score in *SpeedFreak* for two years running."

"It was only you and me playing, Emmett," he says, but he smiles a little. "Not a huge competition. As a matter of fact, I didn't realize you thought it was a competition. You know there was never any contest."

I have to laugh, and he does too, which feels good.

"Well, excuuuuuuzay MOI!" I say in my best French accent. We'd both been taking French at school, and I had an A+ average, but last week, Principal Ally announced that the foreign language program had been cut. "So," I start, "are you going to take French when you go to Rowell? It'll probably be really good there, with, like, native speakers or whatever. " I try to sound 100 percent eager and interested, instead of 80 percent sad.

Luke doesn't answer for a minute. "Maybe, I mean . . . probably." He gives me a sideways glance. "Sorry about the program getting cut at Heart High. But you're still the French award winner in the family. I'm sure I'll keep calling you for help with the accent marks and stuff." He sighs. "It's going to be different up there, that's for sure." When he pats my shoulder, it feels like he's trying to transfer some weight off his own. I wonder what he has to worry about. He's got a whole new world ahead of him!

I know what to do. "So . . . how many film fests should we plan? Billy and WeeDee want to do a whole one on Westerns."

Luke frowns. "They're kidding, right? I know I haven't hung out with them in a while, but, come on . . . Westerns?"

"Yeah, that's what *I* said," I say quickly. "I mean, we'll still have to vote, and Billy and WeeDee may not get it, but I bet they'll agree with you. They always do."

"Mmmm," says Luke. "So, what else do you have planned for the summer? You've got debate camp as usual. That's two weeks."

Did he not hear me? "Hello? We've got more important things to plan. I don't even know if I want to go to debate camp anymore." Luke has been a CIT at the local Y for the last two years, but I stopped going to that camp when I was nine. "Maybe I can come back to the Y," I say. I'd be willing to sacrifice for some dynamic duo antics. Maybe he could even put in a good word and get me considered early for a CIT gig too.

"I wish I'd been taking pictures around the neighborhood," says Luke suddenly, looking around. "So many of the old spots are gone." We wait in the crossing near Crabby Gabby's Coffee. I've never understood the name choice, but there are always people inside. "Not many old-school places like this still around," says Luke. "I hope it doesn't end up like Imagination Books and Harry's Shoes."

"Yep," I say quickly. I don't miss that he changed the subject. Maybe he really does feel bad about abandoning me. I see an opportunity. "Same for Mike's. Who knows how long the diner will be able to hold on. This might be its last summer, the final hurrah, the waning glory days of grease. We should take advantage of *our* last summer together by going every day. Grilled cheese and tomato sandwiches forever!" Mike's is this old-school diner, and we get root beer floats every time we go. Luke always gives me the ice cream out of his so that I get double scoops. Even though he could just order a root beer, he always orders the float to give me the extra scoop.

Luke sighs. "Ugh, my stomach hurts just thinking about it, bro."

Great. Well, what *does* he want to do? I kick at a rock as we walk.

"Hey, Emmett. Hey, Luke." I recognize the voice without looking up. But I do anyway and immediately trip. Tonya Carter is tall, dressed like she just did a photo shoot, and smiling at me. Well, at me and my brother.

Luke laughs. "Hey, Tonya," he says. "Congrats on the math award. And thanks again for all your help." Tonya is a math genius who's been tutoring Luke all year. He says she knows what she wants in a man, and it's definitely not me, but I live in hope.

"No prob," she says. Then she pats me on the head. On. The. Head. Sigh. "Hey, Little," she says, falling into step next to us.

I want to pretend that her calling me Little means we've got some special pet name situation going on. "Er-ar-ahem—blergh" is what I say. Whenever Tonya talks to me, it's like someone emptied a jar of peanut butter into my mouth. Luke and Tonya exchange a LOOK, which I can only describe as amused, and that shuts me down even more. "Wh-wh-whaffle," I add.

We're in front of the new Starbucks. It just opened last month, but the crowd of white people sitting inside look like they've been parked there for years.

"This is me," says Tonya. "Summer job." She hugs Luke. "Drop by and say hi before you head out of town. I'll beat you at chess one last time."

Luke points to me. "Little bro here won a regional chess tournament this year."

"Awwww, congrats, Little!" she says, patting me again even though I hold out my arms for a hug like Luke's.

"Um . . . grank . . ." It's like a jar of peanut butter *and rocks*!

Tonya smiles and goes inside.

Luke gently knocks me upside the head. "Grank? Is that some kind of secret nerd language? Like how are you even a debate champion?" He laughs.

"Ow, shut up," I mutter, and we keep walking. I can feel the sweat patch growing on my back, under my backpack. Now I can smell the chlorine in the city pool before we see it. I hear the kind of screams and yells that mean people are having fun. I swallow and keep my head down as we pass. The story goes that Dad was the swim instructor in the family – he taught Luke, and even Mom. Since I missed out, Luke was supposed to take over the job, but I've been putting it off.

Luke glances at me. "I hope your summer list includes things like talking to girls and learning to swim . . . maybe you can meet a lifeguard and do them both at the same time."

I wonder if Luke would think it's silly that I've been taking notes on how he has what Mom calls suave bola. He's so smooth! Luke had a girlfriend when he was twelve, and even though all they did was walk down the hall holding hands every Monday, I'm still behind. "I don't need to swim to meet a girl. I know a lot of girls," I say. "I just have to . . .

make up my mind."

"The problem is what happens once they get to know you," says Luke, laughing again. "And they make up *their* minds!"

We're on our block, and he counts down our usual race to the door. Whoever loses has to clean the bathroom for a week, which is, like, the Chore Vortex of Torment. "Three, two, one . . . GO!" he shouts. It was a couple of years before I realized that he always gives me a head start. I never said anything, though. But today he starts running at the same time that I do, and he's opening the door when I'm still running up the front steps.

"Good thing I just bought a new pair of rubber gloves," he says, smiling, when we're both inside, breathing hard. "See how I'm always thinking? Have fun, little bro. And you're not going to talk me into doing it with you. You and the toilet brush are on your own."

Chapter Three

"Here's to summer!" WeeDee folds two slices of pizza together and shoves them both into his mouth. He raises his arms like he just won a prize, and Billy high-fives him hard enough that he falls back on the park bench and almost chokes on his pizza. We've had a few days to shake the stench of school off; the park isn't quite middle-of-summer full, so we're not getting any side eye for being big (-ish, in my case) kids on the playground. My two best friends are technically older than me. Technically—they don't always act like it. They were Luke's friends first, and since I was always with him, they became mine too. Deep down I know we wouldn't be friends at all if it hadn't been for Luke. But since they're my only friends, I don't think too much about that. The truth is, Luke's been hanging with a different crowd lately. I wonder if they're feeling as left behind as I am.

Today is our first official hangout day of summer. It's always been the four of us, but Luke told me that he was going to be with his girlfriend, Taleisha, all day. I get that he's gonna miss her next year, but this is a tradition!

WeeDee and Billy and me, we haven't changed. This park has though, little by little. The new swings and slide

make me wish I was little again, to be honest. But we have to be extra careful about what side of the park we hang out on, because there are strict rules now about where big kids can be. They don't get screamed on like that time Luke and I did when we were racing through the park. Sometimes even white kids like WeeDee and Billy get a little side eye when they fool around too much in the baby section. There's a group of women doing yoga on what used to be our makeshift soccer field. And the battle between the icee lady and the ice cream truck ended when they both got banned by the new Parents' Association. There's a farmer's market here every Wednesday now. That's cool and whatever, but I miss my chocolate with chocolate sprinkles.

Still, it's the only park left in the neighborhood, and we'd just started a movie marathon at my house when Mom gave us money to buy a couple of pies from Esposito's so she could have the place to herself for studying. *Save the Last Dance* had begun, and normally I'd take the opportunity to demonstrate some real moves, instead of whatever they think they're doing in that movie, but pizza is pizza. Esposito's is the only pizza in town at this point. There used to be three; luckily, Esposito's is the best. Mom always grumbles about how their prices have gone up because of all the new white people in the neighborhood, but she's so desperate to study that she coughed up two twenties.

"Yo, that stroller is pretty sweet," says WeeDee as a red-haired woman with a ponytail walks toward us. The stroller she's pushing does look like it could have power steering and a V-8 engine.

"Yeah," says Billy, from behind a jawful of pizza. "They didn't have rides that smooth when I was a baby. I should ask my parents to get me one now." We laugh, and Red Ponytail frowns at us and walks faster. She joins up with

two more white women and their fancy strollers, and I look around the park. I'm one of two Black people here. Mom's been saying that we're being "displaced and replaced" every day, and right now, I feel it.

"Guys," I say. "Focus. Since we're out here, let's caucus. I have a lot to plan for my last summer with Luke, and if you're gonna to be a part of it, we gotta get organized. He hasn't had time to brainstorm with me, and he'll be pretty disappointed if we don't get it together before he leaves for school."

"Sounds like a real fun start to summer," says Billy. "I'm sure Luke is on the edge of his seat, waiting for this master plan."

"Did you just say *caucus*?" asks WeeDee. I can see the chewed up food in his mouth. "And you're reminding me that I have to pick up an SAT practice book for the summer. Not cool, Emmett."

"We don't need books, we've got Emmett," says Billy. "That's why we keep him around, to give us big words in context and the answers on tests."

"Ha-ha," I say. "Good thing I'm in a jocular mood."

"See what I mean?" says Billy, and he high-fives WeeDee.

"I was being sarcastic, boneheads." I sigh.

"Anyway," says WeeDee, "Luke said he was thinking of getting a real summer job, so he'd have money for school in the fall. He's not gonna have a whole lot of free time."

"He's gonna work at the Y like he did last year," I say. "That leaves lots of time."

"I think he meant another job," says WeeDee.

"You must have heard him wrong. He never told me about a new job. But we *have* been talking about watching movies. I can tell he's gonna miss our movie marathons. We don't have a movie theater in the neighborhood anymore—"

"We don't have a lot of things anymore," says Billy. "All my dad does is complain about how SuperMart is gone and that fancy organic grocery store charges eight bucks for a dozen eggs."

"So I was thinking, well, Luke and I were thinking that we could do the movie marathon thing bigger and better, invite more people, maybe even sell tickets!" I'm coming up with ideas as I talk, and I'm getting excited because I'm sure Luke will love this. "We do this right, it could be a gold mine. Luke will have all the money he needs, he knows that."

WeeDee shrugs and looks away. A baby cries.

"Maybe Triff could join us for movie watching," says Billy, who never seems to miss a chance to bring his new girlfriend into the conversation these days.

"Oh yeah, then Lana might hang out too," says WeeDee. "Wouldn't it be great if they became friends?" He low-fives Billy, then they both look at me and look away. I'm cool with the fact that they both have girlfriends now. Good for them. I stay unbothered, but they keep making a big deal out of it.

"Oh, maybe Luke will get Taleisha—" starts Billy,

"Are we trying to plan a couples' retreat?" I snap.

They exchange a look. "Dude," say WeeDee gently, like I'm an old lady he's helping across the street. "It's just that you're too young for the girls we know and—"

Not brains-wise, though," interjects Billy. "Your brains are way old and huge."

"Wayyy huge. Like disproportionately, since you're, um, smaller-framed, er . . ."

"Can we NOT talk about my big brains and tiny body?" I shout. A little boy on the swings starts to cry, and his adult glares at me. "Sorry!" I call out. I lower my voice.

"Can we just get back to planning so I can update Luke later?"

"Oh, we have to work around summer swim team though," says WeeDee. "Do you want to do it this year? It's really fun!"

What my friends, and my family for that matter, don't seem to understand is that I don't swim. I guess they get the fact that I can't. But they keep thinking that *I will*, one day. That I even want to. And they're WRONG. Dad was supposed to teach me, and he's not here.

"No thanks," I say. "Water and I are like . . . like water and oil. Anyway, *focus*. Film festival. What should our theme be? I asked Luke for ideas, but he hasn't given me anything yet."

"Maybe Luke has found a higher purpose," says Billy.

"A mission! A calling!" WeeDee stands on the bench as he yells, and now a little girl starts crying. Her adult looks like Bruce Banner and stares us down so hard it feels like he just might turn into the Hulk. WeeDee sits down.

"Whatever, you guys need to chill. I know Luke, he's got my back on this. He always does. You should have seen him shut Mac down the other day."

"He told us," says Billy. "I guess it'll be weird for you to handle Mac on your own next year. Not that you can't, of course . . . It's just . . . weird. For all of us."

This is the moment in a movie when WeeDee would say, "But don't worry we got you," and Billy would be all, "Yeah! Of course! Bros forever!" But nobody says anything for a while. I wonder what Luke told them. Maybe I'm the only one feeling left behind after all.

"I do wish we could have talked Luke into one last prank," says WeeDee. "Remember when he had the idea to send Mac that rejection letter from the X-Men? Classic."

I laugh. "He even drew that official seal and everything. Mac couldn't decide whether to be embarrassed that someone knew his secret dreams or excited that the X-Men were real." Billy and WeeDee are cackling so hard they're wheezing. Some more ponytailed moms come in with dogs and strollers. There's a big All Dogs Must Be on Leashes sign, but their dogs run ahead and around in circles while the moms smile. One of them sees me looking and stops smiling.

"It's gonna be so weird when he leaves," Billy says, and looks at me again. "For you
most of all, I guess . . ." He trails off like I'm going to lose it completely without Luke around.

"Since he's not gone yet, maybe we could get back to what we're gonna do while he's here?" I grab the last slice of pizza and push it into my mouth. "And anyway, he's not *that* excited about going to school in Maine. Who wants to eat chowder all day? He's doing it to make Mom happy. Which is why we have big plans for the summer. Last hurrah, blah, blah, blah."

They share another meaningful look. "We know you have big plans," says Billy slowly. "But, are you sure about Luke? Maybe his plans are . . . different."

"You guys just don't get it," I say. "You have *sisters*."

"Low blow, Emmett," mutters WeeDee.

"I'm just saying, we're a team. Batman and Robin," I say. "A double dose of dynamic duo."

"Which one of you is Batman?" asks Billy.

"Double dose duo . . . isn't that redundant? Methinks you're slipping, smart guy," says WeeDee, and I give him an elbow.

We sit and watch squirrels fight for a while. Taleisha comes into the park with a couple of girls. She waves, and I wave back, a little surprised. If she's here, where's Luke?

I turn back to the guys. "So . . . the next film fest theme?"

"Can't go wrong with the seventies," says WeeDee. "*Godfather. Jaws. The Exorcist.*"

"My uncle Davidson was telling me about some cool seventies movies," I say. "*Car Wash, Shaft, Foxy Brown* . . ."

"I never heard of those," says WeeDee. "Are you sure they're from the seventies? Are they foreign?"

"We should make sure we pick stuff that people know. It'll bring back memories for the old people, and the rest of us can laugh at how freaky old people used to be," says Billy.

"Still are," says WeeDee. "My mom is literally taking an eighties-themed retro exercise class as we speak. Oh, I have to put in a good word for eighties mov~ ~s, though. Leg warmers? Neon? *Flashdance? Footl~* ."

"Wait—we could do ？ ~e hip-hop thing for the eighties!" I say. "*Breaᴸ· ~at Street, Krush Groove* . . ." Sometimes, when ı ıu home alone, I watch those movies and try to copy the moves. They were classic! And guys danced *hard* back in the old days. I was pretty disappointed at my first real school dance last year. I thought it would be kind of like a movie, with everyone making a circle around the best dancer (me), but most of us just glued ourselves to the walls and a few shuffled out from time to time to shuffle next to a bored-looking girl. "*The Last Dragon*! That combo of hip-hop and martial arts is—"

"Nah, the eighties has to be *The Breakfast Club, The Outsiders, Pretty in Pink*," says WeeDee.

"Yeah, the classics!" shouts Billy. "*St. Elmo's Fire*, starring the Brat Pack. I saw a documentary about them."

Pretty sure Uncle Davidson considers *The Last*

Dragon to be a classic but okay. "I didn't see that," I say. "Maybe I'll try to watch. And maybe the eighties hip-hop one could be for the town hall idea."

"I guess," says Billy, shrugging. "But I don't know if people are going to pay money to see that."

"What's *The Last Dragon*?" asks WeeDee, but before I can answer, he goes on. "Did we finish two whole pies already?"

"Yeah, we did," I say. "And by we, I mean you two." I lean back when he tries to grab for the little scrap of crust in my hand. "Begone, scavenger! And I gotta go home. Once again, we didn't get anything done. Do you guys want Luke's last summer to just go by without . . . something special?"

They exchange another glance.

"Sorry, Em, we'll focus next time," says WeeDee, patting me on the shoulder.

"Yeah, we're just excited, the whole summer ahead of us, you know," says Billy. "We'll have a real meeting next week. And maybe Luke will be able to hang with us."

"Of course he will," I say. I don't add that neither one of them never actually answered my question. Luke would have gotten them to get it together if he were here. Without him, the three of us tend to kind of . . . wander around like Sims sometimes.

"My stomach hurts," says WeeDee.

Mine too. But I just keep chewing my crust. If Luke hadn't ditched us for Taleisha, then where was he? He should have been here. Maybe it's not just my friends who need a dynamic duo reminder.

Chapter Four

"And that's creepy Maine fact number one hundred and twenty-three," I announce, pointing my fork at Luke. "I have sixty-seven more." And it's only the second week of summer vacation.

Mom rushes into the kitchen, dumping her purse and backpack on a chair, which is a thing Luke and I would get in trouble for quick fast. "Sorry about the time, guys," she says. "I know it's later than I said, but the cafeteria at the hospital was almost empty for once, so I figured I'd do a practice test before I came home. That way I don't have to force you to be quiet."

"Sweet! Maybe we can play UNO after we eat," I say.

She shakes her head. "I have to study, hon."

"And I gotta pack," says Luke. "Plus I told Taliesha I'd call her." He jumps up to get Mom a plate of spaghetti and meatballs.

"It's not like you're leaving tomorrow," I say. "And didn't you just see Taleisha?" I wait for him to come clean, but he just shakes Parmesan onto Mom's plate of spaghetti. Hmmm.

She smiles when he puts it in front of her. "There's salad too," Luke says.

"This looks delicious!" she says. "How did I get so lucky? A son who's such an amazing chef!"

"Probably has something to do with your mandatory Saturday morning cooking lessons," Luke answers. "You told us no son of yours was going to grow up expecting someone else to wait on them hand and foot."

"And then I asked how that would work exactly, waiting *hand and foot*," I add, "You said—"

"Okay, okay," Mom puts up her hand as Luke chokes back a laugh. "Don't talk with your mouth full," she adds, going into Mom Rules mode. She yawns; she's been getting up extra early to study for her medical school exams before she goes to work at the hospital. And then she stays up late to study too. She says it's a piece of cake because she's a nurse and nurses are like the hospital version of decathletes.

I shovel a big forkful of salad into my mouth. "So . . . as I was saying to Luke: *Pet Sematary*. Have we really considered the *Pet Sematary* angle? One of the creepiest films of all time, set in the dubious state of Maine. Where Rowell Academy is. Where Luke will be, possibly surrounded by undead animals. I'm just saying, is he ready?" I try to give my brother a concerned gaze, but I can feel a piece of lettuce hanging out of my mouth, ruining the effect. "Luke has been punished enough. Do we really want to . . . compound the injustice? And remember how he felt about that movie? He couldn't sleep for weeks." I take a page out of WeeDee's book and stand, holding my fork high. "Maybe I should put together a zombie-fighting boot camp for him. I'd make a great trainer."

"Sit down, silly boy," Mom says. She makes a face as another piece of lettuce falls from my mouth. "I *just* said

. . . seriously, don't let your mouth get that full again. And if I recall correctly—and I always do—you were the one who tricked your brother into letting you watch that movie, and then for weeks *you* were convinced that every animal you saw was a murdering zombie."

"Fun times," murmurs Luke.

I sit down and take a medium-size bite of a meatball. "I'm just saying, maybe Maine isn't all that. Aren't boarding schools usually haunted?"

Mom frowns at me.

"You are really wacko," murmurs Luke. He clears his throat. "So. I've been thinking," he says.

"Uh-oh," says Mom. That's our usual response when one of us says, *I've been thinking.* It's an old family joke, but I still laugh.

Luke ignores us. "I need to earn some cash this summer, and Patrick told me about a junior counselor opening at his summer camp. He was going to work there, but he's got into a summer architecture program instead. So . . . he put my name in for his spot."

"The bougie camp?" I ask. "Where the guys dress like golf players?" I laugh again, but no one else does. Luke is looking down; Mom's eyebrows are raised to a level five. There's no danger unless she hits eight. She's probably a little irritated because our summer plans have been set for ages, and she worked hard to make sure we signed up for stuff early. Debate camp, or "nerd summer school stuff" as Billy and WeeDee call it, is free, so the spots go fast. And she says being a CIT is important leadership experience for Luke. Mom says white people can spend the summer doing nothing, but we don't have that luxury.

I have one meatball left; I use my fork to cut it into quarters while Luke talks. "Yeah, that one," he says. "Camp

DuBois. But it's not really bougie, it's just . . . I mean, actually, Mom, you'll like this. It was started as a haven for Black kids who weren't welcome at other camps back in the day. First it was a school and a summer camp, now it's just a camp."

"Mmmmhmmm," says Mom. "And it's somewhere in New York, right?"

Luke nods. "Not in the city, though," he says quickly.

"I know a little about it. It was created to provide opportunities for Black children, *and*"—she looks at me—"it was clear that they meant a certain type of Black child for the most part. It developed a reputation for being a little . . . exclusive."

"Yeah, bougie!" I say.

"DuBois isn't bougie," says Luke. "Maybe that was true in the old days, but it's not now. I've been . . . doing some research. And anyway, Mom, you are sending me to Rowell Academy. In Maine. They barely have any Black people there, bougie or not." I hold my breath, hopeful. Mom starts to say something, but Luke goes on. "Don't get the wrong idea, I'm really excited about it." *Oh well.* "The art program is amazing, and I can handle the whiteness. But the way I see it, taking this job at DuBois will help me handle it. I want to do this. I'm seventeen." Mom opens her mouth again. "I need to earn some money—this pays a lot more than the Y."

"I'm working extra hours this summer, Luke," says Mom. "I don't want you worrying about money. " She glares at me. "Neither of you should."

Still, probably not a good time to ask for an extra twenty bucks.

"If Dad were here," starts Luke. And Mom drops her fork. Eyebrows go straight to eight.

"Don't do that, Luke."

"Sorry," he mumbles. And we sit in silence for a minute.

What?!! I want to yell. *If Dad were here, what??!!* I'd like to know. There's so much that I didn't get a chance to find out. But Mom's face is closed and Luke is looking down.

So I change the subject. "Horror movies are always set in camps, aren't they?" I ask. "I'd be too scared to go to camp, guys in masks with hatchets and stuff."

Mom whips around on me. "And how would you know that?"

"Uh . . . I saw some trailers online," I mumble. Sometimes I accidentally on purpose watch movies with Luke and he accidentally on purpose lets me. I'm not going to be able to watch scary movies when he's gone, though. That Freddy Kruger one had me using my allowance to buy a night light. And I'm not talking about no Candyman when I look in a mirror either.

"Mom, I'm not worried about money," says Luke. He twirls some spaghetti around on his fork. "I want to do this . . . for me. But . . . it does pay more than the Y. So it will give me even more money for school."

"You got a full scholarship," I point out. "They're basically paying you to go there!" Luke's an amazing artist, I'm not surprised. He won the spring talent show with this series of collages he said were inspired by the artist Jacob Lawrence. It was called *Migrations (Forced),* and he mixed drawings and paper and stuff of all the neighborhood places that had closed, photos of people moving out and all the For Sale or Rent signs that seem to pop up every week. Of course Rowell wanted my brother bad. Mom's been so excited too, even though I caught her tearing up a couple of times in the last few days. She says it's a great opportunity for Luke, and Mom is big on opportunities.

"I'm gonna need spending money, funds for trips into town and books." Luke shrugs. "And it's not just about the money, it's the experience. I'd get to be in a . . . Black utopia for a month."

"Right before you head to white dystopia, amirite?" My timing is perfect, and this time, everyone laughs.

After a minute, Mom nods. "Let me talk to Patrick's parents about it," she says.

"They said you can call them tonight. Anytime until ten thirty is fine," Luke says.

"Oh, did they?" Mom's eyebrows might be at eleven. "Okay."

"And I already went to see Dr. Shepherd and got my physical done yesterday. My lifeguard certificate is still good, but I signed up for a CPR refresher on Thursday at the Y."

I'm expecting those brows to be floating in the air above Mom's head any minute. "You did, did you?"

Luke nods. "And you can even interview over Skype . . ."

Mom clears her throat.

"Which I already did, this morning, and uh, I got the job."

Silence. Our cat, Kangol, pads into the kitchen and meows, but then he takes one look at Mom's face and backs out slowly. Cats know.

"Bold move, big bro," I whisper. "Impressive. Also highly dangerous. Alert! Alert! Danger level ten!"

Luke rolls his eyes. "Not now, Emmett."

"E," I remind him. "We're trying to make E happen, remember?" No shade to Uncle Emmett, but it's just that E has a lot more swag. And people are always asking me if I'm named after Emmett Till, and when I say no it's like I make them sad and disappointed at the same time.

"Not. Now," repeats Luke. He and Mom are staring each other down hard enough to wilt the salad.

Mom takes a deep breath. "Okay, Luke."

"Okay . . . like, yes?" Luke breathes. "I'd need to start in two weeks. We get to camp a week before the campers, then they're around for a 3-week session." He's already saying *we*. And he'll be away for a whole month?!

She nods. "If you really want to do this—"

He jumps out of his chair and grabs her in a hug before she can finish. Suddenly Luke looks more like a man than my big brother.

"I'm still calling Patrick's parents," she warns. "I have a lot of questions."

"I know."

"And I need to see the paperwork right away."

"I have it. I didn't sign anything. And I needed your signature on some stuff anyway."

"Oh, you still need me for something, huh?" Mom's smiling now, but her eyes are wet.

Chapter Five

Luke comes back with his paperwork so fast that it's like he traveled back in time.

"I'm proud of you, Luke," says Mom, wiping her eyes. "You made 'big tings' happen for yourself this year."

My grandpa Dwight was born in Jamaica, so Mom tries to keep us tied to "back home" even though we've never been there. That mostly means eating rice and peas, listening to reggae on Saturday mornings while we clean, and watching this show on TVTube called *Big Tings* where people in Jamaica compete for money to start their own businesses. It's a fun show, but I can barely understand what everyone's saying. It's like that time this exchange student from Colombia came to my Advanced Spanish 4 class and none of us could have a conversation with her beyond "¡Hola! ¿Quieres un libro?" "Sí, gracias." Plus once I brought in a mini Jamaican flag for International Day at school, and Charlotte Mason called me out as "Ja-fakin." One thing I can do like a real Jamaican is suck my teeth, and I look at Luke and do that now. He could have given me a heads-up about this. I guess WeeDee and Billy were right.

"You good, E?" he asks, patting my shoulder. Oh, so now he remembers. Now that he's going off to Bougie Wonderland to wear plaid shorts and shirts with tiny alligators on them. I finish chewing my meatball quarter before I answer.

"Yeah. I mean, congrats, bro." I shrug. "Wouldn't be *my* first choice, but go off, I guess."

Luke laughs as Mom says, "Bring my glasses!" He races out again.

Kangol walks back into the kitchen, and I give him a piece of meatball. I feel Mom's eyes on me.

"I know you had plans with your brother for the summer," she says, "but we'll have fun together, buddy."

When I don't answer, she goes on. "Maybe we get Tony's Chicken for dinner tomorrow night. Since we're getting low on groceries, and nobody has time to shop—" She stops herself. "Well, *you* do, actually . . ."

"Tony's sounds great, Mom!" I say quickly. "We should get food from our favorite places all week, since Luke is going to be gone and all. I've heard all about camp food from WeeDee and Billy. It's like being on punishment."

"Hmmmm," says Mom. "A few home treats before he leaves is a good idea—*a few*. But my guess is that this camp is going to have good eats. Fancy Black folks gotta eat fancy too. And then that school, they're supposed to be world class when it comes to cuisine. There are people that rank these things, can you believe that?" I don't smile back, but she goes on. "Yeah, that camp will be a long way from the Y camp I went to."

"Did Dad go to camp?" I ask.

"No," she says, and that's it. After a while, she hands me her plate, a sign that I should clear the table. "He really did go out and do this for himself," she murmurs, almost to herself. "This is a trip."

"A trip that has enormous implications," I say. "Maybe also complications." I didn't mean to rhyme, but I'll go with it. "Especially when we were all planning on an extended . . . staycation."

Mom looks at me. "You know, you do have to get on the ball with the grocery shopping, Emmett. That'll be a nice summer project for us. We'll make the weekly list together, and then you'll go to the store on your own. We'll draw up a whole schedule."

Woot. Yep, sounds like a lot of fun together, Mom.

I keep clearing the table, and I drop a dish into the sink a little too hard.

Mom comes over to the sink. "Talk to me, Emmett."

"E, Mom. We decided to call me E."

"*We* didn't decide that, because *I* didn't," she shoots back, and guides me back to sit at the table. "Now, talk to me. Is it Luke going to Rowell? I thought you were excited for him."

"I am! I mean, it's so cool, and he's an artistic genius, who even knew? But . . . it just feels weird."

"I know this is the type of thing that typically happens to you. You're used to getting the awards. And I wish that I could give you a gift like this too," she says, smiling a sad smile. "I wish I could give both of you the world. The best I can do right now is encourage you to grab every opportunity you can, and create opportunities when you don't see them right away."

"Mom, I swear I'm not jealous or anything! I promise."

She gives me a long look. "Okay, so what's going on?"

I take a deep breath. "We're a team. Luke's always had my back. You should have seen him on the last day of school, with Mac . . . Never mind. First, he's going to be gone

next year, but now the summer too? We had all these plans
. . ."

"And now those plans have to change." Mom nods. "I get it, change is hard. But, you know, you're a pretty capable guy. I bet you can have your own back once in a while." She makes a muscle. "And your mom will be right here." She frowns. "What happened with Mac? Do I need to call his parents? That boy . . ."

I groan. "Please, Mom, it's fine. Luke handled it."

But Mom's eyes are anxious and tired.

"Mom, don't worry, okay? I'm going to be very busy with debate camp, and WeeDee and Billy and I will have a bunch of fun film festivals too. The summer is going to be great! So much going on!" I try to smile big. "Booked and busy!" I add, trying to say it just like one of our favorite celebrities so I can make her laugh.

She breathes out and smiles. "I'm glad, honey. I'm going to be doubling down on hitting the books, and I want both of you to be occupied in productive ways. I'll worry less if I know you're both all set."

Worry less? How does that even work when nothing ever stays the same? Who's going to listen to me practice my debate strategies? Who will big me up? The thing is, Luke and I make each other better. I wanted this summer to be a spectacular example of that. Now I'm wondering if he needs a reminder.

Luke comes back to the kitchen while I'm at the freezer checking out dessert options. I make myself a big bowl of ice cream, but when I turn to ask Mom and Luke if they want some, their heads are bent over a bunch of papers and a catalog. They're talking and laughing, and neither one of them notices when I break the rules and take the ice cream to my room.

Chapter Six

Luke has been running around doing random odd jobs around the neighborhood for the last few days, so he'll have money for the summer, which doesn't make sense to me, since the whole point of him leaving is to make money *during* the summer. But he keeps saying he wants to look like he belongs there. I tell him his new Adidas take care of that, but I don't think he believes me. Anyway, I'm pretty hyped the day he offers to take me to the diner for our favorite Don't Tell Mom Dinner Before Dinner—chili cheese fries and chocolate shakes. Then a root beer float to go, he drinks the root beer and I get the scoop of ice cream. There are two old guys quietly bickering at the booth near the window, and a woman frowning at a plate of pancakes on the table in front of her.

"So, you can still tell me what you think WeeDee and Billy and I should watch this summer," I say. "I mean, we have to vote, but I bet Billy and WeeDee will agree with you. They always do."

"Mmmm," says Luke. "So you got debate camp. What else do you have planned?"

Did he not hear me? "Movies, I guess. Actually I had this idea, like to do a community film fest at the town hall or something. Since we don't have a movie theater anymore. But that was when I thought you'd be around to help. I don't know if I can count on Billy and WeeDee." I sigh. "Dumb idea, anyway."

"I love it here," says Luke, looking around the diner. "Not many old-school places like this still around. I hope it doesn't end up like Imagination Books and Harry's Shoes."

"Yep," I say quickly. "It's like everything we've ever known . . . is dying out. "

Luke sighs. "Really putting a positive spin on things, bro," he says.

"You know I'm right about the diner at least. Remember when there used to be lines on Saturday morning?"

"And that time I told you to pretend you had to pee so we could cut the line?"

"Mom fell for it—"

"But Dad knew," Luke finishes. "And he didn't say anything, just smiled." This is the most anyone has talked to me about Dad in a long time; I hold my breath, not sure if he'll continue. Even the way Luke says the word *Dad* feels brittle, like if I push, it will shatter.

I clear my throat. "I just believe in supporting our community, not abandoning it. You're the one who's always telling me to think local, do local—which is not very catchy, just so you know."

"Yeah, it's true," says Luke. "Old people messed up a lot of things. We're the generation that's on cleanup duty."

Michael the greeter/waiter/sometimes cook doesn't even come over to take our order; he just nods at us and tells the guys in the back to get started on two large orders of chili cheese fries, then he gets our extra-thick chocolate milk shakes going.

"I was serious about the swimming," Luke says when our food arrives. I hate when he tries to act all dadly. Especially since he probably knows better than me how it's done. Ja-fakin was one thing; since Dad died when I was only five, my memories of him are so blurry that they almost don't seem real.

I shrug. "I don't know why you keep harping on it, it's not a big deal," I say. "I'll do what I gotta do, all in good time." Which is *never* when it comes to swimming.

"Oh, big time, excuuuuse me," Luke says, and he laughs. I don't. "Just get on those swimming lessons this summer. You promised."

"You promised you'd be here this summer," I want to say, but instead I just say, "I don't think I should be forced to learn something that I'll never do for real. I've been fine without swimming all my life, nothing needs to change." Especially not when *everything* is changing.

"That's what I said about quadratic equations, and . . . well, never mind, that analogy isn't going to work," says Luke, and we both laugh this time. "And what about those hip-hop dance classes you wanted to take? Did you talk to Mom?"

I shake my head. "Nah. You said you wouldn't sign up with me, so . . ." I shrug.

"Bruh. You know I don't dance like that. I told you!"

"Yeah, but I told *you* girls love a guy who's got moves . . ."

Luke rolls his eyes. "What do you know about what girls love? Or is there something you haven't told me?"

Yeah, right. I get almost all my info about girls from eavesdropping on his conversations with Taleisha. Or from

WeeDee and Billy, whose expertise is still in doubt, in my opinion. Billy told me last week that if you're on a food date, if you have onions and your date has garlic, they cancel each other out and you don't have to worry about bad breath.

"So, are you going to reconsider?" I ask Luke.

I've been dancing since I was four. Mostly from watching videos and movies and stuff, but it feels like I was just born knowing how. I wish Dad had gotten to see more of it. There's going to be a new dance studio in our neighborhood this summer, and the director came to our school and did a presentation of all the classes they'd have, including hip-hop, and Acro-dance, which sounded like something I wouldn't even bother mentioning to Mom.

"Nope," Luke tosses a fry into his mouth. "Not a chance. And don't worry, I got my party moves all set. I just don't see why you're not going for it. You've been wishing for a class like this for ages."

"I'm not doing it without you," I say. I usually get Luke to come around to my way of thinking. There's still time for him to change his mind about DuBois. We'll be on stage together soon enough, I know it. Maybe if I start making up a routine to one of his favorite songs . . .

We eat and talk about basketball and comics and whether or not the risk of getting Mom mad at us for eating junk is worth bringing her back her favorite caramel shake.

Luke dips a few fries in the excess cheese and nods his head to the Bounce music playing. I slurp up the last of my shake. Then the last last. Then the dregs.

"I'm pretty sure you're done," says Luke.

I give it one more.

He glares. "Seriously. You're being annoying."

I stop. "Sorry."

"About Mom," he says. "There's something else—"

"What?!" I say. "Is she sick? Have you guys been keeping something from me?"

"NO!" he says loudly. A few people look over at us. "No, Emmett, she's fine. I'm sorry, I forget that it doesn't take much to push your panic button."

"Oh." I play with my straw, trying to put the wrapper back on.

"But that's kind of what I mean . . . I don't want Mom to worry this summer, okay? She's got enough on her plate, this is her chance for the whole med school thing . . ."

"Duh, I know that," I say. "What's your point?"

"Don't do anything to make her worry," he says. "Just . . . you know. Be chill. She's gonna need time to herself, time to study, to rest. Don't . . . be a pest, okay? Not"—he holds up a hand—"that I'm saying you're a pest, because you're not. Seriously, you are the best little brother I've ever had."

"Very funny." I start to throw my spoon at him, then I stop. He's just given me an idea. (Plus, Michael was watching me pick up the spoon.)

"Okay, all joking aside, I'm gonna miss you, big time, little E. It's gonna be weird not listening to you go on and on about . . . everything."

I check to see if Michael's looking, and then I ball up my napkin and throw it at Luke.

"Check, please!" he says, laughing.

"Can we split a banana split too?" I ask. "You know, to help me with the whole be chill thing. Get it? Chill? Chilled? Ice cream?" I wiggle my eyebrows for emphasis, and because I know it'll make him laugh more.

"No, and your superpower is being corny, you know that?" he says, still laughing. "But thanks. Don't say anything to Mom, but I'm a little . . . freaked out about leaving."

"For Rowell? Or for Camp DuBois?"

"Everywhere, I guess." He goes over to the counter to ask Michael for the banana split. As I watch them chat, my idea gets bigger and more solid. It warms up the part of my stomach that had been holding Luke's leaving like an icy, hard ball, so I think I'm on the right track.

Luke comes back with *two* banana splits. "He gave me one on the house as a going-away present," Luke says. "So . . . no root beer float, I guess. And he said I could call him Mike when I come back to visit." Everything's changing! As he picks up his spoon, he smiles again. "Tell me some of your corny debate jokes or something. I want to keep laughing."

Don't worry, Luke. I think I can do even better than that.

Chapter Seven

"So, even if you say you're not hungry, you guys are still going to have to eat some vegetables," says Mom as she pulls the sheets from the dryer. "You're lucky I had planned to eat at the hospital cafeteria already. I'm really getting to like that pea soup."

I keep my mouth shut about our detour to Mike's and keep folding the warm sheets carefully, even though Luke is probably going to just ball them up in his trunk. He'd had gotten a break on cleanup duty to work on packing, so of course he'd gone straight to his room to FaceTime Taleisha.

"We should make a Target run," she adds. "Pick up some supplies for your brother. See if he wants to go down to the mall. I know it's not cool to hang out with your mom and baby brother on a Friday night, but maybe he'll cut us some slack."

"Add a Triple Lindy Deluxe Sundae to the picture and I'd say we'll have him eating out of our hands," I say. "Oh wait—I guess that would be kind of messy."

Mom flicks me with a hand towel. "Don't think I don't know you already had some kind of ice cream at Mike's.

Just get your brother, Emmett."

Wait a minute . . . *This is my chance*, I think. *Everything is falling into place.* "Actually, Mom, you guys go ahead. I'll go tell Luke, but I want to stay home. I'm kind of tired."

She looks at me. "You sure? I'm not getting you ice cream, but maybe we could share a popcorn from the cart."

"You and Luke should have a little time to hang out," I say quickly. "It'll be nice." I hug her and leave before she can get sniffly, or remind me to wear deodorant.

As I walk down the hall to Luke's room, I do a quick imaginary hat tip to the photo of my dad on the wall. It's fading and a little fuzzy-looking, just like my memories of him, but I try to let him know every time I pass that I'm going to make him proud up there, or out there, or . . . wherever dads go when they die before they teach their sons how to swim.

I can hear Luke talking in his low, fake-DJ mumble behind his closed door. Even though I make fun of him, I've tried it myself, but I can't get the right amount of bass in my voice yet. I knock extra loud.

"What?" he calls. I open the door. "I didn't say come in," he grumbles, pointing to the bed. "Sit and zip it." Yep, he's talking to Taleisha, who he insists isn't his girlfriend. Yeah, okay. I guess they just talk on the phone, text, hang out, and kiss ALL THE TIME. I wave to her head on the screen and make kissy sounds. He makes the universal one-more-move-and-I'll   stuff-you-headfirst-into-my-tiny-trashcan gesture. I stop the kissy sounds.

When he's finally done romancing, I get into gear. "I remembered something else about Maine and Stephen King. I heard his mansion is like something out of one of his twisted books! People go in . . . but they don't come out. And remember *Misery*? What if it's based on his own life, but *he's* actually the murderous one? He lures in unsuspecting talented teens with promises of top notch art supplies. Did you think of that?"

"No, Emmett, I am super sure that I've never thought of that. And listen, if you tell Mom I let you watch that one too, I'll murder you myself," Luke says, pulling a large suitcase from under his bed. "And *Misery* took place in Colorado, actually."

I change tactics. "Speaking of Colorado, did you know that Maine is literally the whitest state in the country? Just a fact, bro."

"I do know that," says Luke, looking serious. "And I'm preparing myself for it, remember? That's why I'm going to DuBois for the summer." He makes the Wakanda Forever sign. "Extra fortification."

Or, I think, *you could just stay home next year. Then you won't need vibranium or antiracism superpowers or anything.* Am I the only one who has sense in this house?

He holds up a pair of tube socks. "Do you think I should buy some dress socks? Maybe boarding school kids don't wear tube socks."

I shrug. "I guess. They probably wear jackets and ties to bed too, right? Oh yeah, I'm supposed to ask if you want to go to Target," I say, not looking at him. "But maybe you want to stay home and pack some more."

"You think I can get Mom to spring for some new Nikes? What if those kids don't wear Adidas?" His eyes widen. "This is why I need summer money. What's the prep school shoe? How am I going to find out?"

I pat his shoulder. "Chill, big bro. Deep breaths. You got this. You've got plenty of time, we'll figure it out." *We'll have plenty of time to scheme together.* "Remember that time you did your whole mitosis research paper at your locker before the second bell rang? That was epic!"

"That was a last-minute mess," says Luke, shaking off my hand. "I'm trying to do things differently now, Emmett. New school, new start, new me."

What about the old us?

"There's something I'm worried about, though," says Luke.

I knew it! He couldn't forget that we were a team, like peanut butter and jelly, hot dogs and buns, potato chips and chocolate (trust me).

"It's Mom," says Luke.

I look at him in surprise. "Mom? I thought we covered that. Keep her chill. Don't be a pest. Trust me, I'll be invisible," I say. *Literally, if I pull this off.*

"You're gonna have to look out for her since the man of the house is going to be away. Can you handle it, little bro?"

"I don't know what you're talking about." I say, flexing my arms. "I can handle anything."

"Yeah, okay. Anyway. Look, Mom's like, moving into her *next phase* or whatever, she might start, like, going on dates or something. Give her space, but watch out for scrubs."

DATES?! I feel my eye start to twitch. "Hey, yeah, hospital scrubs, right? Mom is going to medical school, so I'll need to make sure that she's fully stocked in the scrub department . . ." I didn't want to think about DATES.

"I don't mean those kinds of scrubs, and you know it," says Luke. He looks at me. "Don't you?"

"Yeah . . . I was just . . . joking." We sit in silence. "Do you ever wonder if she'll get married again?" It's the first time I've said those words aloud, even though I'd thought about them a gazillion times. They fall into the space between us with a hard thump.

Luke doesn't say anything for a long while. "Let's not get ahead of ourselves," he says quietly. "Or ahead of Mom, for that matter. Ix-nay on the m-word. But . . . she might go out on dates, and I won't be here, so you know, you've got to be cool about it."

"Because she's grown," I say softly.

"And?"

"Has every right to grown folks' business."

"And no matter what, she loves us and that won't ever change," Luke finishes. "Got it? But . . . you know, keep me posted, though. For real."

My eye is twitching even more. "Hey, WeeDee and Billy had another idea for a summer prank, and it will only take five hundred dollars, a car battery, and a small amount of copper wire—" I start quickly, but Luke holds up a hand.

"You know that goes for me too, right?" he asks.

"What? Being grown? I know, I know, don't rub it in. But officially you're not an adult, you know. You're still seventeen."

"I'm talking about the still loving you part. Just because I'll be at Dubois this summer, and Rowell next year—"

"In head to toe plaid, walking like you have a stick up your butt . . ."

He continues. "Where I am won't ever change who we are, okay? We're a team, and . . ." He stops, and his voice cracks a little.

"I know, big bro," I say. "We're a team, no matter what." *I got your back.*

Mom pops her head in, and the expression on her face is the same one she has every Christmas morning before we open our big present.

"Sorry, Mom," I say. "We started talking. Luke wants to go to Target."

"I just got off the phone with Patrick's mom," she says. "She can't stop raving about that camp. DuBois really does sound amazing." She comes in and hugs me to her. "Let's look into it next summer, Emmett. I'd love for you to have an opportunity like this too."

Opportunity.

"Okay, well, I'll see you guys later," I say.

"You're not coming?" asks Luke.

"Are you sure?" Mom asks again. "I'm pretty sure I can be talked into the triple Lindy."

"Nah, I want to FaceTime with the guys about the film fest," I say quickly. "We said we'd talk after dinner about the lineup. I, um, forgot."

"The fact that you refuse to even preview *The Last Dragon* is still unforgivable," Luke says.

Mom laughs. "I'll work on him while you're gone, Luke. It *is* a travesty." She hugs me again. "Okay, well since I'm on this new let-my-sons-make-their-own-decisions thing—within reason . . ." She shrugs. "Let's go, Luke. Emmett, keep your phone on and close."

"Got it!" I give them a big smile and a thumbs-up. As soon as I hear the door close and lock, I get on the computer.

The Camp DuBois homepage has a slide show of smiling people in all shades of brown. It does look like Black utopia. I click on *Prospective Camper Information*.

I'm creating opportunities.

Chapter Eight

"I'm really proud of you," says Mom, for the seven hundredth time. I nod and keep my eyes on *The Last- Last- Day of Summer*. Luke has been gone for three days and it feels like three hundred. If a mom says the same thing seven hundred times in three hundred days, what percent . . . oh, never mind. Now that my letter has come from Camp DuBois, I know I can't keep my secret for long. I don't feel quite as proud of myself as I did the night when I'd done my secret Camp DuBois application. Mom might be the one punching a hole in the sky when she hears my news, but I'm hoping that Luke will help keep everything on a positive note.

"You were so mature about your brother leaving for the summer," she goes on, coming farther into the room even though I hadn't exactly invited her in. She looks around, wrinkling her nose. "It smells like corn chips in here," she says. "Have you been eating snacks in your room?"

"Nope," I say. Technically I'm telling the truth. I'd just opened the bag when I heard her coming toward the room. I hadn't had a chance to start eating. Now, it's stuffed under my shirt.

"You ready for debate camp?" she said. "You know, I saw Mac Traister's mom in the grocery store last night, and she was saying that he was on the waitlist. That place is really in demand."

"I've been thinking . . . maybe I should give someone else a chance," I say slowly. "I've gone for two years in a row."

She laughs. "And we work hard to get you signed up early! It's not easy to find quality programs like that for free. I'm so grateful for the opportunities you boys have had." She sits on my bed and sighs. "And I'm glad that you'll be occupied this summer. Like I said, I know it's not a fancy camp, but between two weeks of debate camp and maybe some work out in that garden and whatever shenanigans you have planned with WeeDee and Billy . . ."

"They go to camp too, remember?" I say. "For like half of the summer." I put my book down and look at the clock on my nightstand. "Hey, it's about time for Luke to call, right?" Perfect timing. It's like he knows I'm gonna need a rescue in 5, 4, 3, 2 . . .

Mom's phone dings, and she answers the video call. Luke's face fills her screen, and I sit next to her so we can both see.

"Heyyyyy!" he says. There's music in the background and a lot of activity behind him.

"How's it going, honey?" Mom yells. I wave. Luke looks around and quickly moves to another, quieter room.

"All good here, just checking in like I promised," he says. "But I can't talk long."

"Sounds more like a party than training," I say. "Guess you're having a good time."

And I will too, soon enough.

"Yeah, okay, you got jokes, little bro," he says. "We

just finished a three-hour Black history workshop. You know about the Oklahoma City sit-ins in 1958?"

"Ha, sit-ins were in 1960," I say. "We learned that in history, maybe you should have been paying attention."

Luke laughs. "You might be talking about Greensboro, North Carolina. Woolworth's, college students. I'm talking about kids, some of them littler than you, in 1958. Sorry, brain, perhaps the student has become the teacher."

"Ohhhh . . . I forgot for a second." I clear my throat. "You just caught me off guard."

Luke shrugs. "I didn't know about it either till I got here. Seriously, thanks, Mom. I'm learning so much, it's fantastic. Now Emmett's not the only scholar in the house."

Mom smiles. "I'm glad it's going well. And you've both always been scholars, you just expressed it differently."

"Yeah, I get good grades," I blurt out. My words fall out of my mouth and seem to sink to the floor.

Mom gives me a look. "How's the art apprenticeship going, hon?" she says to Luke.

"We're going to be doing all these great projects with the campers," Luke says. "And everything is in the context of Black culture and Black history . . . It's totally different from how we did stuff at school."

"Sounds great," I start, but he's not finished.

"Brace yourself, little bro, I'm going to school you when I get home. And I'm making a book list for you too. I'll text you later so you can start getting them from the library." He looks around as people start coming out of a room behind him. "So, you guys okay? I gotta get going soon. What's the news?"

Mom nods. "Studying, work. You know the drill." She looks at me.

I clear my throat. "Well, I do actually have news. I,

uh, it turns out I'm going to be joining you at Camp Dubois in a few days."

This time my words hit the floor with an almost audible thud. No one says anything. I clear my throat. "So great, right! We'll have our Brother Summer after all, Luke! Yes!" I wave a fist.

"What are you talking about?" asks Luke.

"I, uh, applied . . . They had some last-minute openings . . . I wrote a really good scholarship essay!" I don't look Mom in the eye. "I had to fill out some parent forms, Mom, but I'll show you all the paperwork—"

"You. Did. What." Mom's jaw is so tight, I can barely understand what she's saying, but her tone and facial expression make things pretty clear. "What did you just say to me?"

"Um, I, well." This is harder than I thought.

Luke is staring at the screen, motionless and stone-faced. In fact, he's so still that I think the screen is frozen for a second. But then a man whose fade is so tight he must live at the barber's comes into view.

"Hey, Luke, break's about to end," he says. He's taller than Luke, so he leans down to look into the phone screen and waves at me and Mom. "Oh, is that your family! Hey, fam! He's doing good!" He pats Luke shoulder and moves away.

"I knew you'd pull something like this," Luke mutters so low I can barely hear him. "I knew it."

"What?" I say. "I thought you'd be happy, dynamic duo at DuBois! Hey, that kind of rhymes!"

"You're talking about alliteration," he says. "I guess I'm the smart one on that too now." He shakes his head.

I don't dare look at Mom. Judging by the steam emanating from her right now, I may not live past this call.

"That night . . . when you went to Target . . . I did the online application for Camp DuBois. The uh, parent signature just had to be typed in, and I figured you'd be happy about me taking initiative so, I . . . I filled it all out. I had to write an essay, but it was short. Hey! Remember when I won that essay contest in fifth grade? Anyway, so I wrote an essay and I made a video and I sent that in too, and I wrote them about how Luke was going to be working there, and . . ." I trailed off as Luke finally looked up and gave me serious fire eye.

"You put me in the middle of your mess?" He's looking at me like he doesn't know who I am.

"You knew about this, Luke?" Mom's anger might have enough power to lift her out of her chair. At the very least, the look in her eyes might knock me out of mine.

"No!" he shouts. "Mom, I have no idea what is going on right now. And I have to get back to work." He shakes his head again. "Nice job, bro. You couldn't just let things go the way they were supposed to for once. Mom, I'll call you later." He doesn't say goodbye to me, and the screen goes black. I turn to Mom.

"It was supposed to be a surprise," I say quickly. "I thought if I went with Luke to camp, then you wouldn't have to worry about me. I, uh, got a scholarship and everything. Like how Luke got one to Rowell."

Mom takes a deep breath. "I need a minute," she says in a scary-soft voice.

Is a minute all it will take to obliterate me? To huff and puff and blow me off the face of the earth? Is it cold in here all of a sudden? It's June, but I feel like I want my winter coat. And a blanket.

This is not going how I planned.

After a while, Mom takes a deep breath. "What were

you thinking? Why would you do something like this?"

I'd had an answer all planned for this kind of question.

But in my head, the context had been verrrry different. We were supposed to be in the middle of a family celebration right about now, where she'd be talking about my *initiative* and how *proactive* I'd been, such a *creative thinker*, which are words I hear a lot around here on most days.

Right now, though, Mom looks like she's thinking words that she would never say out loud around us.

"I, um, well. You guys were saying what a great opportunity it was for Luke, and you, um, just two days ago you did say you wished I could go too . . . so I created an . . . uh, opportunity . . ."

"Emmett Franklin Charles." The way she says it makes my name sound positively criminal.

"But Luke did the same—" She holds up her hand.

"Don't even try it," she spits out. "Do not try to compare what your seventeen-year-old brother did to get a job to this . . . this . . ."

"Proactive plan?" I suggest.

"You are *thirteen years old*! You still have to get permission to breathe audibly!"

"You know how my report cards always say I show a wisdom beyond my years? I'm thinking that puts me at a theoretical fifteen."

"Really?" She scratches her hair and for a split second I can see how tired she really is. Like, bone-tired. Like I made her that way.

"Sorry," I mutter, looking down. "I'm definitely thirteen."

I get an earful for another fifteen minutes at full volume and lose my phone and computer privileges for a week before she says she has some studying to do and sends me to bed like I'm five.

I mean, I did this kind of cool thing, this thing she wished for me, all on my own, like independently and maturely, and I'm not even going to get props for that?

I'm not gonna brush my teeth. So there.

***

I have to call Luke three times before he picks up. He's laid out across his bed on top of his worn navy-blue comforter, with a tablet in his other hand. He doesn't look into the camera, but I start talking anyway.

"Mom's really mad," I say slowly.

He just raises his eyebrows and types on the tablet.

"Huh. Not exactly chill . . . more like *shrill*, amirite?"

Still no answer.

"Texting Taliesha?"

No answer. Just typing.

"Maybe if you smooth things over with Mom for me," I start, but the look he gives me is almost a duplicate of Mom's and I stop talking. I don't get it. Why is Camp DuBois good for Luke but not me? I did exactly what Mom's always talking about, opened a window for myself and climbed through—and everybody's mad.

"Why'd you keep it a secret?" Luke's voice is so low I have to practically put the phone inside of my head to hear.

"Well, you—"

"Don't try it, E," he says. "Don't even try it. You knew what you were doing was wrong, that's why."

"If you're going to answer your own questions, then . . ." I trail off. Then I sigh. "Okay, I mean . . . I guess I wasn't sure what Mom would say. I mean, we never went to sleepaway camp before." We weren't even allowed to sleep over anyone's house until Mom had met all the household adults at least three times, and after four supervised hangouts. WeeDee and Billy still think that's hilarious.

He looks straight at the camera, and it's like he's in front of me. "That's all?"

What does he want from me? "I thought you'd be happy, to be honest. I know I'm not as old as you or whatever but . . . I'm responsible! And it's camp! It sounds really good! Does no one in this house want me to have any fun?"

"You ever think about how your fun affects me?" he asks. "You try to put it on me, all, 'Well, but Luke did this. '" I start to speak, but he holds up a hand. "Did you think about what Mom would do if she thought I put you up to this stupid thing?"

Well, when you put it that way . . .

"Okay, so . . . no, I guess I didn't think about that part," I whisper.

"Yeah, okay," he says, rolling his eyes. "Whatever. It's late. I gotta get up early tomorrow."

"Are you going to talk to Mom?"

He doesn't answer, just picks up tablet and starts texting again.

"So . . . I guess I'll see you soon, maybe," I say. "Depending on what Mom says."

He hangs up.

Well, that went well.

Chapter Nine

Sometimes being the "baby" comes in handy, I'm not gonna lie. After Mom talked to the people at Camp DuBois, Patrick's mom, Patrick's dad, Patrick; had endless pots of tea with aunties Carolyn, Frances, and Renée; read every online review of Camp DuBois she could find and then cross-referenced each one; and talked to Patrick's mom again, she finally decided that I could go to camp.

Basically, she said that going to camp might help me not do things like sneak my way into camp again. Parent logic.

When I told WeeDee and Billy the whole story they were all, "Be careful what you wish for" and started telling me all the camp horror stories they'd left out before. Apparently, there's more than bad food and your underwear up flagpoles to worry about—there are also giant spiders, brown water, immortal vampire mosquitos, and lightly supervised goons. They introduced me to Camp Crystal Lake. (If you don't know, be glad. You will never look at a hockey mask the same way again.) I know that Camp DuBois isn't really that kind of camp; Luke's been saying all this time that it's more like a "summer workshop for passionate young artists," which sounds like something out of a brochure, but I'm a little nervous anyway.

Mom still went full consequences because of my "deceptive practices," though—I have to take over all Luke's old chores and do all our jerk neighbor Tyler Day's yard work while he drinks lemonade and sends pictures of me doing his work to everyone from school. No video games, online games—even magnetic chess was off the table. My phone ban will be temporarily lifted during my time at Camp DuBois, but I can only use the phone to call Mom. So, basically still a ban. Mom manages to add at least one new consequence every day, which doesn't seem fair, but I know it would be pushing my luck to complain, so I just keep my head down and scrub the bathroom till it shines.

What I hadn't thought about was getting to camp. It turned out that Mom was not trying to just send me on the train even though that's exactly what Luke did. She couldn't take time off from work, so Luke has to come home to bring me back with him. Which . . . hasn't made for much conversation between us, he's continued to ice me out since he got in last night. He grunted at me and then stomped to the kitchen and talked to Mom. I tried to wait up for him, but I fell asleep and dreamed that I got lost trying to find Sesame Street. This morning he was gone—Mom said he'd gone to see Taleisha. We're supposed to meet him at the train station in a couple of hours, during Mom's lunch break. None of this has the celebratory air I was going for, but I know it'll all work out.

Mostly, I'm real glad that Dubois Day has finally arrived. And I think I've got some new muscles from of all this work. I mean, I didn't have old ones, but who was checking? (Me.)

I'm still a little freaked out about Mom being some kind of bachelorette or something while we're gone, but I'm trying to be chill. It would help if I could talk to Luke about it, but he's been pretty quiet for the last few days, hanging up fast when I try to join Mom on the phone. Things to do tend to work out for me; Luke paves the way, and the path just smooths out. And I'm ready to ride that train into infinity. I leave tomorrow. What could possibly go wrong?

***

I could get used to this. Luke opted not to sit with me; he's directly across and staring out the window. I push my seat back a little farther. No one is sitting behind me; the train to New York is almost empty, and I've even changed seats a few times, just to see if the view changes (it doesn't really). Mom had cried outright when we were boarding the train, and I'm not gonna lie, I got a little sniffly myself. I know Luke noticed, but so far all he's said to me since we waved good-bye has been, "If we have to sit together, I got the window." Still, he hasn't glared at me as much since we settled into our seats; I suspect that Mom gave him a "talk" behind my back; she probably told him to ease up on me and do his big brother duty. I take out a deck of cards and lean toward him, and after he stares at them for a minute, he nods. After we play a couple of silent rounds of Spit, he loosens up. He takes out the DuBois brochure and points to a little shed.

"That's where you're gonna be living," he says, smirking. "There's a special place for trolls."

"Ha-ha," I say, and since I'm grateful that he's talking, I act like it really was funny. I look around. "This is pretty nice, right? The seats are cushy enough to sleep in, I'm about to get a good nap."

"You know rich people got like full on hotel rooms

on the train, right?" he says. "Like that *Murder on the Orient Express* movie but modern. There's a whole first-class world going on in the next car. Waiters walking up and down the hall with trays of shrimp and champagne. People get satin sheets and chocolate on their pillows. That's also how *I'll* be living as a counselor at DuBois, by the way."

"Will the rest of us walk in front of you the whole time, tossing rose petals like *Coming to America*?" I ask, rolling my eyes. "One, you're a *junior* counselor. And I'm not five anymore, Luke. This isn't like how you used to tell me you could get inside the TV to be on any show you wanted."

"Yo, that was hilarious," Luke says. He barks out a laugh. After a brief moment of side-eye, he hugs my shoulder. "You are a piece of work, bro. You don't even know how lucky you are that this all worked out."

"Yeah, I know. Thanks, Luke. And I mean, it did work out, right? This is our summer, right?"

"Anyway, I'm just saying. This is only the beginning. I'm on my way to first class all day, every day. Did you see these art studios?" He pulls out the glossy Rowell School catalog for the gazillionth time. I don't point out that printing out five hundred pages of We Are an Awesome School isn't the most eco-friendly way to do things. Or that I'd been using the catalog as a step stool to reach the Christmas presents that Mom hid in the back of the cabinet over the stove. Or that I didn't really want to hear again about how he was going to be a million miles away in September.

"Take that, Ally-Cat," grumbles Luke. He has a right to be bitter; Principal Ally really did have it out for him and every other Black kid who didn't have the "gifted and exceptional" seal of approval. She's pretty much a big reason why he's not coming back to Heart High for senior year. Well, that and the fact that he got a full scholarship to a fancy school. I know it's like that long sermon we heard in church one day, what she meant for evil turned out good for Luke, because that's how he ended up getting the Rowell scholarship. I'm still trying to work out how it's good for me, though.

"Rowell is my big chance for a fresh start before college," continues Luke. "No bad memories."

And no me, remember? "Um, Luke? I know, I . . . kind of messed up and all, but . . . I'm glad we'll be at DuBois together this summer. It'll be like nothing's changed. We'll get to be a team for a little longer." He rolled his eyes, then grabbed me in a crushing bear hug. "Ow!" I said.

"You're forgiven, E," he says. "I get it. I keep forgetting how young you are."

Okay, he doesn't have to go there. But I'm glad he's talking to me, so I keep my mouth shut.

"And I think this experience will be good for you," he says.

"Why do you and Mom have to talk like it's Root Vegetable Summer or something? When you were going to Camp DuBois alone it was all *fun, fun, fun,* now you guys make it sound like . . . medicine."

"I just mean that it will be fun *and* a learning experience for you, little bro. Relax. Not everything is not some Big Moment. Sometimes life is just . . . life. Change happens."

"Yeah, yeah, I know," I say. There is usually never a better time to panic than when someone tells you not to panic.

Things That Could Destroy Me at Camp
- *giant spiders*
- *vampire mosquitos*
- *HOCKEY MASK-WEARING GOONS*

Deep breaths. Luke will be there, that's the whole point. It'll be all good.

He looks at me. "I'll be working, though, so, you know I can't really hang out with you."

"Yeah, but I can help you out and stuff," I say.

"Just go have fun, little bro," he says, leaning back and crossing his arms behind his head. "You know what I said before still stands. Make a good summer for yourself, you can still get yourself a girlfriend—hey, and now you'll *have* to learn to swim, we learned in training that everyone gets lessons . . ."

I punch him in the arm. "Yeah, yeah," I say. "Wait—I thought swimming was optional."

"Yeah, I guess." Luke waves his arm and rubs my head like he doesn't know how much time I spent every night making sure my do-rag was tight. The waves in my hair straight up look like the Caribbean Sea.

"Will you tell them that I don't swim?" I ask.

"Tell them yourself," says Luke. "E, I'm glad you're coming to DuBois, but being here is my job. You've got to . . . make your own experience. I can't get in your business while I'm working, okay? Seriously."

"Yeah, yeah. Don't worry, I got plans of my own." I mean, I haven't said anything to anyone, not even Luke, but I've been dreaming about some things—sharing s'mores at the campfire with my first-ever girlfriend, winning the camp dance contest like in the movie *Step to Me Summer*, which we make fun of every time it comes on but still watch the whole thing.

Luke and I spend some time flipping through the catalog pages together; I'm wondering if the kids in the pics were actual campers or just actors paid to look happy, and if there really was a sundae bar in every dorm. But I don't say anything to disturb the good vibes we have right now. From the looks of things, Camp DuBois isn't exactly going to be fish sticks and Tater Tots. Still, I'm glad that I buried Boo Boo and Mr. Elefancy (when I was two, I figured that a stuffed elephant wearing pants was fancy) in the bottom of my suitcase. They were my favorite stuffed animals when I was a baby; I only keep them around because I know Mom's sentimental about them.

"Mom's really grinding for this med school test," I say. "I can't believe she'll finally be a doctor."

"Well, she's just getting started," says Luke, putting down the DuBois brochure and taking out his Rowell School packet. "It's a long road ahead and a lot of work."

"She just seems so . . . happy we're leaving, once she stopped being mad," I grumble. "She skipped over sad! I'm almost offended. It's not like we're babies she had to take care of every second. She can study with us around."

"You know how it is," says Luke. "Now she gets the whole summer to focus. Camp DuBois really hooked her up."

"I guess," I say. I'm still a little salty.

"Ha," he says. "They've been showing this same kid on every other page. Didn't even bother to let him change out of that corny striped shirt!"

"And those khakis, tho," I say, shaking my head. "Is that Maine fashion?"

"He's either a real superstar or he's all they got to be the Black friend in the group shots." He shows me, and we both laugh, but then he gets quiet and puts the packet away. After a minute, I take out the little notebook where I've been writing down all my get-ready-for-camp ideas. It's not easy to keep track of things without the Notes app on my phone, but Mom hasn't budged on *consequences.*

I look at the list I've started of all the things I plan to do.

- *DJ workshop*
- *Basketball*
- *All-you-can-eat sundae bar*
- *Rock climbing*
- *Graphic novel*
- *Film screening*
- *Fencing! (Say "en garde!" at least once, no matter what.)*
- *Street style dance*

This really could be very, very cool.

Chapter Ten

By the time we pull into the station, my stomach hurts (turns out there was a deal on the hot dogs, I went a little overboard even though Luke warned me that there was probably a bad reason for the deal), and I'm back to making lists.

Things That Could Destroy Me at Camp
- *Bears*
- *Axe murderers*
- *Bears that know how to use axes*
- *Axes left around to give axe murderers of many species ideas*
- *Raccoons (I saw a documentary —those things are vicious!)*

"What are you doing?" asks Luke. "We're here!"

The first thing I notice is all the green. So many trees. So much grass. Roberts, New York, looks like one big botanical garden.

"Yo, you feel that? That's ... *air*," says Luke, breathing in big gulps as we walk down the steps of the train platform.

Taxis are lined up, and an old white guy leans out of one saying, "Heading to Camp DuBois? Hop in."

"Is camp the only thing in town?" I ask as we pile into the back seat, but the driver doesn't seem to hear.

This town is definitely deeply green—and also blue. As we drive, I see signs for Gigli Beach State Park, Old Apple Beach, Slide It! Water Park, and Splash City, USA. I open the window on my side and breathe deeply.

We move off the highway onto smaller roads. There are cute houses with two cars in the driveways and more trees. A few people are out taking care of their yards; all the yards are full of flowers, and all the people are white.

The driver's name is Traxler Wexler, according to the hanging laminated badge. Kind of a tongue twister. I practice saying it under my breath, "TraxlerWexlerTraxlerWexler."

"There's a lot of apple picking here in the fall," says Luke. "Apparently people come from all over. Those must be some good apples."

"Mmm-hmmm," said TraxlerWexler. "Yep, summers here are popular too. Go a little south of here, toward Betway, you'll find a festival next month. Right around Visiting Day."

"How'd you know we were here for Camp DuBois?" I ask. We pass through what must be the main part of town— lots of people, walking, hanging around outside the cute houses and little shops that look kind of fake in that ye olde way. I still don't see too many people who look like me.

TraxlerWexler shrugs. "Most of you guys are."

Luke's head whips around.

TraxlerWexler must feel his side eye, because he stutters a little. "I . . . uh, I mean, most young African American kids coming here . . . around this time . . . I mean, usually it's for DuBois . . . I just, you know, figured." He trails off.

I try to catch Luke's eye, but he's stone-faced and staring straight ahead.

We ride on in silence. I look out of the window; the streets get smaller again, and the fresh air smell gets stronger.

"We're here!" Luke says suddenly. I hadn't realized that I'd dozed off. We are pulling into a driveway that's as wide as Macaulay Boulevard back home.

"Whoa!" I say as we drive up to an imposing building that looks like a mini version of the White House. It's even better than the pictures. There's a huge fountain in front of it, and I half expect to see a butler standing around with a white cloth napkin over his arm.

"It started out as a school," says TraxlerWexler. "Kind of a fancy one." He shrugs. "Some people thought those kids needed all this froufrou folderol. In my day, camp was about getting some sun and exercise. Learning to swim."

"Yep," says Luke. "And *those kids* probably swam in segregated pools. How old are you, exactly?"

Oooh, Luke's bringing a little fire. I stop trying to remember what *folderol* means and glance at him. He's already . . . bigger somehow.

"Huh" is all TraxlerWexler says, and he keeps driving. We go in a giant U, gravel crunching discreetly under the wheels. We pass two basketball courts and some large birds, maybe geese, just chilling on the grass. I see a couple of guys who look like they're about Luke's age, sitting on the steps of a brick building. I'm both a little disappointed and relieved that they aren't wearing polo shirts and ironed khakis. TraxlerWexler starts talking again, telling us about renovations, landscaping, and other boring stuff.

"He sure knows a lot about DuBois," Luke whispers

to me. "Maybe he's just real light-skinned."

I smother a laugh, because TraxlerWexler seems as white as can be.

Finally we're at a big building, and he stops. We get our stuff out of the trunk, and Luke gives him a tip, which surprises me because he's still stone-faced. He doesn't say thank you. As TraxlerWexler drives off, Luke just sighs.

"He was kind of weird," I start, but then the two guys on the steps wave in unison. Luke nods at them and says a casual, "Hey." The one who's wearing a T-shirt that says BLERDS UNITED WILL NEVER BE DEFEATED across the front walks over.

"New campers?" he asks.

"I'm a JC," says Luke quickly. "I was just here for training, I had to go home to get my baby brother." He points at me like I'm a squirrel that's just run up on him out of nowhere. "He's a camper. First-year. Newbie."

Yeah, okay, Luke. You spent last year trying to grow a mustache and it still looks like you have crumbs on your upper lip.

"Oh yeah, my bad, I remember," says the boy. "I'm Justin." He looks at me. "I can point you in the direction of sign-in and everything." He turns back to Luke and frowns a little. "I'm sorry . . . what's your name again?"

Ha!

Luke isn't dark-skinned enough to completely hide the blush.

"Uh, Luke Charles . . . I'm a junior counselor? And art assistant?" He fumbles around for his acceptance letter. Last week I'd asked him if he thought he should laminate it, and he'd looked like he was actually considering that.

"Oh, sorry, my bad," says Justin. "I'm in the sports division, one of the soccer coaches. Haven't met everyone yet." He starts walking. "We're all heading to the same building," he says.

"I like the shirt," says Luke as we shuffle behind Justin.

"Thanks," says Justin. "It's the unofficial motto here at DuBois."

The breeze moves gently through us, and more geese stroll nearby. I see a small pond and a lake in the distance. A few of the geese honk at us, like we're intruders. As more cars are pulling up, and the squeals and shouts of reunions surround us, I feel like the geese might be right. I think about Boo Boo and Mr. Elefancy again. Not even Luke knows that I still sleep with them under my pillow every night. I wonder if there's a way I can play them off as ironic decorative touches on my bed here.

We walk into the biggest mansiony building. It smells old and important and rich, like damp wood. The entranceway is big, and I half expect servants to be standing around, but there are just families and cheerful staff members directing them to different areas. Most of the activity is happening in a room with a big sign hanging from the ceiling that says THE LOUNGE. When I go in and take a close look, I see that the big puffy chairs are a little worn, and there are spots on the cream-colored walls where the paint is chipping. I hug myself; the air conditioning game is strong.

"Emmett, you should head straight ahead to the registration table," says Luke, pointing, like he's not going with me. "They know Mom's not here, all you gotta do is get your schedule and pick your electives. There's not much left because most of the campers already signed up for stuff. I'll try to catch up with you after you register, okay?"

"Oh, okay, but I—" He's already out of earshot. I

watch him copy Justin's walk as they leave.

There are signs all over the place, so I find the registration table pretty easily. It's in a giant, crowded room with a fireplace. I get a packet that says I'm in the "Young Lions."

"Do we have to turn in our devices?" WeeDee had gone to Forest Camp last summer and he said they'd locked everybody's phone in the office on the first day. I'm ready with a five-point argument against that medieval practice, just in case.

The woman at the table smiles. "Oh, no, you can keep whatever you have. And you can sign phones, tablets, and other devices out at the office." Wow! I look over at the kid next to me, who puts his phone down on the table between us. I cover my phone with my hand; his looks like something from the future. Then I realize that it is.

"I didn't think those were coming out until next year," I blurt out.

He glances at me. "Yeah, they're not. My dad is a VP there."

My phone isn't *that* old, but compared to this kid's, it's a vintage flip-phone. If this guy is the norm around here, then I kind of *want* them to confiscate my phone. For the first time, I'm a little glad that Mom's consequences will keep it put away for the most part.

Registration is a little overwhelming, and because I registered late, a lot of electives are full. No fencing for me. Or DJ workshop. When I get to Street Style, which sounds like a blend of b-boying and krumping, it says *audition waitlist* on the screen.

"What does that mean?" I ask the woman at the desk.

"Oh, Micah's not taking any more elective students, but there's one spot left for the Street Style major. Every year at least ten extra people think they want to sign up, so he leaves a spot open, then runs auditions for it."

"Just one spot?" I ask. "That's cold . . ."

"Remember, a major means three periods a day," says the woman. "A double period of class, then a period of independent study—in a dance class, that means rehearsing on your own, research, stuff like that. Majors are a commitment."

I can hear Mom's voice in my head so strong, it's like she's right next to me. *Sign up, sweetie pie, you love to dance!* I know, I know, opportunity.

Mom, please, shhhhh, I whisper back in my head. Oops. Maybe not in my head, because I notice the boy with the nice phone giving me a funny look; he's been listening to the whole conversation. I'm not sure what makes me look more like a punk—signing up and showing how much I care, or not signing up because I'm scared of competition. The Mom-voice keeps nudging me, and people are waiting to use the screen. I start to sweat when I hear someone mutter, "Come on." The auditions are tomorrow during the free period, so maybe I can practice a little before then. I put my name down and silently tell my stomach to settle.

I wish I could sign up for film, because I'm all about watching movies, and maybe I could get more ideas for a film fest at home, but it's full. I add the Great DuBois Baking Show mostly because I think it will be cool if I can whip up a nice surprise for Mom when I get back. Most of the other classes I want are full, so I settle for chorus (I've always heard that girls love a brother who can sing), badminton, and ceramics (it's art, so I figure I'll get to see Luke). There are two classes that everyone has to take: Black to the Future, which sounds corny, and Superhero Secrets, which sounds really cool until I hear a boy grumbling that

Superhero Secrets "is the kind of thing corny kids think is cool."

It also says that swimming is required (yeah right), so I think about how to get out of that without Mom finding out while we wait to meet my counselor. No way am I getting in a pool in front of all these people. I grab some chips and pretzels and look around. I guess they did some Photoshopping in the catalog, because even though it's definitely nice, once I look closer, some things are not exactly as sparkling and fancy as they looked on paper and on the website. Still a major upgrade for Luke and me, though; it's all a little overwhelming. I get a free DuBois T-shirt too; I have a choice between three sizes too small and four sizes too big. I don't see any other campers wearing one, so I know I can just stash it in my trunk. I go big. And I kind of want to go home.

Chapter Eleven

As I stand there taking deep breaths, trying to look bored but excited, smart and athletic, and like a genuine mack all at once, one thing stands out, big time. Black people everywhere. I have never even seen this many Black kids in a room together at school back home. And even though we're all Black, I can see skater kids; artsy kids; straight up preps with those alligator shirts; hippie types tie-dyed out; and guys wearing red, black, and green and calling girls *queens* . . . I wonder what type they think I am. Luke told me on the train that I'd find my people here, the Blerds, but I don't even know if I *am* a Blerd. As I look around at everyone, I wonder: How is a Black nerd different from a white one? Or an Asian one?

The phone boy strolls over with a man who I assume is his dad. They both look like they wear their do-rags every night.

"Are you okay?" asks the boy. "You look like your stomach hurts or something."

"Excited-bored" clearly isn't working. "Oh—yeah. I was just remembering that I left my newer phone at home."

"I'm Lamar," says the boy. "This is my dad. I told him you liked the phone."

"Hi, I'm Emmett."

"After Emmett Till?" Lamar's dad asks. "Heavy name to bear."

Sigh. "No, uh, after my mom's uncle Emmett; he was a barber."

"Huh," says the dad. We stand around awkwardly. I swallow down the mix of anger and sadness I always feel in the presence of a boy and his dad.

Luke comes over. "What up, E? How's it going? I've been helping out with the Bear Cubs. A lot of tears." When I give him a blank look, he adds "They're the youngest campers. You probably got Young Lions, right?"

Lamar looks at Luke, clearly impressed. "I'm Lamar," he says. "Do you play ball?"

"Yep," says Luke. "And I hear it's junior counselors against campers every Sunday night, if you're up for it."

"Sure!" says Lamar. "What are you a junior counselor in?"

When he finds out that Luke is an art counselor, Lamar immediately asks his dad to sign him up for an art elective. He asks me if I want to check out his phone too. I smile. My brother's cool lasts forever like vibranium. And his powers extend to me if I stay close enough.

Luke pats my shoulder. "Looks like you're all set, E," he says. "I'll see you. I'm going to help greet new campers."

Lamar's face falls. "Yeah, I'm ready to bounce too." He starts looking around. "I think I see my roommate from last year."

"Don't you want to see my dorm room?" I ask Luke.

"I'll try to come by later," he says. "I've gotta work, remember? You'll be in good hands. All the counselors are great—they hired me, right?" He gives me a fist bump.

"Yeah," I mutter, "I just—"

"Hi, I'm Marcus," says a voice. "Emmett, right?" He daps up Luke and then me, smiling like he wants our vote. "You're in my house, Emmett. Follow me."

Luke pats my shoulder with a little push. "Have fun!" He hurries away.

Marcus walks like he never gets lost. "We're living in those houses?" I say, pointing to a bunch of small stone houses as we cross the lawn.

He shakes his head. "No, we call each floor in the dorms a different house. I'm the head counselor in Walker. " He glances at me. "Not Madam C. J. Walker, by the way. It's David Walker. People sometimes think the beauty empire." I have no idea who either of those people are, so I just nod while he keeps talking. "I started as a camper here when I was around your age," he says. "Good times."

I have to jog a little to keep up. Now that we're out of the main building, beads of sweat run down my back.

"I'm almost fourteen," I say, crossing my fingers and standing up as straight as possible.

"Ah, got it. I was wondering why you were in my house. You're just a "Little"."

What kind of training did these counselors get? Not enough to know that some of us might be sensitive about being called a little.

I thought the Bear Cubs were the youngest group. I'm a Young Lion," I say, but he doesn't seem to care.

"When I started here, I'd just won the Cordex National High School Science Competition, and I thought I was all that." He laughs. "So, Emmett, what are *you* into?" Marcus asked as we walked. "Astrophysics? Athlete? Animator?"

"Uh, does it have to begin with the letter *A*?"

"Good one. Comedian? Are you an acting student?"

"Uh, I do debate. I've been school champion three times..."

"Great! That's like a requirement around here. We have about fifteen state champs this year."

All righty then. "I like to watch movies . . . I, um, recently founded Cinemathique, a film club in my community." I mean, I'm trying to, sort of, so it's not really a lie, right? And I wish Mme Francine was here to give me points for coming up with a Frenchy-sounding name on the spot. Marcus is looking at me like he's expecting more, so I start quoting my own application essay. "I'm, uh, looking for that space between the lines, where I can find my deepest self." When I was writing the essay, I hadn't *plagiarized* exactly, but I'd taken out this book of essays that we'd used in English class and used it for inspiration. I'd laid it on a little thick, but the people who read applications like that kind of thing. "The summer is always a time of discovery, you know? It's like you can take a deep breath because school and all that . . . um, folderol is over, but you're also holding your breath in anticipation of what's to come. It's an awkward position. A liminal space, if you will."

I'm using vocabulary words now. Please make it stop.

"Uh-huh." Marcus stops at a room and looks at me. "Folderol. First time away from home?"

I nod, and for a second he looks like he'll burst if he doesn't laugh. But he remembers that he's a counselor and not supposed to laugh at campers, so he keeps it in, and I hold my head high.

"I went on a school camping trip for three days, though," I say, wishing my voice didn't have to squeak right at that moment. "I was also ten at the time, which is quite the coincidence. Like, with you, I mean, when you went here." I force my mouth closed. "Um . . . I guess I'm a little nervous." Now I *do* seem like I'm about ten!

"No worries, bruh," says Marcus as we step into a building with a sign over the door that says ROBESON HALL. Marcus pats my shoulder in what he probably thinks is a gentle way. "Welcome to Robeson Hall. You're on the third floor, which is . . ."

"Walker?" I say.

"Yeah, right, Walker."

"Not the beauty empire," I add, like he wasn't the one who told me that.

He gives me another funny look. "Yeah. So this is a warm, welcoming community. Diverse but tight knit. You'll meet kids from the States, the Caribbean, even the Continent. There are kids from eleven states and six countries this year. We represent the Diaspora here at DuBois. "

"The Continent?"

"Africa," he says, smiling and making a fist.

"Right," I say. "I knew that."

"Do you have any questions?" he asks.

"Uh, do we have trips into town or anything?" Now that I'm on DuBois' campus, which is the Blackest place I've ever been, I'm not eager to get off. I'm thinking there might be more TraxlerWexler types.

"We don't go into town much," Marcus says, after a pause. "And if we do, you guys will be well-supervised."

That reminds me that I have to let him know that Mom's alter ego is actually Concerned Black Mom, and she's about to be unleashed. "Uh, so my, um, mom, said you would know about this . . . you're supposed to call her? I have her number here . . ."

"Right!" he says, nodding and taking the paper with Mom's phone numbers, Skype name, Facebook page, and email address on it. He goes on. "And, Emmett, don't worry about being a geek or a nerd here. There's no popular crowd. No hierarchy, just community."

Marcus doesn't look that old, but he sure sounds old and clueless about how kids really are. There's always a hierarchy.

"Is that a slogan or something?" I ask. "No Hierarchy, Just Community? And people call me E."

Marcus just smiles as he unlocks a room door. "So, this is your spot," he says, waving his arm around the room. "Looks like your roommate's here already . . . Let me see . . . oh yeah! Charles. I remember now."

I hope that the fact that we share a name is a good sign. It sure does look like Charles is here. Two giant trunks sit in the middle of the room, along with five suitcases and four instrument cases. There are also two twin beds, two desks with office-looking chairs, and a little couch near the window.

"Yep, Charles is an interesting guy. I think you two are going to get along."

Why, just because his first name is my last name?

"Hey, you'll be like . . . the Charles Brothers, get it?"

"I already have a brother," I say, but he's not listening.

He looks at his watch, which is an old-school watch with hands and roman numerals and everything. "House meeting downstairs in thirty minutes. I'll see you down there?"

"Um, is that a question or a directive?" What is wrong with me?

Marcus laughs. "You're a funny little guy. See you in thirty."

"Uh, don't forget to call my mom," I say. I look at my watch. "I'm supposed to call her in fifteen minutes, but that needs to be after she talks to you. She's kind of intense about that kind of thing."

Marcus grins. "I gotchu. She just 'wants to ask a few questions,' right?" He takes out his phone. "It's handled," he says, like he thinks he's really ready for Mom's smoke.

I shrug as he heads down the hall, and all I hear is "Hi, Ms. Charles, so good to—" before I hear Mom, all loud: "Is this my son's counselor? I've been waiting for your call! I just want to ask a few questions!"

I have to laugh.

Chapter Twelve

I watch Marcus leave, walking a little slower than before, then I shut the door and take a deep breath. The beds look a little thinner than mine back home, but not like the boot camp slabs that Billy and WeeDee warned me about. The wooden closet is all along one wall, and as I walk over, the door opens and a boy pops out.

"AHHHHHHHHHH!!!!!" I scream. I knew it! Horror movie! "AHHHHHHHHH!"

"Sorry! Sorry!" says the boy. He is wearing a polo shirt that's tucked into khaki shorts. His whole self looks freshly ironed. "I didn't mean to frighten you. I'm Charles Thompson. Your roommate."

"BRUH, WHAT ARE YOU DOING?!" I look to see if he's hiding a hatchet behind his back.

He holds up his hands. "Sorry! I'm really sorry! It was just awkward, and when things are awkward, I get . . . more awkward." His glasses are all fogged up, and he takes them off to wipe them on his shirt, which is the most normal thing he's done so far.

There's a knock.

"You okay in there, Emmett?" asks Marcus.

I stare at Possibly Charles, Possibly a Camp Killer, for a long minute. I gulp. "Yeah . . . sorry, I thought I saw . . . a raccoon. But . . . it was, uh, nothing. I'm fine."

"Okay," says Marcus. He chuckles. "You'll probably be seeing more of those. Good idea to get used to them."

"Yep, cool, cool, thanks," I say. A few seconds pass before his footsteps fade.

"I am really, really sorry," says Charles, stepping forward with his hand out. "Thanks for not saying anything. It would have made me look weird in front of Marcus, and I'm pretty sure he already thinks I'm weird."

"It *is* kind of weird!" I say, folding my arms. "What's up with"—I gesture to the closet—"that?!"

"I was hanging up my stuff and then I heard you coming and I was trying to decide if it was better to let you have a moment to yourself, or to be here welcoming you since I figured you were a new camper since they always pair up vets with newbies, but I wasn't sure and then it was too late and I panicked and just jumped inside." He looks at me. "I overthink a lot. And I panic a lot."

Hmmmm. I can relate, I guess.

"I'm Emmett," I say.

"I heard." He nods and holds out his hand again, so I shake it.

"Charles," I finish.

"Yep, that's me," he says, still shaking.

"No, I mean, my last name is Charles, I'm Emmett Charles." My hand hurts.

"Oh! I'm Charles Thompson, but you can call me Charles." He finally lets go; I sit and notice a stack of big hardcover books.

"My vintage encyclopedia collection," he says, smiling

and proud like he just said, "My vintage car collection" or something. "I also have a small selection of dictionaries in multiple languages and a sampling of atlases, if you're interested in the changing geography of our world."

I think about how Marcus said Charles and I would get along well. Hmmmm. Also I have the uncomfortable sense that this dude is more me than, well, *me*.

"I thought everyone was a nerd here," I say. "It was even on a guy's shirt. Blerds united and all that. No hierarchy, just community?" I sigh. "I was kind of looking forward to just being . . ." I grinned. "Ordinary."

"Oh, don't worry about that," said Charles, plopping down in the other chair. "Everyone is amazing in this place. And of course there's a hierarchy. We're kids. You're a newbie, so there's a learning curve. But it's abundantly cool, that's why I keep coming back, kind of a Wakanda of Black excellence for three weeks."

Well. Okay, then.

Charles keeps talking. "But it can be intimidating your first time. Oh, and pro tip: Steer clear of Derek Huff."

Just the way he says, "Derek Huff," tells me a lot about the kind of guy Derek must be. But I'm not worried. I've got Luke, which means I've got points before the game's even started.

Even though we'd gotten off to a rocky start, Charles is cool. His stuff is in the middle of the room because he'd waited until I arrived to choose a bed. And he knows the same version of extreme advanced Rochambeau that I do so that makes it easy for us to decide. Once we get that out of the way, we start to unpack. He has a whole trunk full of sheet music. Two of the instrument cases hold a bassoon and a keyboard. He's also got a vest with all these pockets for his harmonicas.

"What do you play?" he asks.

"Oh, I'm not a musician," I say.

"Oh, okay. Sorry, I just assumed. Almost everybody here plays an instrument a little, like on the side."

"Oh . . ." I say. "Well, I can breakdance. I'm going to be in Street Style." I point to his bassoon. "I had a bassoon solo dedicated to me last year at my school, and the marching band did a half time salute to my third straight regional debate win." Yeah, I'm flexing a little.

"Nice," says Charles. "But even more impressive is how you found a way to work in a debate brag."

After a pause, we both laugh.

"You'll fit right in. Like I said, this is an oasis of Black excellence. I mean, there's this girl who plays English horn—she is FIRE! Like, I've never heard anything like it, and I've been playing English horn since I was nine."

"I thought you played bassoon," I say.

"Yeah, I dabble in English horn. When I want to relax."

Oh, he wants to battle? "Aaaaaactually," I say, drawing the word out long, "I'm also interested in film, but the class was full by the time I signed up." I don't add that my film experience is basically just watching a lot of them, or that I'm feeling a tiny bit nervous about living up to everything I said about myself in my application. I *may* have made it sound like I'd done a little more filmmaking than I've actually done, which is none.

"Cool," says Charles. "I don't know anything about filmmaking, but my friend Michelle—she's a playwriting major—has a friend who's into film too. Natasha. She's been to all kinds of film festivals and places where they have red carpets and stuff. Her mom's a famous director. She always wins. Natasha, I mean. I'll tell Michelle to introduce you."

"What do you mean 'wins'?"

"She just wins. Best camp project, most likely to succeed at life, the Blackity Bowl—you'll see."

"Uh, sounds good," I say. Not intimidating at all. And what in Black campness is a Blackity Bowl?

Charles jumps up, his eyes a little wild. "You're supposed to call your mom! And then we have house meeting! I hate being late!"

I stare at him.

"I'm sorry, I heard when I was inside . . ." He trails off, pointing to the closet.

"Uh." I look at my phone. "Thanks. I have two minutes, plenty of time."

"Yep, just want to be of help," he says. "I'll go on ahead and save us seats."

"Yeah, no worries. Thanks for keeping me on my toes." I like Charles. I mean, he kind of makes me look pretty cool. And he is definitely, as Marcus said, interesting.

Suddenly I wonder . . . what does that make me?

***

"Are you sure you have enough underwear? You didn't pack any with holes, did you? And I went through a lot of trouble to find those little Spiderman shorts you asked for."

"MOM!" I hiss, looking around and turning down the volume on my phone. She's so close to hers, her head fills the screen. "Did you call Luke already? I'm sure he wants to talk to you too."

"Luke is busy working. I'll text him later. You're sure you have everything? How do you feel?"

To be honest, I'm kind of glad she's a little worried. She'd practically packed our bags for us, and it seemed like she was itching to get started on her big summer study session. Or was it something else? I couldn't get Luke's dating talk out of my head.

"You never told me if Dad went to camp," I say.

"He didn't mention it," she answers, and that's it.

"Well, did he ever—"

"Don't forget to spray the disinfectant before you put sheets on that bed, Emmett," she interrupts. Okay, I get it. No matter what else is changing, we're sticking with the status quo when it comes to talking about big things. I guess only opportunities, achievement, and other big tings are allowed.

"Mom, you know I'll come home if you need me," I say. "I bet Luke would too."

She laughs and rubs her hair back. "I'm the parent here, I'll be fine. I'll be hitting the books and getting ready for that test. It's just so fortunate that this worked out."

"Well . . ." I say. I don't want to be all I told you so, but, "You always do say to take initiative."

"Don't play yourself, Emmett," she says, but she laughs. "Seriously, buddy, I'm happy for you both. My boys are growing up. Enjoy. " She waves her hand. "All that. I want you to have fun."

She says some more mushy stuff, and I pretend to hate it. Then we say goodbye and she hangs up quickly, probably because she's already crying for real. A squiggly tickle bubbles up in the pit of my stomach, and I swallow a few times as I put my phone in my pocket.

Charles pops up next to me. "Um, ready to go to the house meeting?"

"BRUH! Where did you come from? Seriously, do you have an invisibility cloak or something?"

"I'm like a panther," he says, twisting his body around awkwardly. I can't hold back a laugh because Charles is about as un-panthery as you can get. I'm relieved when he laughs too. He points to the puffy-but-shabby dark green couch near the doorway of the lounge. "We're over there."

"Thanks," I say, following him to the couch. When we plop down and sink deep into the cushions, we both laugh. And even though a couple of kids give us funny looks, I've got someone to laugh with, so I don't mind.

Chapter Thirteen

The house meeting in the lounge is short and all about the rules. Most of the kids from this dorm are musicians, but I hear a couple of kids talking about Street Style, so there are dancers too. Marcus wasn't kidding—I meet a girl from Jamaica who introduces herself as "Clarinet, first chair, all-state" as if I know what that means; then another from Jamaica, Queens, who says she's a "social media influencer" and offers to sell me some likes; a boy from Chicago who says he can hook us up with the best popcorn ever; and a Nigerian kid everyone calls Prince who plays guitar. I try to throw *debate champion* into conversation just to keep up, but around here, that's about as special as saying *grocery list*.

There aren't enough chairs for everyone, so I move to the floor and watch a couple of ants try to transport a corn chip without getting stomped. Once Marcus finishes reading from his scripted welcome, we move outside to the lawn, which is a relief, because it's clear that the AC is only for the main building, probably to make a good impression on the parents. Outside, all the houses are gathered on the grass, and I watch a bunch of reunions—hugs, jumping up and down, shouts and cheers. A really short woman wearing a headwrap and big hoop earrings keeps clapping and trying to herd us into a circle. Finally she puts two fingers in her mouth and whistles, loud. It's an impressive whistle that stops everything. The sun is starting to go down, and there's a late-afternoon glow that makes it seem like we're in a dream. We all slowly move into a roundish formation.

"I'm going to find Michelle," says Charles. "BRB."

Of course he says *BRB*. As I sit down on the grass, I listen to a few whispered conversations about who's back, who isn't, who's changed, and who hasn't. Apparently Lamar's phone made his stock rise instantly, and Charles' friend Natasha thinks she's all that, but she's not, which probably means she is. I can tell that there are a few other newbies like me; we're busy trying to look like we really want to sit alone, not talking to anyone. If this were home, I'd go up to one of them, but here, I feel different. Local debate and dance celeb and neighborhood spelling bee champ isn't all that. My plan had been to stick with Luke, but I don't see him anywhere. A bunch of adults in blue T-shirts that say BLACK EXCELLENCE in red are standing in the middle of the circle, and older kids—oh, there's Luke!—are on the perimeter, trying to kind of herd us in like a flock of hyper sheep. Black sheep, heh. I wave Luke over, but he just holds up a hand in response.

Charles comes back with a girl. A cute girl. She's wearing a hoodie that says I'M NOT A SNACK, I'M SOUL FOOD!. I smile.

"This is Michelle," says Charles. He's doing a terrible job of whispering behind his hand. "The one with THE FRIEND I WAS TELLING YOU ABOUT."

Charles and I are going to have to talk.

"Uh, hi, Michelle," I say. "I'm Emmett, you can call me E." Nothing else to see here, folks. "I'm new."

"No kidding," she says, sitting down and pulling Charles with her. "Sorry, was that rude? I don't want to be rude. Sometimes, because I hate fake nicey niceness, I go too far to the other side. The rude side. Was I rude? I'm sorry. What do you know about Amy Garvey?"

I blink, hoping I don't have to come out and say "Who?" And then I see that Charles is staring at Michelle with a face that would go right next to the word *lovesick* in the dictionary. Probably a dictionary that Charles has in our room.

"Um, not . . . much?" I say, but it doesn't matter because she's going so fast I'm not sure if she expected an answer at all.

"I'm working on a musical this summer, about Amy Ashwood Garvey and Amy Jacques Garvey—*The Two Amys*. These women, known primarily as Marcus Garvey's wives, were so much more. Really essential to any true study of our history and the diaspora."

I think I'm supposed to know who Marcus Garvey is, and I'm realizing that people here say *diaspora* a lot. I hope Charles has a Black history encyclopedia in one of those trunks. I don't know if the sweat running down my cheeks is from the humidity or my nerves. I try to remind myself that I got myself here all on my own, so I must be impressive too, just in a . . . different way. Michelle is talking about something called the UNIA when the adults start doing a Be Quiet clap that reminds me of school, and Luke is doing it too, like he's been here all his life. A tall, dark-skinned man with a black-and-gray beard stands up and walks to the center of the circle.

"That's Dr. Triphammer," whispers Charles. "The

director. He's been here forever. I think he went here when it was still a school. He's nicer than he seems, just . . . cares a lot."

I nod.

"Shhh," says Charles, like I'm the one talking. "He's starting."

"Not like we haven't heard the same speech for the past three years," Michelle mutters. But she sits back and smiles like she's getting ready for something good.

And it is pretty interesting . . . Dr. Triphammer tells us about the history of DuBois, how some kid named Wanda Morgan from New York City had wanted to go to camp in like the 1900s, but they were all white-only, so she grew up and bought some old fancy school and turned it into Camp DuBois. And apparently now, DuBois gets accused of "reverse racism" every year. It's open to anyone, but "so far, the only ones who register are Black folks," says Dr. Triphammer, and everyone laughs and cheers. As I look around, I think about how sometimes I'm the only one at some of my activities. Even if I complain, Mom still makes me go. I guess it never works the other way around. I can't imagine WeeDee and Billy's parents telling them they had to come here. I can't imagine WeeDee and Billy asking to, either.

"Wanda Morgan and her husband were Black millionaires at a time when that was most unusual," he says.

"Like it still isn't?" yells out someone.

We laugh.

He smiles. "Good point. But the main thing isn't how many ducats they had, but what they did with that scrilla." We collectively cringe at him using slang older than our parents, and he bulldozes on with his speech like it's inevitable. "As you can see, we are situated on seventy-five gorgeous acres of land on Lake Hunter, and our buildings are a mixture of art deco and minimal traditionalist styles, which we work hard to preserve and maintain. Segregation meant that facilities like these were not available to Black people in the 1920s—"

"Except when they wanted us as servants!" someone yells out.

Triphammer nods. "The Morgans lived on and bought this property and the surrounding land, little by little, over a period of fifty years, lifting as they climbed, building a school and then a camp for Black children." Several campers are mouthing Dr. Triphammer's speech along with him, and he doesn't seem to mind. "I know I tell this story every year. It's a tradition, and an important one. Our heritage as a people is rich, dynamic, and multifaceted. We have endured great pain and experienced soaring triumphs. You are here to have fun, make new friends, and experience new things. You are also here to dig deep. To find the Morgan Mission in you—'sowing seeds for mutual progress.'" He gets up on a large rock; it takes him a few seconds to steady himself. "Show UP!" he yells.

"Show OUT!" yells back almost everyone else.

Charles turns to me. "Unofficial DuBois chant."

"Uh, yeah, I figured," I say.

We chant it three more times, then the barbecue starts. There are grills set up next to giant picnic tables that are decorated with green-and-gold paper tablecloths, and all the plates and cups and utensils are green and gold too. Charles and I get on the line that seems the shortest, but it doesn't matter because the DuBois staff is like a machine and we're moving pretty quickly. The burgers look as good as they smell—they aren't gray! They even have veggie burgers that don't look like they're made of clay. There's fresh corn roasting, and the hot dogs are foot longs. I let my hot dog stay on the grill until it's black on the outside, just the way I like it, then load it up with mustard, ketchup, and relish. Charles and I pile our plates high and grab seats at the end of a picnic table.

A group of guys is already there, laughing and loud-talking in that way people do when they want to be noticed. Been there, done that. Lamar is there, and he gives me a quick nod.

"Like, why does it have to be all about progress and I have a dream by any means necessary and blah, blah, blah, we the people?" says the loudest boy who also has the best haircut.

"You mixed up about ten different things in that one sentence, Derek," says another kid, and they all laugh. Charles and I join in, quietly. Derek looks over at us.

"Whaddup, Chucky," he says.

"It's *Charles*," says Charles. "And hello, Derek." He says *Derek* like it's not a real word, more like a bad smell. From the way time seems to stop, I can tell that Charles is being pretty brave. He takes a big bite of his burger-hot-dog combo sandwich. There's a pause, and it's heavy, and something's not quite right. I look at Charles, but he just looks straight ahead and chews. Something tells me not to look at Derek for too long.

Finally Derek laughs again. "My bad. Good to see you, Charles."

I can feel everyone take a deep breath of relief. Little conversations start up again.

"Is that the one you were talking about?" I whisper to Charles. "What was that about?"

"Yes. He can be annoying, but he's harmless," says Charles. Then his eyes light up like he's been plugged into an electrical socket. "Michelle! Over here!" He scoots over on the bench so hard and fast that I almost fall off.

Dr. Triphammer stands and claps his hands to get our attention. Then he turns things over to the program coordinator, Ms. Marshall, who talks about this opportunity to immerse ourselves in pursuit of our existing passions, explore new ones, and spend each day nestled in and nurtured by DuBois's award-winning facilities and staff. I hear some kids grumbling about how DuBois is "not as good as it used to be." We sing the DuBois song, which is to the tune of that Beyoncé song that is based this old song about letting go that uncles and aunties always jump up and do the Electric Slide to at weddings.

> *Camp DuBois makes me happy!*
> *This you can bet.*
> *Fam right beside me,*
> *And I won't forget.*
> *I really love it,*
> *You should know.*
> *I want to cheer Camp DuBois,*
> *It's my second home.*

Then the counselors get up and do a step show! I try to pick it up, I'm usually good at that, but it's complicated, like the ones my cousin Dwight showed us when we when to visit him in college. A few people are playing drums on the sidelines and the veteran campers are cheering and clapping to the beat. Even Dr. Triphammer is doing some kind of uncle two-step, while this other guy next to him is doing a whole routine with flips, even though he looks just as old as Dr. Triphammer.

Luke is stepping with the other counselors—when did he even have time to learn that routine? I'm the one who picks up moves super fast. He looks smooth and right at home with the others. It's a minute before I realize that I've fallen into doing the school dance shuffle without realizing it. I stop and just clap. I tell myself it's because I'm tired, it's not that I've lost my moves, or that I'm feeling a little . . . lost in general.

"This is my favorite part," whispers Michelle. "For the culture."

The counselors end the step show with big cheers, then they start teaching campers the routine. Some of the musician campers have their instruments with them and start up an impromptu jam session. Charles runs back for his bassoon and offers to let me use his oboe (I pass). Some kids are straight up ignoring everything and just reading books at the picnic tables. It is all kinds of a jumble of awesome, and I'm glad to be here with my brother.

Well, sort of. I try to get over to Luke so we can add our own brotherly swag to the step routine—I really want people to know we're family. But he's surrounded, so a girl with the biggest Afro I've ever seen teaches me the step routine and pumps her fist when I pick it up. Charles and Michelle come over, and we hang together for s'mores and ice cream by the firepit. We compare schedules; I'll see Michelle in baking, and we're all together for Black to the Future and the Superhero Secrets class. I'm really curious about that one. I would never ask out loud, but I wonder if we'll have outfits, or at least capes. Real full-on cosplay would be pretty cool. I tried to get some inside info from Luke, but he kept talking brochure talk at me: "There is a *world* of options. It's not *camp*, it's a summer arts and culture *experience*."

"What's the *A* for?" I ask, pointing to my schedule. I look; they have it too.

"Aquatics," says Charles. "We take the swim test and get placed tomorrow. It's pretty basic. We're all usually in the same group—Michelle, Natasha, me, and some others—so you probably will be too. Unless you're like lifeguard level or something."

"I'm not," I say. And leave it at that. I wonder if Mom is missing me so much right now that I can guilt her into writing me an excuse note for swimming. Then I wonder what kind of son thinks that. It's like I can go from hero to villain real so fast I scare myself.

I only catch a couple more glimpses of Luke as the party goes on. The mosquitos seem to congregate around the citronella candles that are supposed to repel them. I'm guessing they're high-fiving and laughing at our futile attempts to avoid being bitten. A girl wearing a flower crown and a shirt that says NYC FOREST SCHOOL tries to get us to "listen to the fireflies' song" while a few guys start a competition to see who can make the most disgusting hot dog. When Dr. Triphammer finds out, he makes them eat everything they made, including the chocolate marshmallow surprise that this boy named Darius created. Just when I'm trying to keep the smile pasted on my face, the DJ plays this old-school song about candy; some staff people working the bbq grills really do start the Electric Slide, and even though everybody laughs, a lot of people join in, not just old people. Even Luke does, and so does Charles, looking like he's doing a completely different dance. He waves me over, but I pretend that I'm still eating.

By the time we're heading back to the dorms, the squiggly feeling at the bottom of my stomach is almost gone, and I only blink a couple of times when I see Mom's good night text with a row of heart emojis. I don't write back anything about swimming. I just send three hearts.

Chapter Fourteen

Something is being slaughtered.

"Axe murderer!" I yell, jumping up. But I'm all twisted up in my sheets and fall out of bed. "Don't touch the mask! He'll kill us all!"

Charles opens an eye. "Shower screams," he says, like that explains anything. "Gimme two more minutes." He puts the pillow over his head and turns over as the "shower screams" continue.

I get up and go to the window and see a bunch of people jumping into the lake, screaming and screeching. "It must be FREEZING. Why would anyone do that?"

"It's a tradition," mumbles Charles. "New counselors jump into the lake on the first morning after campers arrive. It's freezing, and there's always someone who chickens out."

My expression must show what I'm thinking, because he gets up and says, "Yeah, it's silly. And they still take a regular shower after." He shrugs. "I told you, we got all kinds. Anyway, some campers take a morning dip too, after we have the swim test. As long as you're level three and up, and everyone our age is at least level three. So if you want to join in one day, no judgment."

Mom would probably grow super wings and fly right to New York if her spidey-mom sense told her I wasn't taking a real shower with soap and a washcloth and running water. Ugh, swimming again. I keep my mouth shut and we get going. There are only two showers on our floor, and Charles warns me that last summer, they had run out of hot water pretty fast. I spray on a good amount of the Lemon Chill Rock Steady body spray that Luke gave me for my eleventh birthday. I've been making it last, but today I go all out. Never get a second chance to make a first impression, right? Charles and I get dressed, and I wish I'd brought more sneakers. These barely match my outfit and it's only the first day.

***

Now that the screams are over, it's pretty quiet on campus. As Charles and I walk to the dining hall for breakfast, he points out the different buildings, including what he says used to be a planetarium. There's a man watering flowers in front of the main building, and a security guard who already looks bored rides past us in a little cart. I send a few pics to Mom, and she writes back, *Beautiful!* and then *Get off that phone!* Two counselors are taking the covers off rowboats by the lake, and I feel a familiar twinge of wishing I could just know how to swim without actually having to go through the process of learning.

Charles and I are in the middle of an amazingly delicious breakfast (I have a full tray of Belgian waffles that I've drenched in buttery maple syrup and stuffed with thick slices of bacon), and I'm still half-asleep when Michelle and another girl walk over.

"Hey," says Charles. "You guys are late. Breakfast is almost over." His omelet looks like it was made out of a whole dozen eggs and a wheel of cheese.

Michelle shrugs. "I'm just getting an acai bowl. Speaking of bowls, we're late because Natasha was prepping for the Blackity Bowl. We all know she's the Serena Williams of the tournament. I started quizzing her as soon as we got back to our dorm last night. Gotta respect the grind." She sniffs. "What's that smell?"

Maybe I didn't go hard enough on the body spray.

Charles turns to me and loud-whispers, "Natasha's the one I was telling you about." He has no chill whatsoever.

"It's like . . . a mixture of roast beef and dead roses," says Michelle.

The other girl smiles, and it seems like the gap between her teeth sparkles. "Hey, Charles. What exactly were you telling him about me?" She looks unbothered. She nods at me. "Hi, I'm Natasha. That's weird, it smells like . . . bologna-flavored lemonade over here."

"Hi," I say. "I'm Emmett, you can call me E." I give her a nod back. Pretty smooth, I hope. But when I look down, there's a piece of bacon on my lap. "What's the Blackity Bowl?"

"It's a trivia contest on the last night of camp. Pop culture stuff."

"Who was the first hip-hop group to win a Grammy?" rattles off Michelle.

"DJ Jazzy Jeff and the Fresh Prince," answers Natasha. "1989. 'Parents Just Don't Understand.' Fresh Prince is also known as Will Smith. I mean, he *is* Will Smith.'"

"See?" says Michelle. "My girl is at the top of her game." She looks around and holds her hands up. "We welcome *all* challengers!" Natasha mouths, *We?* but she just says, "Ugh. My stomach, I need to eat."

"Seriously?!" says another kid across the table. "That's all kinds of wrong. 'Parent's Just Don't Understand' was not real hip-hop, even in the olden days."

"It's truth, though, parents *don't* understand," says a boy. "So it sounds like real hip-hop to me."

"What does that even mean?" asks Michelle.

"Who defines what's real?" says the flower crown girl from last night.

Natasha shrugs. "I'm just repeating the facts." She turns to me. "I need to beat my dad's record this summer. He won the bowl three times in a row when he came here. This could be my fourth win. So, what are you into?"

"Uh . . . I like watching movies . . . Sometimes I get pictures in my head . . . scenes . . . like movies . . . films . . ." My tongue feels all swole and heavy.

Michelle looks from Natasha to me, then back again and raises her eyebrows at me. "Natasha is the Ava DuVernay of film at DuBois," she says.

"I thought about taking film . . . full . . . I like movies." I can't stop babbling.

"I'm a film major!" says Natasha, glancing at Michelle. "Documentaries are my specialty. Hey, maybe I can interview you for a potential piece on new campers. *DuBois Through New Eyes.*"

"See what I mean?" says Michelle. She taps Natasha's arm. "Before you guys get deep into it, let's grab some food. I've been waiting for these croissants since last summer." They leave, talking super fast and laughing.

"Natasha won the Camp Showcase last year. She made a movie called *Legacy* about how her parents went here," says Charles. "She'd already recorded interviews with them before she got to camp!"

That gives me an idea. If I wanted to make a film project about Luke, I'd have to interview him. We'll have to hang out then, he'll want to see me win. I pick up the waffle-bacon sandwich I'd made. "I've never had breakfast this good!" I swallow and a twinge puts a lump in my throat. "Except for my mom's, of course." I hope Charles doesn't laugh.

He doesn't laugh, but this other kid across the table does. It's Derek. My GOON antennae are definitely up. "Aw, you miss your mommy's cooking!" Derek says. I pretend not to hear him.

Maybe Charles is pretending too. He just says, "Every summer they bring in the person who won that big cooking competition show *Sliced*." He shoves about seventeen pieces of bacon into his mouth. "Former *Sliced* contestants run the kitchen, and the rest of the staff are from famous Black-owned restaurants around the country."

"Not this year," says Derek. "I heard they couldn't afford it. This place is getting janky." He glances back at me. "And apparently, they let everybody in now. You look like one of those brownnosers who tries to be an 'intern.'"

"Well, the food is still good, and everyone's nose here is some kind of brown," says Natasha, sliding into the seat next to me. "Literally."

Charles just shrugs, and I keep my eyes on my plate. I know guys like this, and the best thing for me to do is stay quiet.

Natasha leans over and smiles at me. "Waffle sandwich. Good idea," she says, pointing to her own.

"Derek, you need to stop, your attitude is getting so old," says Michelle, settling into the seat next to Charles, who immediately starts choking on his juice. She turns away from the Derek kid and continues. "I'm excited about that Black to the Future class, y'all."

Derek mutters, "Of course you are," but only the guy sitting next to him responds with a laugh.

"Me too, but I wonder why it's only once a week," says Natasha, holding up her waffle sandwich. It has sliced bananas and chocolate spread inside. She has good taste. "That means we only have it three times." Her cornrows are all swooped up into cute little buns.

"All I know is that it means three less free periods," grumbles Derek. "And that it's going to be corny."

Natasha ignores him. "And Triple M is back, so you know the street style routine at the Camp Showcase is going to be fire . . ."

"REACH!" booms Charles. "STRETCH!" Michelle and Natasha laugh along with him. "EXTENSION!" I guess that's him imitating this Triple M person. "BOOM! BAP! BOOM! BAP!"

"Who's Triple M?" I ask. I don't mention that I'm on the Street Style wait list.

"Oh—you have to call him Mr. Micah McDowell," says Natasha. "You've got to say the whole thing until he gives you permission. He's . . . quirky. But he's a choreography legend."

"According to him," says Michelle with a smirk. "But shhhhhh! Remember, this is Emmett's first time," she added. "You can't hit him with everything at once. Let him be innocent for a little longer."

Ohhh-kay.

"Are you in Street Style too?" I ask Natasha.

"No, I'm in Advanced Dunham," she says, like I'm supposed to know what that means. She glances at me. "Katherine Dunham dance technique. It's a thing."

"Tash is the Misty Copeland of dance at DuBois,"

says Michelle.

"I thought she was the Serena Williams of the Blackity Bowl," I say. "And the Ava DuVernay of film."

"Yep" is all Michelle answers.

"Soooo back to Superhero Secrets," Natasha goes on. "You think we'll be talking about the Marvel Universe?"

"Uh, they said superhero, not convoluted, overrated drama," says a girl with a slight British accent. "Like you said, we've only got three sessions. I bet we'll talk about proper heroes with clear story arcs like John Stewart. The DCU is so underappreciated."

I never thought about the definition of the word *scoff* before, but the way a bunch of kids react to that statement seems pretty much on the nose.

"A, B, C your way out of this convo, Amina, as my mom would say," says Natasha. "And that's a stretch, saying DC even has a universe!" They're both laughing so I can tell it's not actual beef. Sometimes things get real quickfast in the comics community. Everyone starts arguing about different comics; I'm glad I'm not the only one ready for some serious cosplay. I want to say something about Night Man, which is Luke and my favorite graphic novel series, but I still feel a little brand-new here, so I just listen.

Michelle points to the rooster-shaped clock hanging over the dining hall doorway. "We better hurry up and eat. Breakfast is almost over." She and Natasha introduce me to some of the other kids at the table. In the space of five minutes, I meet a kid who's won six National Science Awards, a girl who's taking a break from her Broadway role as Young Janet Jackson, and a boy who's working with NASA to redesign spacesuits.

"Is everyone here unbelievably amazing?" I ask.

"Well, there aren't any dandiprats!" Charles says.

I just look at him. I refuse to ask what a dandiprat is. Or which ye olde dictionary he pulled it from.

"Black excellence, the next generation, blah, blah, blah," says Natasha. "That's pretty much the main reason why my parents send me here every summer. I cannot forget I'm a 'legacy.'"

I must look confused, because she adds, "My parents went to high school here. They went to *prom* together." She pretends to gag. "So gross."

"Young bougie love!" sings Michelle, and Natasha elbows her.

"Your parents—I think that's kind of romantic," Charles says to Natasha. He leans toward me and loud-whispers, "You see how I worked in *dandiprats*? I've been memorizing words from my *Archer's Antiquated Dictionary*. Do you think Michelle will be impressed? This is my second year of trying to dazzle her."

"Bruh." I pull him away from the table. "You've got to play it cool," I say. "I can help you out, big time. This is my specialty." I mean, it's Luke's, but I've been taking notes.

"You have a better dictionary than Archer's?" he asks, worried. "I was assured that it was the most comprehensive source of—"

"No, with the ladies." I nod in Michelle's direction. "I've learned from the best." No need to add that I'm still learning.

"Oh, is it that obvious?"

"Bro, you just said—Never mind, don't worry, we'll talk. I gotchu. My brother's got skills."

"Does he give lessons or anything? Maybe I can talk to him during my free period," says Charles, brightening.

"I've been soaking it all in since I was a baby. Don't worry, I can help you out," I say, patting him on the back. We sit back down. Natasha is gone.

"Oh, um, where's your friend?" I say it real casual.

"Natasha?" asks Michelle in a loud voice. "She has a headache, she went to the nurse. She'll be back." She winks at me. "Don't worry."

Was I that obvious?

"So"—Michelle holds her arms out wide—"I'm thinking that in this scene I'm writing, when the two Amys meet, they'll call each other by their maiden names. It'll be this big dramatic but also feminist moment—'Jacques!' 'Ashwood!'"

"A type of guillotine was also called a maiden," says Charles to no one. "In Scotland. I'm up to the sixteenth century in my *Dictionaries of the Centuries* collection."

"No offense, Mich," says a kid named Troy, "but a musical about Marcus Garvey's wives sounds boring."

"That's what people said to Lin-Manuel Miranda about *Hamilton*," snaps Michelle. "Begone with you, unbeliever!"

"Yeah, begone!" Charles interjects loudly.

Michelle and Troy stare at him.

"You're funny, Chucky," says Michelle, punching his arm.

Chucky. Ouch. I speak up. "Hey, Charles, let's go grab another drink."

"No thanks, I don't—Oh, OH, YEAH, yeah, okay," he says, standing and making the least subtle exit ever.

We walk over to the drink station. "Look, we need to get you on the fast track," I say. "It's clear that Troy dude is trying to push up."

"I thought so, too! Did you hear the way he said *Mich*?" says Charles. "I have an exact replica of a sixteenth century suit of armor at home. Should I get my mom to send it up here so I can show that flatigious knave that I'm not to be trifled with?"

I put both hands on his shoulders. "Absolutely not."

"Good," he answers. "Because she'd say no. And I don't really want to do that anyway. That suit of armor is really heavy."

"We're just gonna make sure that Michelle sees the real you but a little brighter," I say. "Let's start with your walk. When we start back, take long steps, really striiiide," I say, demonstrating as I grab a few plastic cups. "And give him a nod as you sit down, like, *I see you, playa, but I don't see you.* You know what I mean?"

Charles nods.

"Oh! And this works too!" I'm enjoying this. "Do you know what she's drinking? Luke says it's always good to offer a girl something to eat or drink, and it's even better if you seem like you've been paying attention to what she likes."

"She always drinks fifty-fifties," says Charles. "Half lemonade, half iced tea. Minimal ice. Should I make one for her? Extra large?"

I nod. On his own, he adds a twist of lime, which I think is a smooth move.

"You're a natural, C," I sat. "All right, let's head back. Smooth. Suave. Silky."

"C?" he makes a face.

"It's better than Chucky," I say, shrugging.

"I'll stick with Charles," he says firmly, and starts marching back to the table like he's leading a band. One step at a time, I guess.

"For you, *milady . . . my queen*—uh, Michelle," he says when we get to the table, with a big flourish. A flourish so big that he waves the cup of fifty-fifty right over Michelle's head and into my stomach. I watch it spill down the front of my pants like it's happening in slow motion.

"Arrggh!" I yell. Maybe even yelp.

"Confound it!" shouts Charles. I have a fleeting thought: *He keeps it real, doesn't he?*

Michelle and Troy jump up. "Let's get some paper towels," says Troy.

"I'm deeply, deeply sorry," says Charles. I just nod. Michelle and Troy come back and of course Natasha comes back right at this moment too. I try to dry myself off as much as possible, but it's clear that unless I really want to spend the day looking like I'd wet my pants, I'd have to go change. The distance from my table to the door seems insurmountable. Insurmountable? Great. Now I'm thinking in Charles.

"I'll walk directly in front of you," says Charles.

"I think that'll just call more attention to this whole . . . situation," says Michelle.

"I think maybe all of us standing around him like this is calling more attention to the 'situation,'" says Natasha, making air quotes. "Let's just act natural." They all get in the most unnatural poses imaginable. Charles tries to balance a tray on his head.

"Guys, I appreciate the support, but I'm guessing that a circus troupe looks more natural than this," I say.

Charles put the tray down. "I was going for the distraction strategy," he says. "I do something even more ridiculous to call attention away from your . . ."

"Pee pants?" suggests Derek. A girl a few seats away giggles. "Hey, check it out, everyone!"

Please don't let me be this guy!

"Wow, Chucky," says Derek in a low voice. "You're a regular weirdo. But *this* dude"—he points to me—"this dude is just regu*lar*."

I pretend to ignore him and his Mac-like ability to get to me. *Why is it that the jerks always know what your weakness is? And why is it that I never have any mental vibranium on the ready?* Natasha would probably be mad about me mixing my comic universe metaphors. "Just act natural," whispers Charles. I am still frozen in place, with Charles, Natasha, and Michelle standing around me.

Even Natasha has given up on that. "I mean . . . we can't stand like this forever," she says.

I mean, *I* could. Her hair smells like cake.

"Yeah," says Michelle. "This is getting uncomfortable. I'm not good at being still."

"You're more like a whirlwind," says Charles dreamily.

"'Look for me in the whirlwind,' yes, come through with the Marcus Garvey quotes!" cries out Michelle, jumping up and down. "I could hug you!!!" Charles almost falls over, *aaaand* my human wall of protection has crumbled.

"E!" calls out Luke's voice. I look up to see him jogging toward me. Yes! Luke to the rescue. When he gets close, he leaned in and whispers, "Just go with it, okay?" Before I can even nod, he'd lifts me up onto his shoulders. "Hey, everyone! My brother E here won the school debate championship back in May!"

Ragged claps. I hope he's got more, because I already know that's pretty routine for this crowd.

Luke continues. "He's going on to even more in the fall! I'm so proud of him." Nice work. He makes it sound more important than it is by keeping it vague. He's a master. Then he simultaneously deepens and raised his voice in a way that makes a subtle shift from encouraging to slightly menacing, which is hard to do without coming off like a bully. He's practiced on me a lot. "So . . . who's gonna help me cheer him on now!"

A few claps and even whoops, the loudest from Charles. Luke starts some rhythmic clapping, more kids join in.

Luke lifts me onto his shoulders, and starts in, his voice booming. "E! E! E! E!" As he cheers my name, he keeps up the clapping and carries me toward the door. "Do you, E," he whispers. I start to smile and raise my arms like I've just won a boxing match. The cheers and claps get louder.

As we walk by Derek, I hear him ask someone, "Why exactly are we cheering this kid? For being a debater like a hundred other people here? And how can that guy be his brother? *He's* actually not a punk." But the cheers drown him out.

Luke gets me outside fast and closes the door behind us. I can hear everyone go back to their food and conversations.

"All right, go change," Luke says to me. "Only you could have gotten into such a mess." But he's smiling.

"Thanks!" I say. "That was AWESOME. I'm a little nervous. People are kind of intimidating here. Also I keep hearing that the swim test is mandatory and I have badminton now. I'm sure I'll look awkward."

"Everyone looks awkward playing badminton," says Luke. "And will you look at that. It's *almost as if you didn't think this through.*" When I don't say anything, he goes on. "Look, you wanted to come to DuBois, so—" He holds up his hands.

"Yeah, but—" *It was to hang out with you!* I want to say, but he's already looking back into the dining hall. "Oh, wait, so I met this girl, she does film, and I had an idea for something you and me could do together, have our Brother

Summer that we planned—"

"E, I gotta get back to work . . . I was just grabbing a quick bite and saw what happened. I'm feeling a little . . . Well, this isn't easy for me either, so, you know, try to stay dry, okay?"

"Um, yeah, about that swim test—"

He sniffs. "Is that Black Tiger or Lemon Chill? I remember those days. Did you spray on that whole can? Yo, think of the environment, if not the rest of humanity." He pats my shoulder and goes back inside before I can say anything else. I hear the cheering rise as he steps into the dining room. They're yelling "E! E! E!" again, like they don't even realize that it stands for me. Or maybe in spite of that.

Chapter Fifteen

I can't believe I was worried about looking awkward in badminton—Luke's right. It's impossible *not* to look awkward. A girl even walks by the nets and says, "AWKWARRRRRRD" as we're taking practice shots; it's like we're in a teen movie. I guess it's a small consolation that we all look corny. Except Natasha, who is apparently also the Serena Williams of badminton. I try to think of something complimentary-but-not-thirsty to say. I really wish I'd brought more sneakers. Natasha is wearing a tank top that says UNBOTHERED in sequins. I notice something new about her every time I see her, it's like I can't take in all of her magic at once. She doesn't seem to sweat at all.

A birdie hits me in the head. "Ouch!"

"My bad, heads up," says a voice. I look, and it's Derek. "I was just trying to help you out."

"Yeah, thanks," I say. I pick up the birdie and line up with the rest of the class.

I can feel his eyes on me as Natasha gets in line behind me and taps my shoulder.

"Hey," she says.

"Hey." I play it cool, like I've just realized that she's there. Another birdie smacks me in the face.

After the period is over, we walk around, picking up the birdies on the grass. I feel rivers of sweat running down my sides even though there's a cool breeze blowing and we really didn't do all that much. I'm going to have to do three coats of deodorant while I'm here, or at least right before I know I'm going to see Natasha.

"So I heard you going hard for Green Lantern at breakfast," she says. "I'd love to do a superhero movie one day."

I clear my throat. "Uh, yeah . . . So, do you really think Superhero Secrets is going to be about comics and stuff?"

"I mean, yeah, if Dr. Triphammer's smart. Because that would be so good," she says. "I'm a huge Night Man fan."

I guess my surprise shows, because she rolls her eyes. "Seriously?! You're looking all shook because a girl reads Night Man? I like Cobra Woman and Ayo too, so . . ."

"Sorry," I say quickly. "It's not that I don't think girls read comics. It's just . . . Night Man's pretty low key. Not that many kids I know read it. I only know about it because of my older brother."

She nods. "Yeah, the early volumes are so-so, but once Monifa's story starts, it really gets going."

"Monifa is awesome! She needs her own movie."

"I know, right?!"

We dump our armfuls of birdies and rackets into the sports shed. I really am sweatier than I thought. Maybe I'll try four coats of deodorant. It doesn't hit me until I'm almost at my dorm that I just had a semi-real conversation with a girl that I don't know and I wasn't awkward or anything! Mostly.

"Welcome to Black to the Future," says a woman in a just-loud-enough voice. The auditorium quiets down quickly; there's something about her that makes me sit up straighter. Charles is next to me; we're a team now, and I guess Marcus was right, because it doesn't even feel strange that he's telling me about his plan to get fluent in three West African languages before he's sixteen, just because. He's traveled to Africa once, on a band trip to Senegal. DuBois is the farthest from home I've ever been.

A man walks in and joins the woman in front, and they stand there together in silence until we're still in our red cushioned seats. No AC in here, but there are giant fans blasting, so they both have to keep almost-shouting.

"Thank you for your attention," says the man. "I'm Gordon. Show UP!"

"And I'm Charisse," says the woman. "Show OUT! And no, we're not brother and sister, girlfriend and boyfriend, father and daughter, or mother and son, or whatever story y'all decide to make up this year." After a pause, she smiles, and everyone laughs. Out of the corner of my eye, I see Luke and Lamar walk in, both dressed in DuBois shirts and Adidas everything else.

"So now that that's out of the way, let's get down to business," she went on. "Gordon and I have been members of the DuBois community for twenty years—"

"Yo, y'all must be vampires, or Black really don't crack!" yells a voice from the back of the auditorium. We laugh again, and Charisse goes on. "No, it doesn't. But the point is that we started here as campers, just like you. And like some of you, I didn't come from a world of privilege that resembled anything remotely close to this."

Some whoops and cheers.

Gordon jumps in. "And we know that some of you, like me, do come from exactly this world of privilege." More whoops. "And there are many in between. So this is going to be a space to examine what it means to be Black in today's world."

"And what it means to the future of our community," finishes Charisse.

"Sounds like a Ta-Nehisi Coates kind of class," whispers Charles. He doesn't hear me ask, "Who?" because Michelle plunks down on the other side of him, and I notice the sweat spreading from his armpits immediately, like a reverse superpower.

Charles and Michelle start whispering about reparations, which for once at this place, is a word I know, because when Mom saw my history textbook and a line about how "Because they were often treated with respect and good care, slaves sang as they worked" she called the principal and aunties Carolyn, Frances, and Renée and the school board and the city councilwoman and the local paper and bought me a book called *Slavery: Its Infinite Impact*. Unfortunately, I'd only read the introduction before I went back to practicing for the spelling bee, and then I forgot about it.

"We're going to show you a brief presentation, then we'll pause for questions," Gordon says.

After a Powerpoint that has a lot of charts and statistics on it about things like "resegregated schools" and "internalized racism," a sea of hands raises, and I'm glad, because my head is spinning right now. I don't know what I was expecting, but I know it wasn't like . . . Black Power Prep School.

"Is this place some kind of college boot camp in disguise?" I whisper.

"Disguise?" answers Michelle. "Pretty much all of us here have been in college prep since second grade, right?" Michelle and a few others laugh, but when Natasha snaps in agreement, she's not smiling.

"Why *did* y'all add this class?" a girl asks Charisse and Gordon. "I come here to work on my dance technique and have fun with my friends. I know DuBois is all about Black excellence, but it's still summer!" The murmuring around me sounds like a lot of people have the same question.

"Well, we had the Black History elective every year," points out Natasha.

"Yeah," says the girl. "But we just had to memorize a bunch of dusty facts, not get all . . . *deep*."

Gordon and Charisse nod. "Yep, we're trying something new," says Charisse. "And there is a long legacy of intersection between social justice and the arts, by the way, especially in the Black community, so your—excuse me—ignorance of that is exactly why we think it's important to do this."

"Do what, exactly?" asks Natasha, in a voice that makes her question sound genuinely curious and not rude.

"We're just going to talk in an informal way, and we hope that will get you thinking about how these ideas can intersect in your own work."

"Like Lorraine Hansberry and *A Raisin in the Sun*," calls out Michelle. The community theater group in my neighborhood did that play last summer, but I didn't see it.

"Nina Simone," says a boy who I've already noticed is always singing and humming under his breath just so people can tell him he can sing.

Charisse nods. "Yep, Travis. For those of you not familiar, you should be. Nina Simone was a singer, pianist, activist, and so much more. I'm sure your parents have some of her music."

I look over and Luke is nodding, so I guess Mom does.

"Nina Simone spoke about the artist's responsibility being to 'reflect the times.'" Charisse reads from her phone: "'An artist's duty, as far as I'm concerned, is to reflect the times. I think that is true of painters, sculptors, poets, musicians. As far as I'm concerned, it's their choice, but I CHOOSE to reflect the times and situations in which I find myself. That, to me, is my duty. And at this crucial time in our lives, when everything is so desperate, when every day is a matter of survival, I don't think you can help but be involved.' Let's just start there. What do you think that means?"

We get into small groups to talk about that question and it ends up being pretty cool. The I-came-here-to-dance girl is in my group. "So, you're gonna tell me if I draw a rose, that's some deep political thing?" she asks. "Or even the *Conjuring* movies? *Everything* is political?"

"Yo, Hannah, maybe it's the choice to do it," asks another kid. "The art we decide to create has political implications." A debate starts, but it isn't like the debates I'm used to winning, where it's mostly a battle to fit as many words into as little time as possible. This is real talk, and it feels itchy like that suit I only wear for funerals and weddings.

"So if I choose to make a challenge video and post it online," says Hannah. "I'm being *political*?"

"You sound stupid," says a boy.

"No, *you* do," Hannah shoots back. For a few seconds the debate goes into a second grade style I-know-you-are-but-what-am-I vortex, but Natasha pulls us out.

"I think that's a good question, and my answer would

be yes," she says slowly, raising her voice a little. "Because you're kind of showing what's important to you and what you think people want to see, right?"

"Everyone's saying *political* and we haven't, like, *defined* it," says a boy.

Too bad Charles is in a different group; he'd get all dictionary in a second. Somebody looks up the definition on their phone, and we decide to write down *motivated or caused by a person's beliefs or actio*ns.

Gordon walks over. "Toni Morrison once said that 'all good art is political,'" he murmurs, then glides away.

Who's Toni Morrison? I keep my mouth shut because no one else asks.

"So is bad art not political?" asks Hannah the dancer.

"I guess I see the point that everything we create is influenced by the world around us, so, like, it makes a difference if I write a story about homeless people in a rich country when I live in a country that doesn't care about homeless people," says a boy.

"This is giving me ideas," whispers Natasha at one point. "As a filmmaker, I have an opportunity to work through a social justice lens."

Wow, she picked up the lingo fast. "I wanted to sign up for filmmaking, but it was full," I say. "But whatever, like I said, I'm here to hang with my brother and have fun. I don't have anything like this at home."

"But it's like they're saying . . . then what?" asks Natasha. "What will your legacy be?"

"I'm thirteen," I say. "I'm pretty sure I don't need to think about that now."

"I don't think we should have to," says another girl, nodding. "Like why does everything have to be so heavy all the time?"

Counselors and junior counselors are group facilitators, which means they keep us on track and try to keep us from joking around too much. I see Luke with his group and wave, and he waves back without smiling. I'm guessing that Derek, who's in his group and all up in his face, is getting on his nerves. Charisse and Gordon walk around and listen to the conversations, but they don't say much. They flash questions on a big screen, things like "How can art empower communities?" and "Which Black lives matter more, and whose stories do we tell?" and tell us these are the things we'll be talking about this summer. Whoa. And the thing is, people like Natasha and Michelle really are talking like they have real things to say. I feel like I'm in one of those dreams when I didn't know there was a test and it's too late to study.

Our group's discussion kind of peters out, and Marcus gets on his phone, so I stand to stretch my legs. Luke is leading a conversation about Jacob Lawrence and the Great Migration. He's taking every point that Gordon and Charisse had made and breaking it down, connecting it to people like Faith Ringgold so even the youngest kids start nodding their heads and buzzing about their own projects. He's waving his hands a lot while he talks and squats down low to listen whenever one of the little kids talks. Even though we're in a totally new environment, Luke seems so confident and smart and separate—less like my brother by the minute. He'll definitely be able to tell me about this Toni Morrison guy. I try to catch his eye when Derek says something pretentious about knowing Auntie Kara Walker, but Luke doesn't look my way. He goes over to Gordon and Charisse and gets into a huddle with them. I stand close to them until Marcus notices me.

"Hey, Emmett, you good?" he calls out. He steps

away from the counselor he's been talking to. She escapes immediately, rolling her eyes, but he doesn't notice.

"Yeah, I'm fine," I say. "Just going to have a word with my brother." I point to Luke.

Luke excuses himself from Gordon and Charisse and comes over. "What's up, E?"

"I heard you talking about those artists," I say. "You were really schooling everybody!"

"I did get an art scholarship to Rowell," he reminds me. "It's kind of my thing."

"Who's Toni Morrison? He sounds like fire."

"*She* was an amazing writer. Nobel Prize winner. You'll read one of her books in high school, probably in Ms. Hartwell's class. Hartwell's ignorant, don't let her ruin it for you. She's still mad *Huck Finn* isn't required reading anymore."

I'm just glad I didn't make myself look stupid just now by saying *he* out loud to anyone but Luke.

"What about Kara Walker? Who's . . . that?" I'm not taking any chances on gender pronouns.

"She does all kinds of amazing paintings, silhouettes, large installations . . . I'm planning to do an independent study on her next year. There's a kid here who knows her— he actually calls her auntie!"

"Maybe he was making it up," I mumble. "Some people do that."

"Hey, is Marcus your counselor?" Luke asks. "He's cool. You're in good hands." At the moment, Marcus is up in another counselor's face, making a lot of big gestures, and judging by the look on her face, he might want to invest in some mouthwash.

I shrug. "I guess. His hands seem to be more focused on other things." I try to wiggle my eyebrows, but Luke's not looking at me. He pats my shoulder.

"I gotta get back to my group," he says, and leaves. Marcus comes over and guides me over to some other kids who are talking about old school hip-hop groups like Public Enemy and X Clan.

"My mom likes to go on and on about the nineties conscious rap," says a girl. "But I know gangsta rap was big then too."

Charisse is taking notes. "Oooh, we should have a debate about hip-hop and what people think is for the culture, who decides what's harmful to the community . . ."

"How about what's fun?" Hannah says "It's all just *music*! It's not that deep."

"We can talk about regional rap too," says Gordon coming over.

"My dad still won't acknowledge anything outside of New York City as hip-hop," says a girl.

Charisse says a few lines that sound familiar.

"What's that from?" I ask. I've heard Uncle Davidson say those lyrics. I'm thinking it might be Boogie Down Productions, but I'm not sure. Not trying to look like I don't know anything about hip-hop either.

Her eyes are about to pop out of her head. "Really, dude?" She frowns. "We can't go Black to the Future without knowing our past," she says, and a couple of kids nod, like they aren't just as clueless as me. "You've got to know your roots!"

"BDP—Boogie Down Productions," whispers Natasha. "'The Bridge Is Over.' 1986 or 1987. I need to review the classic hip-hop category."

Argh! I *did* know it.

"And just so you know," says one of the other counselors. "Big ups to Jamaica. Hip-hop was started by a

Jamaican named Kool Herc in the Bronx because we always start the party right." He whoop-whoops, and a bunch of people join in. I want to, but I hear *Ja-fakin* in my head, so I just smile and raise a fist halfway.

"Who wants to present on this?" asks Charisse. "I'd love to see somebody dig into the roots of rap. Maybe shout out to female MCs—y'all think Nicki Minaj is an OG. What do you know about MC Lyte? Sweet Tee?"

"How old *are* you?" asks a girl, and everyone laughs. "I think my *Nana* was friends with MC Lyte."

After we talk for a while longer and end up shouting out a bunch of different lyrics, Gordon claps us all quiet. "I'm hearing some great questions on top of questions, and that's cool. You're not going to find answers here in one meeting. Maybe not by the time camp is over."

Charisse says, "Maybe not ever. But we believe that the questions are important." A boy raises his hand. "And no," she says, "there isn't going to be a test." The boy slowly puts his hand down, and we all laugh.

"We're encouraging you to continue the conversations informally," says Charisse. "During your free time, at meal times . . . I know this is a change up, but the world is changing, and some of us believe that DuBois has to change too." She looks like she wants to say more, but just adds, "Take advantage of being in this space; it's precious."

"You said informal, but I don't see any snacks," mutters Hannah. "Informal gatherings of Black people *showing up and showing out* should always include snacks, is all I'm saying." She nudges me and rolls her eyes. I smile, but not too much, because Natasha is nearby, and I'm not trying to look like a lightweight. The truth is, I don't know what I think, except that I need time to think about it. Luke is rounding up his group, and as we file out of the room, he sees me and waves, a smile on his face. Other people notice, and I know that's why he did it. Troy waves and says, "Hey, E," and we walk out together with Charles, Michelle, Natasha, and some other kids. I turn to Luke and wave back.

Chapter Sixteen

"Everyone has to take the test," says the woman with the clipboard. Her hair is pulled back into a tight bun, and her lips are so tight I'm surprised words can even escape her mouth. She looks like the type of person who always has a clipboard. "Even people who say they 'don't swim.'"

I can feel the air quotes in her tone. I can feel the line behind me getting restless. I can feel my stomach doing flip flops. Under normal circumstances, I'd say that this pool was impressive. There are two diving boards at one end, and the three foot, five foot, and nine foot (!!!) markers all look freshly painted. The water is clean and allegedly not too cold. But I'm still shivering in my old blue swim trunks. This is not going how I expected, and I don't see Luke anywhere.

"Ensuring swimming proficiency is one of the most important traditions at DuBois. You will be assessed. You will be placed in the appropriate group for your skill level." She moves her lips into something almost like a smile. It looks like it takes a lot of effort. "Don't worry, the test isn't a big deal. You just swim across the baby pool."

I want to explain that I know I can't swim, so why

waste everyone's time and laugh muscles on a swim test, but I can't get the words out and she tells me to take my number and move on.

I walk over to the "baby pool" and offer to forfeit and just be named a beginner, avoid public humiliation, but nooooooo, they wanted to "assess" us each individually. I stand in the back and try to keep a low profile. Any hopes I'd held that a camp full of Black people might have a plethora of non-swimmers are dashed within minutes. The people I met from my dorm jump right in, laughing and easy. Everyone from sixth grade on up seems to be about to get their lifeguard certification. Even these two girls who say they spent too much time on their first day hairstyles to ruin them finally put on DuBois swim caps and get in. I see Luke, standing in front of a group of little kids.

"Luke!" I call out. "This swimming thing, they're saying I have to do it. Can you talk to somebody for me?"

He glances over and frowns. "E, man, I'm working right now. Take the test."

"Maybe I can postpone?" I say, figuring I can come up with a way out if I buy a little extra time. "You could give me lessons during your breaks."

He doesn't answer, just shakes his head and moves his group over to the pool.

My turn goes just as badly as I expected, and after I splash around, swallow an enormous amount of water, and ignore the giggles, I'm assigned to Novice 0.

Charles, Michelle, and Natasha look away as I approach them, and I grab my towel without saying a word. I walk over to my Novice 0 groupmates, who are standing next to the little pool, which is three feet deep. They incidentally are not much bigger than three feet tall themselves.

"I have to pee," says a boy as I approach.

"That's what the water is for, Lance," says a confident kid next to him. "Don't worry, we're getting in soon."

"Ewwwwww!" cries a girl, stepping forward. "I'm telling!" She fast-walks over to the instructors.

"You look big," says Lance, the need-to-pee boy.

That's a new one for me. I shrug.

"He's a junior counselor swim helper, dumbhead," says the confident kid. "One of the cool guys."

"Actually," I say, "my brother is a junior counselor. He's over there." I point to where Luke is standing.

"Your brother's cool," says Lance. "He showed me a shoe-tying trick this morning."

That was *my* shoe-tying trick. "Yeah?" I say. "He taught that to me when I was a baby."

"You still look like a baby," says the confident kid.

"I thought you said I looked big."

"Lance said that. And that was before. Now your brother looks big."

What grade are you in?" I ask.

"First," they answer in unison.

Great.

"Are you our teacher? Or are you in this group?" asks Lance. "I still have to pee."

I'm rescued from having to explain by our instructor, whose name is Brant. He gets us into the water and starts us on "froggying," which is as mortifying as it sounds.

"Yoooo, that's the new kid I was telling you about," says a voice I already recognize. My stomach tightens up: Derek. I stumble in the water, and he laughs. "Bruh. You really can't swim like that?" He starts laughing and his buddies, who in comics would definitely be called henchmen, join in.

"D, he might be on scholarship or something," says

one of his friends in a not-low-enough voice. "There are kids here who've never *seen* a pool." The friend holds up his hand in my direction. "Ignore Derek," he says, like he's not dissing me to my face, just in a fake polite way. "There are other Fresh Air types here, I'm sure. You're doing great!"

I don't answer, and they barely pretend to stifle their laughter.

"Move on, guys," says Brant. "Shower and change, you're going to use up your free period."

As they walk away, still laughing like cartoon villains. I stand there, stupid and still, in three feet of water. Water that feels . . . suspiciously warm all of a sudden.

I look at Lance. "Did you just—"

A whistle blows. "Everybody out of the baby—I mean little pool!" yells Brant.

Lance starts to cry.

Chapter Seventeen

I have free time after the Great Pool Disaster, and I'm in no rush to see anyone. I wonder if Charles is waiting for me at the dorm, and what he'll say if he is. Or worse, if he talks a lot and tries to pretend that I'm not a joke . . . Ugh.

I'm relieved when the room is empty. The dorm is pretty quiet in general, and I shower and change into my Adidas audition outfit. While I practice in the mirror, I keep picturing Derek sitting next to the judges while I audition, making cracks about pee pants and baby pools. I've got to learn to swim.

I throw myself facedown onto my bed (ouch). It's not that I can't swim. I mean, okay, I can't swim. But I haven't tried to learn. I just get all tight whenever I get near water. Swimming makes me think of my dad. One of the last things we'd all done together was go to the Y with the Olympic-size pool for family swim, and he'd been in a great mood all day, running and jumping into the water over and over. Then we'd gone out for pizza and Mom had even let us get soda—real Coke, not just okay-with-grownups ginger ale—but by the time we'd gotten into the car to go home, Dad had gotten quiet. I asked him what was wrong a couple of times, and he didn't answer, and when he looked at me it was like there were ghosts behind his eyes. Luke had pulled me over to him and whispered "It's just Low Dad time, okay? I'll read to you when we get home." And he did. He'd read *Clean Your Room, Harvey Moon!* sixteen times until I fell asleep.

There's a fast knock at the door.

"Hey, Marcus," I say. "I'm good." Just in case he has a script for some kind of Inspirational Counselor Conversation.

"It's me," says Luke. I open the door for my brother. He's got a giant bag of chips and a couple of milk shakes.

"I didn't know they had shakes here," I say. "And isn't the dining hall closed?"

"I know people," he says, and we sit on the floor next to the bed. "I heard it was rough out there after I left."

"You heard? Great. So everyone's talking about my swim fail?"

"No, I just know Brant, and he knows you're my brother, so . . ."

Being known as Luke's brother is supposed to be my badge of honor, not Luke's shame. "What did he tell you?"

"He just said you didn't pass. Look, be glad you'll learn to swim here, it's way past time. Brant is a great guy, and from what I hear, he's an amazing coach. He'd probably even help you out during free periods if you ask."

"Why can't *you* help me out?" I say. "I'm a fast learner and . . . you know how to teach me." A whine creeps into my voice before I can stop it. "Remember, you were going to help me learn to swim this summer anyway."

"This is a *job* for me, remember? Not a vacation," he says, looking away from me. As he looks around my room, I realize that he hasn't even shown me what his room looks like. I wonder if the junior counselors have fluffier beds or fireplaces or something.

"Listen, you brought yourself here—and I backed you up. I used a lot of capital taking on Mom for that. So, come on, make the most of it."

"You're acting like I'm a problem or something," I say. "So okay, what about helping me get out of the class."

"You can't escape this time. " He sighs. "And you know, you came here to do stuff, right?"

I nod, but I don't say, *I came here to be with you.*

"What do you have next?"

"I'm auditioning for Street Style," I say. "I was going to do my old-school New Jack Swing routine. I heard the teacher likes vintage moves."

"You'll kill it!" Luke says. "Listen, I gotta get back. I just wanted to make sure you were okay. You got this audition, E. And the swimming thing—don't worry about it. You can do it."

"Do you want to see me run through the routine? It's only three minutes, and I—"

"E, I'm sorry." Luke pats my shoulder. "Ask Marcus to watch, or one of your little friends. I gotta go, there's a kid who's going to help me out in the art room, set up projects and stuff, put out supplies. He's gonna be like my intern, isn't that sweet? Anyway, I've got to meet with him."

"*I* could do that," I say. "Why didn't you tell me you needed an intern? I didn't know they had interns here." I point to the shakes and chips. "We didn't even open the bag!"

"Share with your roommate, I've got to go," says Luke, heading toward the door. "Have fun at the audition. Like I said, you got this." He leaves, closing the door quietly.

"Thanks for the snacks," I say, too late. *One of my*

little friends. Yeah, okay. And what did he mean by I can't escape, *this time*? I take the top off a shake and finish it in one big gulp, and put the other one in the mini fridge for Charles. When I open my door, I see Marcus down the hall. He waves, and I wave back but don't say anything. If Luke can't help me, I'm on my own. I take a deep breath and open the bag of chips. If there's one thing I can do, it's dance. I hear Luke's voice in my head. "I got this," I whisper to myself. "I got this."

***

It takes me a few minutes to find the right studio, so when I get to Street Style auditions, class has already begun. I try to sneak into the back, but the person who I'm assuming is the teacher (he hits me with some serious side eye) isn't having it; he points me to a seat up front. I see that girl Hannah from Black to the Future, and she gives me a not-so-sympathetic smirk. I'm not exactly late, because he's doing a demo class before auditions, so those of us trying out can get a feel for what the class is like. It seems like the main difference between his class and military boot camp is just music—they are moving *fast*.

There are three of us on the audition list, and one guy crosses his name off in the middle of class, and then I hear a girl doing the old preempt, talking loud about how she has an ankle injury and really shouldn't be dancing on it. I know that strategy, and her technique is pretty good, but the teacher (I confirm it's him when one of the junior counselors calls him Triple M) just looks at her. He's wearing a hoodie and cutoff sweatpants, and he bangs a giant wooden staff on the floor with every eight count. "Anyone who dares to do jazz hands or spirit fingers in this room after today will run five-K a day, is that understood?" he growls.

In what feels like five seconds, class is over and it's time for auditions. Sprained Ankle Girl says she can't stand up. Triple M points to me with his stick.

"Your turn, Sparky," he says. Sparky? I hope that doesn't stick. I get up slowly, and go to the computer to start my music. It starts with an old-school joint called *Rump Shaker*—Mom had told me that it was a new jack swing classic, and since she was around in the olden days for that music, I trusted her. But now . . . I swallow. Was I about to make a fool of myself? I miss my cue and have to start the music again. I hear a few giggles.

"If you need a moment," says Triple M in a silky voice, "you don't have one. Start or begone." He smiles an evil smile. "And just so you know, we don't *need* another dancer. We're just fine as is."

5-6-7-8. I start.

***

I! Killed! It! I started with the routine I'd done in the spring talent show at school, but then Triple M asked me to freestyle and I went right into my own version of an updated Milly Rock that flows into some of the stuff I'd seen online from a seventies show called *Soul Train*. *Soul Train* was like *the* Black people dance show—and the outfits people wore were *out* there! Anyway, I imagined I was an action figure in the toy section of a store who comes to life after closing time. I was a little worried that it would seem too kiddie, but everybody laughed at the right moments when I pretended to be exploring the store and trying not to get caught by a security guard.

I think a few of the kids in the class had heard about my swim test fiasco, because there'd been some whispering when I walked in, but the whispering after my audition is totally different. Excited. Impressed.

Triple M is stone-faced the whole time I dance, and my heart is pounding as I try to catch my breath when I'm done. Then he just says, "Welcome to street style," without smiling. I'm in! See? Even though Luke had been all stressed and weird, he'd said his magic words and gave me the power to do my thing.

We start a new group routine right away and it's hard, but I go all out, and I even stay after to go over some moves with a few other kids. I'm the most me I've been since I got to DuBois. Triple M tells us that since it's our major, we have a double period of class every day, plus an independent study period where we're supposed to rehearse, do research (in dance?), and "create and marinate."

"And as many of you know, I will choose a select few for the dance battle on Camp Showcase night," he says. "You have just under three weeks to show me what you've got."

"Is the dance battle like a competition?" I whisper to the girl next to me. She gives back the slightest of nods, not taking her eyes off Triple M.

Ooh, a chance to win an award! I'm on it.

In the second half of class, Triple M has us watch clips of that movie *Beat Street* that Uncle Davidson had told me about. It has a bunch of people in it that I never heard of, but Triple M says they're hip-hop legends, so I pay attention. The moves are tight, the colors are amazing—the graffiti is like nothing I've ever seen. Whenever I've watched old movies about New York City, everything is gray and ugly and scary. I'm going to add this to the film fest list. Triple M says that when he was a kid he got trained by the Rock Steady Crew, who were big time breakdancers, apparently.

"B-boying, krumping, there's a history there that you

need to know," says Triple M, and he's mad serious, like a priest in a scary movie. "In this class, we're not going to be just about showing off the moves you *think* you invented"—he kind of glances my way—"we're going to delve into the foundations of hip-hop culture as well."

"Y'all better just give Atlanta our props," yells out a girl. "We transformed hip-hop culture—Dirty South foreva! Right, Triple M?"

He gives her a look that lowers the temperature of the entire room.

"Uh, excuse me . . . Mr. Micah McDowell," she says. "This is my last year at DuBois, and I, um, heard, that seniors . . ." Her voice drops a little, but the boy next to her nudges her, and she goes on. "That seniors can call you Triple M . . ."

It gets downright Arctic fast. He doesn't even have to say a word.

"I apologize, Mr. Micah McDowell," she murmurs.

It turns out that we're going to be doing reports and presentations and stuff in this class too. "What is this?" whispers Hannah. "Can Black people get a little fun out of life?"

Triple M (Mr. Micah McDowell) tells us about a guy named Crazy Legs and asks for a volunteer to do a presentation on him in one of the next class sessions. I raise my hand, partly I want to get on Triple M's good side and partly because I'm realizing there's this whole world that's part of my world that I never knew about. I kind of want to know more, even if there's not going to be a test. Maybe Charles has a hip-hop encyclopedia I can read.

"Okay, Sparky," he says. "Next session. Two-minute oral report on Crazy Legs, and please be prepared to show us a routine of your own creation in his style."

"Uh, by tomorrow?" I ask. And should I say something

about Sparky?

"Is that a problem?"

"No . . . nope, not at all, Mr. Micah McDowell . . . sir."
I feel like I should be saying Your Highness.

"It shouldn't be. Class dismissed. And whoever is trying to asphyxiate us all with that horrific Lemon Chill body spray, do not even think about coming to my class tomorrow smelling like fruit-flavored bologna."

Chapter Eighteen

The next day flies by, with intro sessions in the Great DuBois Baking Show, which is forty minutes of reciting kitchen safety rules; ceramics, where we sit and commune with our lumps of clay by rolling and smooshing them around; and a free period, during which I hide in my dorm room and practice interesting things to say to Natasha. Charles leaves to practice his interesting music in a soundproof practice room.

Aside from Derek, who snickers loudly every time I see him, nobody mentions my swim test. I almost forget about it until Charles, Michelle, and Natasha use our second free period to go out in the little pedal boats. At first, they pretend they just want to watch other people do it, but I know they're being nice, so I tell them that I want to rehearse in one of the dance studios anyway.

I find one that's empty and start making up a routine inspired by the New York City I saw in Beat Street. I start with the six-step and am out of breath so fast. I'm going to have to hit up the gym in order to do anything for more than two minutes this summer. I can tell Street Style is gonna be a whole lot more than popping and locking in the hall between classes. Triple M asked a couple of seniors to demonstrate air flares and my eyes almost popped out of my head when this girl did fifty.

I get so into it that I almost miss dinner, but as I'm trying to refine my toprock, Charles comes to get me.

"Nice toprock," he says.

"Yo! How'd you know what it was? You didn't mention that you breakdance too," I say. "Why aren't you in Street Style?"

"I don't, but I have a really good *Encyclopedia of Hip-Hop Culture*," he says. "Two volumes. Feel free to check it out anytime."

I knew it! I'm grateful, for the sake of my presentation, even though I can't imagine learning about hip-hop from a book, but whatever. I sign up for more studio time during the week and we head to the dining room. It's make-your-own-tacos night; there's also a pasta buffet and my motto is "Why not both?". That was one of the meals that WeeDee and Billy had warned me about (and they'd taught me the "Beans" song that they said was a "classic"), but here at DuBois, everything is fresh and spicy, and there is even a Baja option—fish tacos with lime and coleslaw. It's petty, but I have to flex and take pictures of my food and text them to WeeDee. I like the idea of DuBois camp being so much better than their bare-bones barracks and canned gray beans "with no flavor and maximum aromatic fart potential," according to Billy. Michelle and Natasha go off to train for the Blackity Bowl, and I know I need to work on my presentation, but first I ask Charles to come with me to find the big Afro counselor to teach me the step routine from the first night.

By the time I get back to the dorm that night, I'm

exhausted. Charles marches off to the library after our step lesson (I really have to talk to him about toning down the walk), so I have the room to myself for a while. I stretch out across my bed, feeling the three helpings of ravioli alla genovese and four slices of strawberry pie that I'd wolfed down at dinner. I'd only caught a glimpse of Luke on my way back to the dorm; he'd given me a quick thumbs-up before he went back to talking to some crying little kid. I check my phone again; no messages from Mom, which surprises me. I decide to FaceTime her myself and check in.

"Hey, sweet potato pie, are you okay?" she says, putting her face way too close to the screen.

"Yeah, I'm fine, Mom, only don't say the word *pie*," I say, holding my stomach. "Just checking in, since you didn't." That last part comes out sounding accusatory, and okay, I guess it is.

She takes a breath and smiles. "I'm trying to let my babies grow up. But don't think you're too grown. How's it going for Luke? I doubt I'll hear from him. I know he's got a lot on his plate."

I have a lot on my plate too. "I guess he's okay," I say. "I don't see him that much." I decide to leave it at that. "But things are okay here." If you don't count my swimming fail and pee pants, it's cool. "The food is really good." I guess I *had* a lot on my plate today. I crack myself up.

She smiles. "I'm so glad you're enjoying it, honey. You're officially off punishment, by the way."

Woot! "Thanks, Mom. Oh—I got into Street Style," I say. "The dance class. I'm already thinking of entering the dance battle at the end of the summer."

"Yeah, boyeeeeee!" She backs away from her computer and starts doing the robot.

"MOM!" I don't even want God to see her doing that.

"I knew you would! So proud of you, sweetie—oops, honey!"

"Thanks, Mom. How's studying?"

"I'm getting so much done," she says, smiling wide. "In fact, I'm about to go out on an ice cream break with some people."

ICE CREAM! BREAK! WITH! PEOPLE! I remember what Luke had said.

"What people?" I ask.

"My study group," she answers. "I met some people who are also taking the test in September too. And I'm not the only elder! There's a man named Brian who's my age; it's great."

Worse and worse. "What's so great about it?" I ask coldly. "And do you really think you should be doing that sort of thing?"

"What, studying so that I can realize my lifelong dream of becoming a doctor, or eating ice cream?" She laughs.

"I'm just saying . . . you banished us so that you could study, so . . . maybe go easy on the breaks."

"Well, excuuuuse me," she says. "Did you forget that you literally went behind my back and got yourself into this camp?"

Oh. Yeah, I guess I did.

She's not done. "A few days away from home and you really do think you're grown. Don't think I can't snatch you up right through this phone!"

"Mom! I'm thirteen! You can't talk like that anymore."

"You're still my baby, Emmett. And you're just thirteen, barely out of twelve."

"Mom, I'm practically fourteen—"

She goes on. "Not even close. And I'm your mother

and will talk to you—Okay, wait. Pause." We had a family rule to say "pause" anytime a discussion was in danger of getting heated.

After a minute, I speak up. "I'm sorry . . . I just miss you," I say. "And I *am* fully thirteen. Can't deny that"

She rolls her eyes. "You *should* miss me!" We both laugh. "Seriously, it's your first real time away from home, it's normal to be homesick. You'll adjust, I promise. And I'm just a little on edge about school. It's kind of hitting me, what I've taken on, and I . . . it's a lot."

"You can do this, Mom," I say. "You're brilliant. Remember, you take after me." We laugh again, and it fills the distance between us in a way that makes me feel warm and a little scared at the same time.

"So is that place as amazing as it seems?" asks Mom. "And what is it like, being in the midst of all of that Black excellence? That must be so much fun. They haven't had the likes of you before, I'm sure. Go easy on them, okay?"

Ha. I'm not exactly the smartest kid in the room anymore. "Oh yeah, I am," I say. "I'm trying not to unleash all my superpowers full force, just yet."

After a few more minutes of conversation, I hear a horn honk in the background. "That's probably Brian and the rest," says Mom. "Gotta go get my banana split on. I'll talk to you soon, okay, pumpkin? Oh! I saw WeeDee and Billy yesterday. They both got jobs at the mall. They seemed so grown up, which is not something I thought I'd be saying about those two."

We talk for a minute longer, she makes kissy faces at me through the phone, and after I double check to make sure that no one outside can see me through the window or anything, I make them back.

We hang up, and I text Luke to see if he can come by

with some more contraband snacks. Then Charles marches in.

"You really don't have to keep walking like that," I say. "Maybe just when Michelle's around."

He relaxes. "I thought it would be good to practice, but honestly, if she can't love me at my Steve Urkel, then she can't truly love me at my Black Panther either."

"Who's Steve Urkel? Actually, never mind. Anyway, you're right," I say, strolling in a little circle. "If you don't have swagger, then you just don't." I smile, to let him know I'm joking, and he rolls his eyes and laughs.

Then he gets serious. "But . . . there is a dance at the end of camp, and, uh . . . you might have noticed that I'm not the best dancer. Can you help me? We've got two and a half weeks."

"I'm your guy!" I say. "I told you, I learned from Luke, the Master of the Mack. And today's Street Style classes were so good. I bet I can incorporate some of the stuff I'm learning there! You already got the terminology. We'll take it to the next level, a couple back flips out on the field, maybe?"

He gulps. "Uhhhh. There are levels to this?"

"Okay, let's not get ahead of ourselves," I say. "Want to show me a few moves?"

Charles nods, takes a deep breath, and counts to eight. Then he gets into a pose that looks like something between doing a two-point stance in football and being really constipated.

"Huh," I say. "Okay, um, let's get some beats going." I open the music app on my phone and start my Swag Style playlist. "Go, Charles! Go, Charles!" I chant. "Show me what you got!"

And, well . . . he doesn't got a lot. He jerks from side

to side a few times, then starts high stepping, lifting his knees on the one and three. Then he shouts, "Wave your hands in the air!" while he makes window-cleaning motions.

Oh, man.

Finally, mercifully, he stops, and looks expectantly at me.

"Well . . ." I start, and clear my throat. "So . . . um . . ." I close my mouth and then open it again. "Wow, that was . . ."

Charles starts laughing. "I KNOW!" he says. "And those were my smoothest moves! I've been practicing since last summer." He falls back onto his bed, laughing, and after a beat, I join in, until we're both out of breath.

Then I show him how to clap on the two and four, which takes a while. "Bruh, how are you a musician?" I ask. "Like shouldn't your bassoon skills translate to your feet or something?"

"Very funny. At least you're not like those kids at my school who are always asking me to show them how to dance 'Black.'"

"What do you do?"

"This!" He starts his jerky robot zombie frenzy again, and we laugh until Marcus knocks and reminds us that it's lights out/volume low time.

"Yo, did you ever see the old movie *Can't Buy Me Love*?" I ask as we're getting ready for bed. Charles shakes his head. "There's the original, and then they had a Black version too. Your moves just reminded of this ridiculous scene from the first version. The main guy does the African anteater ritual at a school dance. Like what did that even mean, African anteater ritual? It was pretty racist now that I think about it."

"Kind of a requirement for old teen movies, right?" says Charles, shrugging. He robots out of the room to get ready for bed.

Talking about movies makes me think back to that film fest conversation with WeeDee and Billy. I felt just as far away from them when we were all together as I do now. Sometimes it feels like I'm in a river, and the current's real strong, and I have a choice between clinging to a rock and getting left behind, or letting myself get swept up in it and carried along without any control. Luke's my rock; when the kids here know that I'm his brother, they'll get that respect look in their eyes that Lamar had when he found out. And then when they see me winning . . . maybe I'll make new friends.

Charles comes back and turns out the lights. "Maybe I'll just do what I do," he says. "I'll play for her. At the end of camp showcase, or even better – the last Night Hike."

"You've got enough instruments for it," I say. "Seriously, that's a good idea. And Night Hike sounds all romantic, that'll work."

"Keytar?" he asks.

"Bruh. I saw you take that out yesterday. What is that even?"

He laughs, and we talk a little more about how to get Michelle to sit long enough to listen to Charles play. He advocates for them all, but I tell him to settle on one of his instruments, and not the keytar.I lay quietly in my bed for a long time, looking out of the window. The sky is inky black and for the first time, I can actually see stars twinkling, just like the song.

When Charles starts snoring, I slip out of bed and grab Mr. Elefancy and Boo Boo from my suitcase for the first time , then bring them back to my bed. I slide them both under my pillow and close my eyes.

Chapter Nineteen

Finally doing my Crazy Legs presentation. Triple M made me sweat about it for two days after he told me to have it done in twenty four hours. I dance first, and I think I see Triple M crack a smile when I made sure to do the signature W move at the end. The rest of the class was all, "Ayyyyeeee!", so they liked it, at least.

My voice shakes a little at the beginning of my speech because of Triple M's laser eye, but I'm pretty excited to talk about Crazy Legs. Between being off phone restriction and Charles' handy hip-hop encyclopedias, I learned a lot. (He also had a book called *Double Snaps* and we stayed up way past lights on reading insults that we'd never dare to use on Derek.)

"His real name is Richard Colón," I say, and Triple M stops me.

"His dance identity is not real?" he asks.

"I mean, yeah, I meant —"

"His dance identity is linked to his other identities, yes?"

I nod.

"Inextricably linked?"

That was a spelling bee word, so I know how it looks, but I don't know what *inextricably* means. It seems like I should just nod, so I do.

A girl raises her hand. "He could say his 'government name.'"

"Uh," I say, thinking fast, "Crazy Legs, aka Richard Colón—" I pause, but Triple M doesn't say anything, so I continue. "Is from New York *and* he's Puerto Rican—"

"Boricua!" yells someone. "Nuyorican Power!"

I wait for the laughs to end, and I go on. "He was in a movie called *Wild Style*, and he went from street dance battles to competitions all over the world. Fun fact: He was a body double for the lady in the eighties movie *Flashdance*, like for this—" I get down and do a quick backspin, which gets me some applause. "I knew about that movie, but I didn't know that."

"Crazy Legs was a leader of the Rock Steady Crew, which was a b-boy crew, and he also won a Bessie Award for choreography," I say, to wrap up. "And he's still alive! He went down to Puerto Rico to help make sure people got clean water after Hurricane Marie."

Triple M rolls his eyes. "Yes, what a surprise. He's still alive, all the way in his fifties."

"Exactly!" I say. "He's still teaching and doing workshops and community activism and stuff."

Everyone claps when I finish, and after class ends I hang back.

"Thanks, Mr. Micah McDowell, for the assignment, I learned a lot," I say.

"Isn't that a coincidence?" he says, slinging his bag over his shoulder. "Because you've got a lot to learn."

"Seriously, that's him really liking you." I hadn't

realized that this girl named Jeimy is still in the room. "He only talks like that to the ones he thinks are really good."

I shrug. "Uh, okay. Thanks." I'm determined to impress Triple M. Somehow I'm gonna stand out at this place—and in a good way.

***

After the first few days, I get into rhythm, especially in Street Style (get it?). Chorus straight up turned out to be a bunch of us who can't sing at all. Many of us are in this class because it was one of the few electives still open at the last minute, and it shows. Or should I say, sounds. There's that guy again who sings everything instead of speaking, just so he can pull compliments, and this other guy, Jeffrey James, tries to do the same thing but he does a lot of runs and sings through his nose—and he's as bad as the rest of us scrubs, just louder.

Today two girls who are sisters and think they're Chloe and Halle are trying to get us to do "sectionals."

"Y'all don't really want to work!" says fake Chloe. Jeffrey does some runs, extra loud.

"You're flat," says imitation Halle. "LA, LA, LA, LA, LA!" she screeches, and I have to clench my fists like Arthur in the cartoon to keep from covering my ears. "Like that," she says, and she even bows a little like she's getting a standing ovation. "Come on, everyone, can we do this?"

Then fake Chloe starts giving instructions that no one understands, and Jeffrey "I Have to Put My Finger in the Air and Wave It Around" James, keeps interrupting and talking over them both.

"Um, did I miss something?" he asks into the air for the third time. "How did they get to be in charge?"

I kind of agree, but at least they're trying. I want to

say that, but Jeffrey's been coming to DuBois for five years; he has clout.

"I know, right? I mean, how?" says Kristin, walking over to stand next to Jeffrey. She says "Yes!" every time he sings a note. Definitely a clout chaser.

Bootleg Chloe and Halle march around and keep trying to organize us; they end up shouting themselves hoarse before class even starts.

Our teacher, Calvin, does the warmup claps and we shuffle into position. I try to slide into the back row, but he waves me up front, saying, "You won't be able to see my direction!" just to make sure everyone remembers that I'm short. "Zing-zing-zing-za! ZING-zing-zing-ZA!" We sound like my cat, Kangol, that time he got locked out in the rain.

After about two minutes Calvin looks like he's going to cry. "Are ya'll even trying?" he asks. "I was planning to have you do the DuBois song for the parents when they pick you up, but this . . . this is a travesty!"

"Maybe it could be a solo," says Jeffrey, and the collective groan that suggestion brings out is more harmonious than any sound we've made yet, for real. Calvin cheers up a little after that, we squawk a little more and then everyone's glad it's over and I head from purgatory to hell.

***

"There it is, team, the Promised Land—aka the Isle!" says Brant, pointing to the lake.

The Promised Land is a stupid little island of dirt in the middle of the lake that level three and up swimmers can swim out to and sit around on. There are a couple of trees, some hammocks, and those long beach chairs that people stretch out and try to flex on. Older kids sneak snacks from the vending machines onto the rowboats and stash food in a cooler over there. The staff pretends not to know. Charles brought two waterproof card decks over, and Dr. Triphammer is giving Spades lessons to anyone who asks— and also anyone who's just there minding their business. It's dumb, really. You can do all the same things right here, without going across some stupid lake. I mean, you spend half the period getting there and back. What a waste.

I pretend not to see Charles wave. He and Michelle and Natasha and Troy are out there.

"Your friends are waving," says Lance. "Why aren't you waving back? Do you need glasses too? Where are your swim goggles? I wear them even for just blowing bubbles. Maybe you should too. Do you know how to blow bubbles?"

"You ask a lot of questions," I say, turning away from the Isle and looking at Brant. "And you shouldn't talk while the coach is speaking."

"I'm telling, you're not being a buddy," says this little girl named Monifa, who would snitch on herself if she thought it would score her some points.

I try not to focus on the screams of laughter coming from the Isle. Like, who wants to just swim out to a dirt circle, sit on a towel, then swim right back a few minutes later? Yeah, okay, me. I do. I mean, everyone else my age (and quite a few younger) is out there every day. It's designed to look like a beach, with big yellow-and-blue umbrellas and long red lounge chairs. I heard there's even imported sand. Whatever. I've been doing a great job of pretending that I really want my friends to go without me. So good, I think I should have signed up for drama. Every day, as soon as my class starts, they race out there. And now Troy's hanging with them, they've all been knowing each other; they don't need me.

I try to focus on Brant's speech on keeping our hips up to float.

"Let the water do the work," says Brant. "Allow it to support you."

Monifa the Snitch gets it right away, and I hear Brant tell her that she can take the test for level two tomorrow.

"Emmett, let me help you," says Brant, wading over to me. He holds his arms out in the water, and I'm supposed to kind of hover over them in a float. It hasn't worked yet; it doesn't today. Monifa giggles, and Lance says, "*You're* not a buddy, Monifa. Right, E?"

I just dunk my whole self under the water. *I'm not here*, I think.

I have a double period of swimming today, so I pretend I don't see my friends when they head back to their dorms after all the fun they had on the Isle. But right as me and the rest of my group are about to start working with our kickboards, Charles jogs by again, on his way to orchestra, his bassoon slamming against his back with each step. I know he won't laugh, but I still pretend to be helping another kid so he doesn't see me kicking and flopping around like a dying fish. Even with Charles, I want to keep up appearances as much as possible. It feels like he's my first real friend of my own, not a Luke hand-me-down, and I don't want to mess this up. Unfortunately, the kid yells, "Get off me!" which is not easy to play off. But Charles just gives me a thumbs-up and keeps jogging.

Great: Derek and his crew stroll by.

"Brothers like that Ernest kid should have their Black cards revoked," he says loudly. Then he turns to me, looking all fake shocked. "How do you not know how to swim?" He laughs.

Charles stops, turns around, and comes back. "His

name is Emmett. You know, you should do a little research on the legacy of systematic racism that complicates our community's relationship to swimming. I have a book you can borrow." He lifts a fist in my direction. "Do you, E."

Didn't expect him to take it there, and it has nothing to do with why I don't swim, but I guess that's Charles' way of having my back? And he called me E, so that was something. Derek is still cracking up.

"Don't you have somewhere to be?" asks Brant, glaring at Derek. Derek and his friends leave, still laughing. Brant turns to me. "Come on, I don't want you to lose valuable practice time. You know you can re-test next week, if you want to. Then you'll still have a whole week to hang out on the Isle with your friends."

I already know I don't want to. And I tell Brant that I have a stomachache now.

He looks at me for a minute, then says "Go to the benches over there, take a few minutes, see how you feel, okay?"

I watch the rest of my class practice, and they're giggling and splashing, and they actually graduate from the kickboards pretty fast. Brant is a good teacher. He looks over my way a few times with a question in his eyes, but I just look down and he doesn't push it.

Right on cue, there's Luke walking in my direction, carrying a bunch of blank canvases. I smile.

"Luke!" I call, and wave. He glances behind him, then walks over.

"What are you doing?" he says. "Are you supposed to be in the pool?"

I shrug. "Stomachache." I waited for him to say something sympathetic, but he just puts his canvases down on the bench next to me so he can wipe the sweat off his forehead.

"It's not the same kind of heat we have at home," he says, "but it's still hot, right?"

I nod. We're going to talk about the weather? "We saw this amazing movie in Street Style called *Beat Street*. Uncle Davidson talked about that, and Triple M—well, I have to call him Mr. Micah McDowell, but everyone calls him Triple M—showed us a graffiti movie called *Wild Style*—"

He takes out his phone and checks the time. "E, I've got to get ready for class."

I pull out the big Little Brother guns and slump down on the bench even more. "I'm having a hard time, Luke . . . there's a . . . Mac-type here too." I let out a heavy sigh. "He's making me miserable and I don't know what to do." Okay, maybe I'm laying it on a little thick, but sometimes you gotta go the extra mile to get some attention.

"What?!" Luke turns and looks me full in the face. "Why haven't you said anything? Have you talked to Marcus?" He looks at his phone again though, so I've got to talk fast.

I roll my eyes. "Marcus? He's too busy trying to talk to every female staff member here to pay attention to me." I look over at Luke. "Plus, he knows you're my brother, so I guess he figures I'll have you to talk to, but . . . you're always busy." I just want to hang out for a little while, like we used to. If exaggerating a little means that I can tell him about how good Street Style has been and how I've been giving Charles tips straight from the Luke playbook, and maybe get some tips for how to get closer to Natasha, well . . ." I sigh again. "I get it, though. You're going off to school in the fall, you gotta do you. I'll . . . figure it out." He looks so worried that I feel more than a tiny twinge of guilt, but I remind myself that this is good for us both. We're a team, and things work best for both of us when we focus on that.

"Emmett, E, listen, I know that I—Oh, good, here comes my intern. He's a genius—and he's into filmmaking, like you. Maybe you guys can talk." He points to a group of kids. "Do you know him?" He's pointing toward Derek and his crew, and I want to tell Luke that his intern doesn't have the best taste in friends, but I don't want to sound petty.

"D!" calls out Luke. "Can you help me carry some of this stuff?"

My mouth drops open as Derek comes up to us.

"Do you guys know each other?" asks Luke. "D, this is my brother Emmett." D? And how did he get cooled up to just D while I got demoted back to the full Emmett? Derek and I nod and mumble in each other's general direction. Derek is almost Luke's height, and when he puts one leg up on the bench I'm painfully aware that I am sitting here in my swim trunks, in all my forty-second percentile glory. Right then I picture a *Dictionary of Humiliation* on top of Charles's stack of books, with a picture of me right at that moment, next to the word *puny*.

Derek is clearly aware of my size too, because for no particular reason he stretches and stays on his toes like someone had just told him to explore the space, vertically. "Can my boys and I work out with you later?" he asks Luke. "The gyms here are unbelievable."

Luke smiles and shakes his head. "This whole place is unbelievable. I love it. Sure, I'll be there during evening rec." He looks at me. "Want to come, Emmett?" I ignore Derek's snort-turned-cough.

"Uh, no thanks, I'm busy," I mutter. You know what's unbelievable? My brother, consorting with the enemy. I look away.

"Hey, maybe you can help me with some photos and

stuff, little guy," says Derek, glancing at me. "I might make a short film about Luke for my camp project."

A film? I look at Luke, who's nodding and smiling. "Yeah, he wants to enter a documentary about me in the Showcase competition! I told him to find a real star."

What is happening here? I'm the film guy, Luke knows that! If anyone makes a film about my brother, it's gonna be me!

"Yo, Luke, let me get those too," says Derek, taking all the canvases. "I'll see you in a minute." He glances at me. "Bye, Everett."

"It's Emmett," I say, racking my brain for a good comeback. "Der . . . Der . . . *Daren't.*"

No. No, Emmett. Just no.

Derek just raises his eyebrows and leaves.

"Thanks, D," says Luke. He turns to me. "*Daren't?* Was that because he got your name wrong?" He chuckles. "You got jokes." He gives me a punch in the shoulder and runs off.

If this were a movie, I'd be throwing popcorn at the screen and booing because it was so unrealistic. But it's my life, and I'm gonna have to do something about it.

Chapter Twenty

By the end of the first week, I decide that until I can figure out how to help myself, I can at least help Charles. Well, Luke can, even if it's indirectly. "You got this, Chuck-dog," I say. I've been trying to figure out a good nickname for Charles, but so far, he's been stubborn and we don't have one. It's funny, we kind of have nothing in common, but we're *simpatico* as Charles, (and only Charles), would say.

"It's Charles," he says, without even looking up from the book he's reading. While we walk. He sidesteps a big rock without looking. I'm supposed to be the smooth one between the two of us, but I just tripped over a giant branch on the ground from last night's rain, and *I* was paying attention. I'm working out some ideas for street style choreography as we head to Superhero Secrets, so to be honest, we both probably look a little weird. "Not Chuck-dog, not Charlie, nothing but Charles."

"Not even C?" I try again. We pass the circus class; it's trapeze day so there's a lot of screaming and some cursing that I guess the counselors pretend they don't hear.

"Not even C. Look, I like my name. Now, tell me

again."

"Okay, I think you should just . . . talk to her, but by talk to her, I mean more . . . Listen. Like, when my brother's on the phone with his girlfriend, he barely even talks. He just says 'uh-huh' and 'yeah, I understand' and 'you right, you right' a lot."

Charles nods. "What about the walk? How am I doing?" He takes a couple of steps like he's in one of those Blaxploitation movies from the seventies that Uncle Davidson showed me. Is that what I look like?

I shake my head. "It's time to give that up, bruh. I was wrong. Do *your* thing, and don't be afraid. Ask her questions, listen to the answers, and follow up."

"How do you know this stuff, E? Is there a book that I don't know about?"

Yeah, right. "I just watch my brother. He's smooth. His girlfriend is always texting red heart emojis, not yellow or pink. You'll see. I've been wanting to introduce you, but he's . . . working and stuff."

We walk past some of the kids from my swimming group, and that snot-filled, "Original Pee Pants" Lance kid says, "Hi, Emmett!" really loud. I think he believes we're actual buddies, not just forced swim buddies. I nod quickly and keep it moving.

"It must be nice, having an older brother at home. But when he goes to boarding school next year, you'll have your parents' full attention," says Charles. "Take it from personal only child experience. That can be good and bad. Your dad will try all kinds of bonding things."

"We live with my mother," I say. "My dad died a long time ago."

"Oh, I'm sorry. I didn't—"

"You didn't know," I say. "No worries. Mom says it

is what it is." I pause and say to myself, *That doesn't even make sense.*

"How, um, old . . ."

"I was five when he died," I say. Charles closes his book, sits down on a rock, and without thinking about it, I join him. "My dad . . . he never went to camp." I don't know what made me say that. Charles just waits. "Well, I think that's true. I'm not really sure. But I do know he liked cheeseburgers. Or maybe bacon cheeseburgers. And Ma says he liked sweet potato fries." I swallow hard. I stand up. "Come on, we don't want to be late."

"I'm really sorry, E," says Charles.

"Yeah," I say, not looking at him. "Thanks for . . . I don't . . . nobody talks about my dad anymore. And I wish they did."

Charles stands and pats me on the shoulder, then we both clear our throats and look out the window. We walk regular to the main building for our first session of Superhero Secrets, in silence. It's not a bad silence though.

We pass Marcus, who is leaning against a tree talking to another counselor. She looks bored. I gotta say, he doesn't seem to do a whole lot of "counseling" beyond banging on the door in the morning to make sure we get up, and again at night after lights out, to remind us to go to sleep. Maybe the junior counselors do all the work? My super-busy brother sure acts like he has a lot of junior counseling to do.

"I wish we had this every day instead of . . . other stuff," I say to Charles as we walk into an air-conditioned lounge. No need to bring up swimming, even though I know he won't be mean about it. "Only three sessions is kind of booty."

Neither one of us has said it out loud, but we've been waiting for Superhero Secrets like little kids waiting for Christmas morning. I'd held the flashlight while Charles pored over his bound comic book collection until late last night. ("But we can leave the graphic novel collection out of this, I feel certain that it's going to be more of a pure old-school thing.") Turns out we aren't the only ones excited. Most of us are here early; even the cool kids are curious to know what this is going to be about. Derek is here, talking loud about how he doesn't want to be. Whatever.

Charles nods. "I'm hoping we get to learn spy stuff, like how to crack secret codes."

Class is in a lounge in the main building, and there are plush chairs and couches and small tables around. Since this class meets by age group, I see a lot of familiar faces, and it feels good when a few people from Street Style say hi to me. We see Michelle and Natasha standing next to a couch and head in their direction.

"I wonder if we're going to get some martial arts training," says Natasha. There's space next to her on the couch, but I take the chair nearby. We get quiet as a man wearing a very shiny suit walks into the auditorium.

"How to be the best *you* you can be," he says. Then he nods and stares around at all of us, like he just made sense. "Ahem. Welcome to Superhero Secrets," he goes on, adjusting his bow tie. He looks a little hot and out of place wearing a suit—with a vest—here at DuBois. But I'm thinking maybe he's going to reveal a super suit underneath?

"Be yourself. Be positive. Never give up. We called this workshop Superhero Secrets because it's about developing leadership skills—"

There's a loud collective groan.

Shiny Suit Man holds up his hand. "Sometimes, you feel bad or you feel like you can't do anything right. Maybe someone else is making you feel that way—"

Murmurs from the audience.

"Or something embarrassing happened to you."

I keep my eyes down.

"Whenever you feel low," Shiny Suit Man continues, "you've got to remember that no matter what, YOU CAN BE ANYTHING YOU WANT TO BE." Then he starts a slow clap, and after we look at each other for a while, we join in, but even slower. How corny is this?

"So. Now I'd like you to spend the rest of the class period asking yourself: HOW CAN I BE THE BEST ME I CAN BE?" Then he sits down and takes out his phone.

We're quiet for a few seconds, but after a while people just start talking. The counselors look at each other and shrug.

"Marcus?" I ask. "So . . . is that all . . . is this . . ."

"Yeah, I guess so," he says, and he kind of smirks before he realizes that he's on staff so he should probably act like something awesome just happened. He claps. "All right, people, you got your assignment, get started on those conversations! There's not much time."

"Thank goodness," says Michelle. She takes out a binder. "I need to figure out how to stage the big dance number to end Act One. The two girls playing the Amys are great dancers, so I told them to make up their own dance, but one is all about ballet and the other one is some kind of tap champion."

"So why not incorporate both into the number?" I ask, looking at her binder. It's obvious no one's doing that weak Shiny Suit Man assignment, so we might as well work on a real one.

"Duh, yeah, I'd like to, Emmett. I just have to figure out how."

She tells me more about her play, and I offer to

show her a few examples of moves and sequences. Out of the corner of my eye, I notice Natasha and Derek huddled up, which I guess makes sense because they're both film students, but I'm a little paranoid. Is he making jokes about me?

Charles sighs. "I can't believe I was so excited about this." He takes out a sketchbook. "His suit gives me some ideas for a story, though."

At the end of the period, Shiny Suit Man hands out a workbook called *How to Be the Best YOU You Can Be* and tells us to have it filled out by the next session. I flip through and see quotes like "Never let another person's comments affect your self-esteem. Stay away from negative things" and "Stay focused on your dreams because they DO come true!"

Maybe this is some kind of secret superhero code, I think. Because nothing would be this dumb.

So much for Superhero Secrets. I guess I'm going to have to discover my powers some other way.

Chapter Twenty-One

I've gotten into a whole rhythm by the time Week Two gets going. I've been sliding away to the dorm room in the evenings while Charles, Michelle, and Natasha go to the game center every night. It hasn't been as hard as it could be to convince them that I really want to spend that time studying Latin. At a camp like this, it's normal to meet sixth graders talking about their practice SAT scores.

"See y'all later," I say. "I'm gonna study a few root words before I join you."

The things is, at DuBois, that could actually be true. Not that I haven't been dying to see the game center, but I'm still a little worried that they're just being nice when they invite me to tag along. I was the one who helped WeeDee and Billy with homework and studying for tests; I had a purpose in the friend group. Here, I'm just regular degular shmegular, so I figure they don't need me. Plus, I'm hiding from Derek. But tonight Charles says he will literally come back and drag me out of the room and since I haven't been working out like I meant to, and he's been reading some book called *Build Muscles While You Sleep*, I'm taking no chances. After dinner, I go back to the room, do a few pushups, then head over to the game center.

And it is FIRE. Tons of video games, including a totally eighties section with pinball and arcade games like *Asteroid* and *Pac-Man*, virtual reality . . . Now I'm really overwhelmed, but in a great way.

"E!" Charles runs over. "You finally came to check it out—isn't this awesome? Actually—what I mean is . . ."

I wait for another antiquated etymological term that I've never heard before.

"REALLY awesome!" He laughs, and so do I. Even if we're a crew of two, we're a crew.

He takes me over to the old-school board game room; I see people playing dominoes, Quoridor, and whoa—Boggle! Haven't seen that in a minute. Card games everywhere too – counselors are playing Spades and some of the older staff are playing Black Card Revoked. Michelle, Natasha and some other kids are in a corner, playing Taboo.

"I love Taboo!" yells Charles. I'm about to tell him to play it cool, but Michelle scoots over to make room for him right next to her, so what do I know. I look at Natasha, who just looks back at me.

"Uh, can I sit here?" I ask.

"Sure," she says, sliding over. We play for a while, then we all just watch an epic game of Clue happening a few feet away.

"It's always Colonel Mustard," says Michelle, shaking her head. "That man is a serial killer."

"Yo, Professor Plum is a little suspect," says a boy nearby, and the two of them laugh.

I laugh too, not because it's that funny, but because I feel good. I have no idea where Luke is, or if Derek was lurking somewhere, but right then, I don't care. I listen to some counselors having an impromptu debate on old school hip-hop ("Novelty Songs: Good for the Culture, or White People Food?"), then I get in on a dance battle scene from a *Step Up* movie three or four, we couldn't remember), with a couple of people from my Street Style workshop. After that, I sit in a circle with Charles, Natasha, Michelle, basketball star twins named Tony and Todd, and a bunch of other people, reminiscing about our favorite polysyllabic words—it even turns into a contest. We are Blerding out, and I love it. There are bowls of potato chips, popcorn, and pretzels all around the room. Candy sandwiches—gummy bears melted down between two chocolate bars—on bookshelves! Some kids are playing group games, some are reading or doing puzzles and Sudoku, a bunch of people are just hanging out. Nobody getting pantsed or clowned either. One less fun thing about being singularly special at home was that singular part. Sometimes it was lonely.

The music is loud enough to promote dancing but not discourage talking.

"What's this playlist?" I ask Charles. "It's really good."

"It's original music, composed by campers in the electronic music program," he says. "Kids in the DJ class curate it. A couple of kids get record deals every summer."

Of course they do. My good mood bubble pops. My debate wins and test scores feel very ordinary these days. "They should change the name to Camp Black Excellence," I mutter. The other side of not being singularly special doesn't feel that great. That nasty voice that's been floating around in the back of my mind pushes its way forward again. *You got your little trophies and certificates, but Luke's the one getting genuine invitations to the big leagues.*

"Want to dance?" asks Natasha suddenly, and I perk up. She points to a crew forming at the edge of the dance floor. Oh. Like in a group. Michelle is waving us over. Nobody from Street Style is close by, so I can really have the spotlight and try out some of the new moves I've been working on after class. I start to say yes, until I glance at Charles, who has a look on his face like a character in a horror movie right before they get sliced. He's not ready.

"Uhhhh," I say. "Not . . . right now. Maybe later, though!" We sit in awkward silence for a while, and I see Luke across the room, having what looks like an intense conversation with Charisse. I turn back to Natasha. "I . . . want to talk to you, actually. About filmmaking."

"Okay," she says, glancing back at the dance floor. "I guess now, in the game room, with the music pumping, surrounded by kids, is the perfect time to talk about filmmaking."

I ignored the sarcasm. "So, I'm thinking about doing an . . . independent project for the Camp Showcase," I say. "I want to make a film, but I don't have access to equipment since I'm not in the class. I was wondering if you'd help me out . . . I could use someone with your expertise. I want to enter the Showcase competition, and you basically . . . win everything. And I really want to learn more about filmmaking." Charles looks at me, then he shrugs and picks up a deck of mini cards and starts building something.

"I can give you tips or something," she says slowly, "but if you're not in the class, you can't use the equipment. It's policy." Natasha frowns. "Anyway, I thought Street Style was doing a routine. You guys always do."

"I am . . . I mean, we are . . . I just really wanted to get into filmmaking, and then I didn't, but, uh, I still want to make this movie. I thought we could work together."

"I'm sorry," she says. "It's the rules. And plus, I've got to work on my film for the Camp Showcase. "

I come on stronger. "So, the film I want to make is about the staff at DuBois. Kind of like a short documentary to highlight how special this place is, some of the uh, staff . . . to help promote it and stuff." I look down. "It probably sounds corny, but . . ." I look over at Charles. "Charles and I were talking about it, and . . ." I trail off. He gives me a that's-news-to-me look, but he doesn't blow things up, just shrugs again.

She stands there looking at me for a while and the awkward quotient rises way up. Finally, she jumps in this really cute way.

"I love it! I've got ideas already. We can make this work. You can be on my crew, on sound!" she says. "The sound assistant, to be specific."

"Sound?" What is she talking about? "I mean, we already have some ideas . . ."

"Even though you can't make a film without being in the class, people in the class are allowed to get any camper for production team roles. So if you're on my crew, you'd still get some of the experience of being in the class. And I'd get a sound guy, which I haven't picked yet. Derek was going to—"

"Derek?" I frown. "*He's* on your crew?"

"Well, he asked, but—"

"I'll do it," I say. I don't care if it's the most boring-sounding job around. If it means taking something away from Derek, then I'm in.

"Oh, wait—I know you've got your own stuff to work on . . . Are you going to try for a solo dance award? Everyone says you're like one of the best dancers here, Triple M is sure to pick you."

"*One of?*" I say, but I laugh to make sure she knows I'm joking. I wave my hand and try to add a little extra bass to my voice like I've seen Luke do. "I can handle it. Easy peasy lemon squeezy. I'm the king of multitasking."

"Are you sure?" she asks, and the way she kind of sings her words is so cute.

I nod so hard my head almost snaps off. Then I do a thumbs-up before I can stop myself. Luke would not thumbs-up. It's like an anti-mack move.

"Thank you!" she says. "And I can help you with your project, it's a great idea. It has a lot of promise, it just needs some planning. Maybe we can sit down and I'll show you how I outlined my film, and you can show me what your plan is," she goes on, sounding like an adult, or I guess just like a girl. "I've been doing this for a while, so I can help refine it. You'll officially be the producer, and I'll be the director—but I really believe in working as a team."

I guess my feelings show, because Natasha sighs. "I know it's not what you asked, but it's what I can offer. I could use the help, and I think your idea is great, but you're gonna need help too. I just need to know you're going to really pitch in. Everyone has to do their part for these films to get completed. The camp session goes by fast."

"Aye, aye, Queen," I say, saluting her. She rolls her eyes.

"It'll be fun, I promise," she says.

"Especially if someone lets me use their camera . . ." I do my puppy dog eyes. Maybe she won't be able to resist this time.

"Ugh, that face is really not as cute as you think it is," she says, screwing up her nose in her own very cute way. "Never do that again. And I will never say yes to breaking the sacred rules of DuBois."

"Say yes to what?" asks Michelle, coming over. "If my girl is in, then so am I, whatever it is!"

"Me too," says Charles. I'd forgotten he was here. We look over, and my eyes bug out. He's built a replica of the main office building, out of cards, in like five minutes.

"E has an extracurricular idea," says Natasha.

She called me E!

"It was Charles and me," I say quickly. And I'm glad I do, because he smiles and nods.

"Ooh, a side hustle," says Michelle. "That's what I like to hear. You know Amy Ashwood Garvey produced musical comedies? She may have been a revolutionary powerhouse, but she also had jokes."

I don't know what's more hilarious, the fact that Michelle just offered that little tidbit, or the sappy expression on Charles's face when she said it.

"Yeah, exactly!" I say. I wasn't going to turn away an ally, even if I had no idea what she was talking about. "Yes to having some fun together." Okay! I'm making my own magic happen. Superhero status, here I come!

We find a big puffy couch and pile on. We start throwing all kinds of questions at Natasha, and we're laughing and joking and even trying trick questions, but she's on it and doesn't fall for anything.

I clear my throat. "Okay, I'm sure I'll sound stupid, but, since we're obviously going to be talking about it a lot ... Michelle, who exactly are the two Amys? Like in real life?"

And Michelle is so happy to talk about them (again) she doesn't make me feel stupid. She tells me all about Marcus Garvey and his movement to make Black people feel good about their Blackness.

"He was originally from Jamaica," she says.

"Me too!" I say, then I stop. "I mean, my grandfather was. I'm not really."

"Of course you are," says Charles. "I'm from Senegal—

well, my grandmother is, and every June twentieth, we have thiéboudienne. I've got a big flag on my wall at home."

"My dad did a DNA test and he says we're Nigerian," says Natasha. "I claim it. Wizkid, Yemi Alade, Burna Boy all up in my playlists."

"You guys don't feel like you're . . . fake or anything?" I ask. "This girl at my school said I should be proud to be an American."

Michelle rolls her eyes. "It's like what Charisse was saying today. We have every right to claim all the parts of the African diaspora that we're connected to. We're all-in-one, and the fact that we have multiple sets of roots is a sign of our strength. I'm gonna claim it all and celebrate it."

"And Black to the Future is giving us a chance to learn more," says Natasha. "Keeps us from being fraudulent if we want to do the work."

"I don't remember Charisse saying that," I say to Michelle. Maybe I'm still not keeping up. I have a lot of *doing the work* to do. And it's not like there's a trophy or a grade at the end.

"Well, she didn't say that exactly," says Michelle. "But that's how I interpreted it in my notes." When we all look at her, she holds up her hands. "What? I'm a writer!"

While we're laughing, I glance over to where Luke is still talking across the room, looking serious, and suddenly I remember another time I laughed like this, and he was laughing too. Pops into my head, vivid and clear, like HDTV. It was when we were at the fair with Dad. I can't catch Luke's eye, so I keep talking and joking with my friends until the lump in my throat shrinks back down to normal. When he finally sees me, he smiles and waves; he never knew the lump was there, so I just smile and wave back.

Chapter Twenty-Two

"Nothing's how I thought it would be," I say to Michelle as I spoon cookie dough onto the baking sheet. "This is not how I am at home." When I'd arrived at the first Great DuBois Baking Show class, I'd been glad to see a familiar face, even if that familiar face had greeted me with "Are you taking this class because you think it will impress girls? Because I'm not impressed." Still, we make a good team, and being Michelle's partner gives me opportunities to gather intel for Charles. I sneak a bit of dough into my mouth.

"This isn't home," she says. "And—Hey, I saw that!" she yells, pulling our bowl out of reach before I can take more.

"Come on, they make cookie dough ice cream for a reason," I say.

"This is not the same thing," she says. "Anyway, make sure those spoonfuls are equal sizes. Yolande and Margaret are the judges today, and Yolande's still mad that he didn't get the part of Marcus Garvey in my show. Our cookies are going to have to be perfect."

"Exactly," I say. "Everything has to be perfect here.

Everything *is* perfect. Except me." Michelle puts a tray of our toffee rocky road surprise cookies into the oven. The surprise part was pretzel bits. I hadn't imagined how much I'd enjoy baking, all aspects of it—the measuring, the mixing . . . it's like chemistry but with a bonus result.

"Nine minutes, start your timer," she mutters. We start cleaning up our area, because the judges look at that too. Apparently too much mess can result in getting the boot from the class and put on bathroom cleaning duty instead. Our baking class is modeled after this British show—our teacher even talks with a British accent. We get a new challenge every day, and class members take turns judging the rest of us on flavor, texture, and presentation. I'd made a slideshow of my bakes so far and shared it with Luke, but I can see that he hasn't opened the file yet. I'd thought about sharing it with Mom, but I want this whole baking thing to be a surprise. I'm thinking that after she passes her medical school test, I'll just casually bake her a celebration cake, like BAM! I'll decorate it too. Luke isn't the only one with art skills.

"You're in Street Style, right?" Michelle asks. "How's it going? Triple M is no joke."

"Pretty good," I say. It's really hard, but it's fun. For the last few days I've tried to be extra helpful, demonstrating steps whenever I can, cheering other people on. "Triple M almost smiled at me once, I think," I say.

"That's a big deal," says Michelle. "You must have skills."

I shrug, but then I do a little spin, forgetting that I'm holding a spoon full of cookie dough. Oops. The junior counselor who's monitoring our oven use rolls his eyes.

"I keep telling Natasha that *Black Girl Magic* is gonna be amazing, but she is so stressed out about coming up with the perfect film," says Michelle. "I know she's trying to do something different this year, but she's built this rep as the film queen, and with her mom being a big time filmmaker and all . . ." She shrugs. "You know how it is."

Not really. "I wish I did. I wanted to take that class. My brother and I had an idea about doing a film festival together, but he's been so busy . . ." I trail off. "It would have been perfect."

"Well, there's something I think you're perfect for," says Michelle.

"I keep telling you that I'm not going to play Booker T. Washington," I say. "I can't make rehearsals anyway, they're at the same time as badminton."

"We can work something out. That's what free periods are for."

"I thought free periods were for being chill."

"In case you haven't noticed, we have no chill around here. Everyone wants to shine. And luckily for you, I'm giving you an opportunity. The ideal role. You've got grit, determination. I think you'd make the perfect Booker T."

"I'm a debater, not an actor. Debate *champion*," I add.

"Whatever," she waves her hand. "Debate champions are a dime a dozen. And today's debate is not exactly about arguing a well-researched point, is it? It's just like . . . talking fast. And performing. Which brings me back to why you'd make a great Booker T."

"Thanks, I guess," I say. "But wasn't he kind of a sellout?"

She waves her hand. "It's complicated. Like you— you're complex!"

I have to laugh. "You don't stop, do you? That really makes me feel good. But I'm not interested. Maybe I can help behind the scenes or something."

"You already did, you know—both Amys loved the steps that you—HEYYYYYYY!" She stops herself and grabs my shoulders, getting flour all over my shirt.

Kojo, our teacher, walks over. "Are you two having a problem?" He draws out the word *problem* to at least three syllables. I shake my head.

"No," Michelle says. "Also, Kojo, I was wondering if we could talk. I know you're from Ghana, and I'm thinking that next summer, I'd like to do a play about an American girl trying to find her roots there."

"How original," says Kojo. "But . . . we'll talk. For now, focus."

"Nice distraction technique," I say after he leaves, trying to clean myself off. "What did you get all hype about?"

"Behind the scenes . . . how about being my choreographer?"

Before I came here, my dancing was mostly fooling around, and to be honest, showing off. At DuBois, it's *work*. Still fun but . . . "Well . . ."

"Come on, it'll be fun! We are an excellent team! It's so much better when you work with people who are actually part of your crew."

It does sound like fun, and kind of important. And she called me part of the crew! Then I remember that I'm also supposed to help Natasha. "I don't know if I'll have a whole lot of time . . ."

"It'll just take a couple of free periods. You can practically do it in your sleep."

That makes no sense, but . . . it *is* another chance to shine like the old Emmett. The real one. "You did just save us from toilet duty, so . . . I can try," I say. Dance is my thing. I got this. Maybe just pull some things from what we're doing in Street Style.

"Thank you! And can you ask your brother if he thought some of his students would be interested in painting the sets?" she asks. "Make it a family affair."

"Sure, if I can get him to spend two minutes with me," I say. I open the oven to check our cookies. They're ready to come out, and I place them gently on the rack next to our station.

"Okay, it's clear you're feeling some type of way right now," she says. "Need a listening ear while we prep for the classic recipe challenge? What is it, by the way?"

I look at the screen in front of the kitchen. The next recipe is up. "Ugh, snickerdoodles. Does *classic* always have to mean 'bland'?"

Michelle laughs. "I guess it depends on your point of view. Which is kind of deep, when you think about it, it could even be an analogy for the stuff we were talking about in Black to the Future yesterday. About who decides what's classic."

"We're talking about cookies, Michelle," I say, laughing as I take out new bowls and utensils. "But if that offer to listen still stands . . . I thought Luke and I would be spending a lot more time together here. He acts like he's not leaving for boarding school at the end of the summer."

"Isn't he working?" asks Michelle. "Those junior counselor positions are coveted gigs."

"Yeah," I say. "He did a lot to get this job."

"Nice," she said, beating the eggs like they had done something to her. "So instead of being a big baby about your big brother, why don't you find something to keep you busy too?"

"What do you mean?" I ask. "And thanks for all the sympathy, by the way."

"You're welcome," she says. "Move over, let me pour this in. Nice job with the butter and sugar, E, good and fluffy. I mean, you're here, don't waste it."

"I keep offering to help him, but he's all, 'I got interns.' I don't know what else to do." I don't mention that his intern is my nemesis.

"Come on, Booker T.," she says, rolling her eyes. "You told us you basically creative wrote your way into this place at the last minute. So be creative. Like, this is literally supposed to be a summer of creativity. You can think of something."

I did do that, didn't I? I guess she's right, I am here. And maybe I can do both—create some opportunities for myself, and keep Derek the opportunist from trying to take my place. "You're a smart cookie, Michelle," I say. "Cookie, get it?" I get our tray of snickerdoodles in the oven.

She flicks some flour at me. "Just for that, you're on solo cleanup duty," she said. But she laughs, and so do I.

Chapter Twenty-Three

"Uno!" I yell. Free period, and I'm chilling with Charles, Michelle, and Natasha in the game center and we've just finished the most epic game of UNO ever. WeeDee and Billy used to think I was joking whenever I suggested a game— they said they stopped playing UNO when they were eight, but my camp crew is not only up for it, Natasha even has a special Jean-Michel Basquiat deck. Now that I know who he was, I'm even more impressed.

We go over to the pinball machine line, which is super long.

"I'm going to go back to the dorm, rewrite some scenes before dinner," says Michelle. "E, can we talk about the opening dance number tomorrow? During third period?"

"Oooh, I'll come with you, I want to go over my script," says Natasha.

"You're doing a documentary," I say to Natasha. "Why do you have a script?"

"It's really more of an outline. My mom wants to see what I have planned," she says, sighing. "She knows this could be my third win in a row, so she's . . . very interested."

"Good thing you got it handled," says Michelle.

She shrugs and looks down. "Anyway, E, be ready. We're about to start shooting soon, and we won't have much time. I can't believe camp is half over already."

"I know," says Michelle. "Some of my cast members still don't know their lines." She looks at me. "Or their dances, but some of them are saying that you haven't taught them the whole routine yet. I know you're on top of this, but I just want to make sure they have time to learn everything. So, third period tomorrow?"

"I have swimming third period," I say, not adding that I haven't worked on the opening number yet. "And I wish I didn't." They're all nice enough to just nod and not make a big deal of the fact that people have been graduating from my swim class every day. Soon it'll just be me, Monifa the Snitch, and Lance Gotta Pee.

"Why do girls always go places together?" asks Charles after the girls leave. "They lock arms and everything. Why are girls so . . . companionable?"

"Probably because we use words like *companionable*," I say. "On that note, we're never gonna get a turn at this." I point to the pinball machine. "Why don't we give up while we're ahead?"

Charles agrees, and we head out.

"I'm going to practice my solo for the Camp Showcase," says Charles. "Want to join me? I bet you can use one of the music practice rooms. We only have a little time left in this period, but you could run through some of your moves. Aren't you auditioning for a Street Style solo?"

But I've got a better idea. I've got a little steam now, and I'm ready to take on the world . . . the logical next step: quit swimming. Because by "take on the world" I mean things that are not a lost cause.

"Imma see you later," I say. "Just got to take care of some business first."

***

The air conditioner in the camp office is blasting so hard, the guy at the front desk is wearing a coat.

"Hi! How can I help you!" he asks. "Hope your Camp DuBois adventure is going well!"

"I need to change my . . . um . . . schedule," I say. His hard-core cheer is throwing me off my game. "One of my classes."

"Oh, I'm sorry it's not working out. We want you to have a positive experience at DuBois. What are you interested in changing?"

Maybe this will be easier than I thought! "Can I join filmmaking?" I ask. "I tried to sign up before, I sort of do some stuff in film at home. There was a waitlist on Opening Day, but maybe someone dropped out . . ."

"Okay, let me see, it's a little late to make that kind of change, we're halfway through the camp session, but . . ." He types on his laptop so fast I think he's faking it. "Tell me your name?"

"Emmett Charles," I say. "They call me E."

"Emmett, what class do you want to replace?"

"Uh . . ." How do I say swimming without saying swimming? "I have this medical thing, I need to stay out of the water, and—"

"Fancy meeting you here," says a silky voice behind me. I feel a cool breeze and turned around: Mr. Micah McDowell.

"I . . . H-hi, Triple—Mr. Micah McDowell . . ." I stammer. Had he heard anything?

"Did I hear you trying to drop a course?" His eyes are like lasers. I blink. He doesn't.

"Uh . . . I wait, what?" Busted!

"I thought that I heard you imply"—dramatic pause—"that you needed to drop swimming for medical reasons. I assume you have documentation. Signed by a parent or guardian. Or you're willing to have us contact a parent or guardian right now to confirm this medical excuse. Or perhaps I heard wrong?"

"Um, no, I was just . . . making sure that I was officially enrolled," I say as the desk guy frowns and opens his mouth. I go on quickly. "I mean, because I'm new, and I just wanted to make sure of things. I've been in the class for a few days now, and I thought it would be a good idea to be sure that . . . all the *I*s are crossed and the *T*s are dotted." He raises an eyebrow. "Wait—I mean, the other way around."

"I see. I'm glad to hear that," says Triple M. Does he ever blink? "Because I'd hate to think that just because your swim test didn't go . . . swimmingly, that you'd quit. Street Style team members don't quit. You are a member of a team and expected to conduct yourself accordingly."

How did he know about my test? "Team player, yep, that's me," I say. I turn to the desk guy. "Uh, thanks for, confirming that for me. I . . . you're doing great work here. Great work." I back away from the desk quickly, tripping over my own feet until I'm safely on the other side of the door.

"Didn't you tell me you were planning to audition for a Camp Showcase solo?" Triple M calls out after me. *Um, no.* "I can't wait to see what you have planned."

From inside I can hear the faint strains of (evil) laughter. Great, way to ruin things after you smoked that audition, Emmett. Now he definitely has it in for me. I'm gonna have to get Luke to smooth things over. And maybe introduce me to some head counselors so that I can have a little staff muscle on my side when Derek and his henchpeople are around.

***

Triple M seems to be in an okay mood by the time I get to Street Style; he only has us do the same eight count twelve times. He starts a unit on African moves and teaches us the Shaku Shaku, which he says is from Nigeria and is played out there but "with all the clodhopping stomptrosities going on in front of me, y'all need to start with basics."

It looks easy, but it takes me a couple of tries. Every time I swing my right foot out, I can't get it back fast enough and stay up on my toes at the same time.

"This is not a Midwestern marching band practice," says Triple M, walking past me. Still, he does ask me to demonstrate at the end, so I guess I've kind of got it. Then it's presentation time. Jeimy talks about the history of merengue, and my hips almost fall off when we get in pairs to practice. Hannah goes next, and even though she gets up with a lot of heavy sighs and grumbling about "homework at camp," she does a fun presentation on the choreographer Fatima Robinson. It turns out that she directed one of my favorite shows, *The Wiz Live!*. After I saw that on TV, I practiced every dance scene for weeks. *The Wiz* was also a movie when Mom was little, and of course she and Uncle Davidson made us watch it; it was pretty good. Hannah's report is thorough, and Triple M actually smiles when she mentions that Fatima Robinson did that sick choreography for this ancient Egyptian–style video called "Remember the Time."

"That was my first professional gig," says Triple M, sliding into a few moves from the video. We applaud.

"Yo, that was a long time ago," someone whispers. "How old *is* he?"

173

Triple M actually tells us a little more about his career—he was a backup dancer, he went on tour with Normani, he even teaches intensives at the famous Alvin Ailey dance school in New York City. "I still take workshops too," he says. "There is always something to learn. I'm headed to a Dance Theatre of Harlem workshop after camp ends."

"Isn't that ballet?" I ask. "What does that have to do with this kind of dancing?"

"Yeah," says Hannah. "I mean, it's cool learning about Afro-Latin stuff and highlife and whatever, but I thought this class was about b-boying and girling—"

"Peopling is probably the way to go," a boy interrupts, and some people give him snaps.

"—so ballet and musical theater moves are not exactly from the streets."

"Different forms of dance inform each other," says Triple M. "And you'd be surprised at how much musical theater and mainstream forms of dance borrow from street culture."

"I wouldn't be surprised," says Hannah. "People always taking our stuff."

"The point is, it's all our stuff, not just street culture. We are up in all forms of the art of dance," says Triple M. Then he makes do barre exercises for the next fifteen minutes.

"Sounds like something to talk about in Black to the Future," I say to Hannah in a low voice. "I'd be down if you wanted to lead a discussion on it." She looks at me for a minute and then smiles.

"Maybe I will," she says.

"If you two are done with your side conversation," calls out Triple M, "maybe you can come up here and freestyle for our enjoyment . . . or ridicule."

Oops. "To this?" I ask. We've been practicing to some classical music that I actually recognize from one of Charles's playlists. Triple M just folds his arms. I take a deep breath and run up to the front with Hannah. She starts battling right away, and I use the opportunity to try out some of the spins I practiced the night before. I know Triple M meant this as a punishment for talking, but with everyone around us saying, "Ayyeee," I legit feel like I'm in *Step Up 8* or whatever number they're up to.

***

After class, I hang back to apologize to Triple M, and yeah, I guess to suck up too.

"Um, sorry for talking. I'm just so inspired by this class, for real. Thank you for that Crazy Legs assignment," I say. "I got real inspired by that too."

He just drinks from his water bottle and looks at me.

"I mean, I am kind of thinking that I could be a choreographer. My uh, brother, he's a junior counselor here, we were planning this film festival with eighties dance movies. I mean, it's been mostly me doing the planning, but he'll be helping me out soon. Anyway, now I know that Crazy Legs was in *Flashdance* it, um, has even more significance. "

He screws the cap back on his water bottle. "Who's your brother?"

"Luke, Luke Charles," I say quickly. "I mean, he kind of has a lot to do, he has his art, and he's going away to boarding school in the fall, but we used to have these themed film festivals on the weekends, so, um, that's how I got the idea. And my uncle told me about all the dancing in movies like *Breakin'* and stuff. Hey—" I get excited. "Were you in that?"

"I'm not that old," he says, rolling his eyes.

"Oh, sorry. Yeah, so . . . I want to spend some time studying those movies, I'm really inspired by this class and Crazy Legs and stuff . . ." I trail off.

"Yep, you said that already."

"I just gotta see when Luke has time to sit down with me. I want to run my ideas by him. I haven't even had a chance to show him what I've been practicing here. He usually helps me rehearse and stuff, but he's been busy with art."

"Or," says Triple M, "you can make the time to sit down with yourself. If this is your thing, then do it. Don't wait for anyone else."

"Luke and I always do everything together," I say. "He wants to help me, he's just been a little busy."

"Didn't you just say he was going away to school?"

"Yeah . . ."

"Are you going too?"

"Um. No."

"So, live your best life, Sparky. Maybe there are some things you do together—" I open my mouth, but he holds up his hand. "Things that you're *both* interested in. Because it sounds like this"—he points to my feet—"is about you. And you're doing . . . okay on your own."

He doesn't know that back home, I was a star. That with Luke bigging me up, I could win every award at the end of the summer. But I don't want to talk back, because the whole point of this conversation was to get on his good side, so I just say, "I guess."

He looks at me for a long minute. "So the eighties, that's fascinating," he says in a way that sounds like that's not what he thinks at all.

I perk up. "Yeah! I was telling these guys back home about *Beat Street*, but they nixed it . . ."

"Both *Beat Street* and *Flashdance* are eighties," he says.

"Yeah, my friends were talking about a John Hughes focus, but to be honest, I wasn't that into it . . ."

"Well, again, now you have an opportunity to think about doing something that's meaningful to you," he says. "Do some research on a couple of other movies, like *Krush Groove* and *Style Wars*, and report back to me tomorrow."

"I'd be happy to do another presentation, sir," I say, not knowing how that's going to be possible in less than twenty-four hours, but knowing that I can't say so.

"This is not for a presentation," he says. "You'll report back to me. And by me, I mean *me*." He packs up his bag. "For a presentation, let's see one on Katherine Dunham in three days. *That* you can do for the class."

"Isn't Andre reporting on Gene Anthony Ray then?" I ask. I know better than to ask who Katherine Dunham is. Oh wait—I think Natasha mentioned her before.

He's walking to the door. "Yes," he says without turning around. "So you can go first." He stops at the door and waits for me to walk out ahead of him. "And I hope you're preparing some ideas for the Camp Showcase," he says. "There are solo opportunities, and I'm looking for someone to choreograph an ensemble number. I'll be keeping a close eye out for someone who has even a soupçon of promise."

Me choreograph for the whole class? In front of Triple M? And what does that have to do with soup? "Uh, right. Yes, I'm definitely preparing. So, thank you, um, see you later, Mr. Micah McDowell," I say.

"Ciao," he answers, and leaves. "I look forward to your presentation."

Guess I'll be hitting a study lounge during rec time, I think. But surprisingly, I don't mind.

Chapter Twenty-Four

Charles's nine-language dictionary tells me that *soupçon* means "a tiny amount." From Triple M, I know that's mega praise and I'll take it. The rest of the day is pretty chill; Italian subs for lunch with fresh salt and vinegar potato chips. I take pictures and send them to WeeDee and Billy with the caption *#notcampbutaworldclassexperience #youwishyouwerehere.* I sit between Charles and Natasha and try to be low-key suave by helping Natasha with Blackity Bowl practice even though Charles is being high-key corny by going on and on to Michelle about some bassoon concerto in B-flat major. I try to kick him a few times, but he just says, "Ow!" and keeps talking until Michelle says, "You know Beethoven was Black, right? Alexander Hamilton too." Then they debate that for a while.

Natasha eats a couple of my chips. "Come on, E, next question," she says.

She called me E! "Uh." I look at the notebook she's given me. "Who is the jazz violinist who—"

"Ginger Smock," she answers immediately.

"—who was the only Black member of the Los

Angeles Junior Philharmonic when she was a teen and played in an all-female jazz trio called the Sepia Tones. Wow, yep, how do you know all this stuff . . . Okay . . . This man obtained almost sixty patents on his inventions, which included the folding ironing board, and—"

"Elijah McCoy!" she yells.

"You're really good," I say. "No joke."

"I have to be," she replies, taking another chip.

"What do you mean? It's just a game, right?"

"Well, it's kind of a big deal, the tournament happens in front of everyone, on the last night of camp," she says. "Before the Camp Showcase."

"Oh, Triple M said something about that to me today. He's looking for choreographers in the class."

"Wow, the fact that he even mentioned it to you means he thinks you're good. He usually only talks to seniors about that. The routine that the Street Style team does is a highlight of the whole show, after the solo dances. The solos are the main event. But still, it's a big deal. Then there's the Blackity Bowl, of course."

"Oh. Wow," I mumble, not sure if I should freak out or celebrate about potentially being responsible for making the whole class look good in front of everyone. "Um, so the Blackity Bowl? Is it really that important for you to win again if you already won so many times?"

"I'm a legacy, remember?" she says. "I have a lot to live up to. And look around. I don't want to be the slacker."

"I know what you mean," I say. "I know I'm new and all, but I'm thinking of entering the Dance Battle." Along with choreographing for Michelle, and maybe for the whole Street Style class. And helping Natasha with her film. Hmmm. "Guess I'm gonna have a lot going on."

"Join the club." She nods and smiles a half-smile.

"Hey, are you ready for me to join your crew?" I ask. "How's *Black Girl Magic* going?"

"You mean in my life, or the film?" She half-smiles. "Ugh, I'm getting a headache. Hit me again before it gets bad."

As we go through more questions, I think about Mom studying and getting ready for med school. I wonder what my dad would have thought of that, of Luke getting into Rowell, of me . . . doing something. I stop again. "I never really thought about living up to anything." Mom had said to have fun and take advantage of the opportunities, like she always says, but what does that really mean?

"Do your parents put a lot of pressure on you?" I ask.

She shrugs. "Not exactly . . . but they do talk about how fortunate we are, how much people sacrificed so we could live our best lives."

"Yeah," I say. "I guess that true. But it's kind of . . . a lot."

She shrugs again. "Life is a lot. Come on, let's keep going. Give me more science, they always go heavy on those."

"Oh!" I knock the notebook off the table by mistake. It slides under, and I dive for it, hitting my head on the way back up. Ouch. I try to pretend I'm smoothing my hair in a feeling myself kind of way as I feel for a lump. "Um, hey, did you say you were taking a Katherine Dunham class?" I ask.

"Yeah, Lynn might be even tougher than Triple M, but I love it."

"I, um, have to do a report on her tomorrow, like a short presentation." Here comes the swole tongue again. "Um, I, uh, maybe, uh, if you have time later, you could tell me some stuff? Or something?"

"Sure," she says. Then she taps the notebook I'm holding. "More science, please!"

So I keep quizzing her, and each question reminds me of how much I don't know but it's okay because it's Natasha and I've got my sandwich and there's something new happening inside of me that feels good even if I haven't figured it out yet.

***

Ceramics has a vibe that I can get used to. Our teacher, Ms. Clay (seriously), looks like a cross between the illustrations of River Mumma in this book I have at home called *West Indian Folktales*, and Mrs. Whatsit in that *A Wrinkle in Time* movie Luke took me to when I was little. She always has bowls of pretzels in the room, and there's a mini fountain in the back that makes little bell sounds when it's plugged in. Today we talk about different African pottery traditions and techniques, and we watch a film about pot making in Burkina Faso. Then we all get lumps of clay and she tells us to make a pinch pot, which is something I did in kindergarten, but whatever. I sit between a guy named Clarence who keeps asking Ms. Clay to check his work and a girl who says she saw this film at some museum last year.

Even though I'm disappointed that I didn't get into one of Luke's art classes, this is some good stuff. If I ever get a chance to tell him that, I will. I like being in that room, with Ms. Clay's jazz music playing—she tells us it's Mary Lou Williams, and when someone makes the mistake of asking "who" she gives them an assignment—an oral report on Black women of jazz. Sometimes these teachers remind me of all the aunties and uncles at our family gatherings. Once, Uncle Todd, who's not even related to us, had me memorize and recite his original poetry at Thanksgiving because "the boy needs to know how to present and represent" (like I'm not already a debate champion, but whatever). With the sunlight streaming in through the art shack windows, I feel like a real artist. The clay feels like hope in my hands, and working with it gives me ideas for new moves. I also realize that my pinch pot work isn't bad; I wonder if I can be an art assistant or something! Yes! That might be a way to work in some time with Luke, show him all the great stuff I've been doing here, that I belong here with him.

It turns out that Charles, Michelle, and Natasha are all spending rec time in the study lounge. A lot of kids use that period as an extra independent study. The grind is real, and everybody seems to like it. I do too, and it doesn't hurt that we share a big bag of flamin' hot Cheetos that Natasha brought from home. While I'm looking up Katherine Dunham, Charles is trying to compose a piece in honor of someone named Chevalier de Saint-Georges, Michelle's working on *The Two Amys*, and Natasha is quizzing herself on Egyptian history. I hadn't expected to be doing so much school-type stuff at camp, but it's cool. We head outside after a while and Natasha shows me some of what she's doing in her dance class; I try to memorize it so I can practice in the room later for my presentation. I know Charles won't make fun of me. We all flop down in the grass under a big tree, and even though we're working on separate projects, it all feels connected. And *I* feel connected—to my friends, to Katherine Dunham, even to that lady who founded this place. When Dr. Triphammer walks by and gives us a thumbs-up, I think back to his speech about how this place was started, and I'm glad it's still here.

Chapter Twenty-Five

Our badminton coach, Jossie, has given up on trying to get people to stop saying *shuttlecock* instead of *birdie* and snickering. She's also given up on trying to get us to play real matches, because we all just want to count how many times we can hit the birdie without dropping it. Some people even make it into an art, spinning and twisting and closing their eyes while the birdie's up in the air. So Jossie just claps loudly every few minutes and reminds us that it's an Olympic sport. "One of y'all could be the Naomi Osaka of badminton if you just work!"

Natasha and I end up next to each other (basically because I put myself next to her), and we trash talk as we hit. She sure knows how to flex; apparently she met Coco Gauff, and Maya Moore came to her house once. I'm surprised when class is over, and Charles comes over to remind me that we still have to do our Superhero Secrets assignment.

"We're, uh, grabbing to-go boxes for lunch," I say to Natasha. Should I ask her to join us, or would that be weird?

"Bon appétit!" she says, putting away her racquet. I

stand there awkwardly not saying anything until she looks at me. Not weird at all, Emmett. "Oh! Um, I'm going to use the lunch period to go over some Blackity Bowl questions, fine tune my production schedule, I've got tons of work to do. And I'm not hungry anyway."

"Okay," I say. "Well, um, I guess I'll see you later. That was . . . fun."

"It was!" she says. "See you!" Even though I'd told Charles last night that Luke is always the one to leave first when he's with Taliesha, I stand there until Natasha's out of sight and Charles has to tap my shoulder.

"Ready?" he says. I nod slowly. "And just so you know, you're about to catch flies with your mouth open like that. You look a little faint, do you need to sit down?"

I start to protest, then I see that he's laughing. "Okay, you got jokes," I say. "Not like you don't look like a sick puppy when Michelle's in the room."

We head to the dining hall to pick up our lunch, laughing and joking the whole way.

***

Make a list of all the things you like about yourself. For example, your eyes, your smile, your toes, everything! Do you like the way that you walk? The way that you talk?

"Who wrote this stupid book," I ask Charles. "Dr. Seuss?" We're laying on the grass near the art shack. I shield my eyes from the sun; I'm not used to such clear skies. We'd stuffed the Superhero Secrets workbook in the desk in our dorm room as soon after the first meeting, and hadn't looked at it since. But the second session is coming up, and the die-hard school nerds in us means that we're trying to do that dumb assignment anyway.

"That's racist," says Charles, not looking up from his book. "Or at least, Dr. Seuss was." "Yeah, okay, but . . . my toes?" We laugh. As Charles continues to read, I take a mental inventory. "And seriously? He was racist?"

"Yeah, Charisse told us about it last year. Totally broke my childhood but good to know. Maybe that's why they added Black to the Future."

"To break our childhoods?" I say. Black to the Future makes me feel like there's so much I don't know. "So what are you going to say that you like about yourself?"

"Huh? Oh . . . I don't know, my music skills, my mind palace, my voice, there's a lot, actually," says Charles casually.

"Mind palace?" I put up a hand as he starts to speak. "What—Wait, I don't even want to know." That came so easy to him, that list. Before I came here, it would have come easy to me too. But now I feel a little off . . . my hair's not bad . . . when I can get Luke to cut it every week. I probably need a new smile. Something a little more mysterious, with less teeth. I don't realize that I'm practicing until a little girl walks by, carrying a giant pipe cleaner sculpture.

"Stop making scary faces," she says. "Everybody's trying to make me drop my work."

"Uh, sorry."

Luke comes out of the center, surrounded by a bunch of kids, and, of course, Derek. I wave; Luke waves back without stopping. Derek doesn't say anything; I guess he doesn't want Luke knowing what a jerk he really is. Instead, he drops behind Luke and makes swimming motions with his arms.

"Ignore him," says Charles.

"Who?" I answer, and I don't say anything else. Charles just nods.

"What are you two doing?" booms a voice behind me. I jump; it's Dr. Triphammer, and he's carrying one of those clear trash recycling bags.

"Uh, reading," I say. "The workbook from Superhero Secrets."

"Hmph," he grumbles. "I didn't realize that that class was going to generate so much . . . paper," he says. "I need to talk to Mr. Oliver about digital tools, maybe iPads for next year."

"That would be amazing!" says Charles. "With the pen thing!" He's right; Dr. Triphammer smiles at him, teddy bear style, but I'm still not sure that he won't start roaring like a real bear in a second. Charles gives him an exaggerated thumbs-up, but knowing Charles, he means it.

Dr. Triphammer leans against the tree and sighs. "It would. Just a matter of funding. The cost of running this place . . ." He clears his throat. "Excuse me. Anyway, carry on. I hope the class is helpful."

"Uh, maybe Lamar's father would know about getting iPads or something," I say. "Lamar, um . . ." I look at Charles.

"Clayton!" says Charles. "Great thinking, E. His family might be willing to donate . . ."

Dr. Triphammer grunts something like, "We'll see," and hands us each a clear plastic bag. "If we all do our part to create a zero-waste environment," he starts, and looks at us.

"Then we'll have a zero-waste environment?" I finish, because it feels like I'm supposed to.

"Exactly!" He hugs the tree, then holds out his hands for a high-five. As he walks away I hear him singing that "Camp DuBois Makes Me Happy" song. Charles and I look at each other, but we don't laugh until he's at a safe distance. I turn back to the workbook.

Self-esteem is about feeling good about yourself, believing in yourself, feeling proud of yourself for who you are. It means knowing that you are trying to be the best YOU you can be! It's not about what things you have, how much money you've got, or how famous you are. A lot of rich, famous people are still unhappy? Why? Because they've never developed their self-esteem!

I shake my head. "I can't believe they call this class Superhero Secrets," I say.

"Shiny Suit Man is probably connected or something," says Charles. "Maybe Dr. Triphammer is his cousin. There's always a cousin."

True. I have about twenty. Ma is always bringing a new one up, like "Oh yeah, your cousin Maria is an astronaut, your cousin Philip ran off and joined the circus."

"Shiny Suit Man?" says a voice.

We look up; it's a counselor named Reggie.

"Uh," I say. Does he know who we were talking about?

"The Superhero Secrets guy?" Reggie goes on. "He's my cousin."

Great.

"Uh, um," Charles and I both stammer.

Reggie laughs. "I'm just playing with you." He sits on the grass next to us. "It *was* kind of weak, right?"

We just stare at him. It could be a trap.

He laughs again. "Don't worry, I won't snitch."

"We just thought it would be . . . different," I say.

Reggie nods. "So . . . make it different!" He sits back like he just solved poverty.

"No offense," I say, "but you sound kind of like our workbook."

"What do you mean, make it different?" asks Charles.

"Touché," says Reggie. "I really have to be careful about being old and corny. What I'm saying is, when I was just a little older than you." He looks at me. "What are you, ten? Eleven?"

"Almost thirteen," I say.

"Oh, okay, so when I was about your age, I got involved—kind of accidentally, but that's another story—in a school election, and I ended up running for president and—"

"And you won, even though you were the underdog," I finish. "And you got popular. We kind of know that story."

"We, in many cases, are that story," says Charles. "Except for the winning part."

"Actually, I didn't win," says Reggie. "But, as clichéd as it sounds, I did end up creating opportunities to help me do better and to do good. I get that this Superhero 'be the best me' stuff isn't exactly meaty, but—tell the truth, were you hoping for like, actual superhero lessons? And capes and superpowers and stuff?"

Charles and I look at each other. Then Charles, who's too honest for his (and my) own good, says, "We thought we'd at least talk about that stuff."

Reggie laughs. "Well, you still can, right? And about what you'd do with the powers you have—okay, that's more corny than even I can take, I'm about to put on a shiny suit myself. Anyway, it just might mean putting yourself out there a little. Taking a risk. That's the superhero part." He gets up. "I've got to get my group from the art shack. See you all around! Maybe we can talk comics next time?"

He leaves, and I can't lie, I do feel a little cooler after a counselor had an actual conversation with me. I also feel like Reggie just spent more time with me than my own brother has in the whole time we've been here. And I met him on my own. Plus, he's a *senior* counselor.

"I was wondering . . ." starts Charles. He clears his throat a few times. "Do you want me to help you with swimming?"

I look away. "Uh, thanks, but I'm good. I just need to . . . focus, it's not that I can't pass the test. I'll take it again, and then I'll be able to come with you guys to the Isle. I got this." I roll my eyes. "Are you thinking you'll get your cape by teaching me to swim? What are you, Aquaman?" I try to laugh a real laugh.

"Nah, I just . . . wanted to help. If you wanted."

"Yeah, I'm good." A few geese stroll over to see if we have any snacks. When they realize that we don't, they stalk away, leaving a few lumps of poop behind like they're cursing us out.

"Okay, this is going to sound wacked, but . . . even though he's a jerk, Derek does have a point about DuBois getting a little . . . shabby," says Charles slowly.

"Does not compute," I say. Charles is really pushing all my forbidden conversational buttons right now. "Did you just say something about Derek having a point?"

"I'm serious," says Charles. "I heard my parents complaining about the camp fees this year. They want Dr. Triphammer to add more academics so they feel like they're getting their money's worth. I haven't told them about Black to the Future; I'm afraid they'll think it's a waste of time. But it's one of the best things to happen to this place in years."

"Seriously!" I'm surprised. "I mean, I don't know what it was like before, but I think it's great. And it's awesome learning all this Black history and culture stuff. It should be part of academics, but it's not, at least at my school back home. I know a lot of y'all go to private school, so maybe you're used to it, but not me."

"Ha, I go to Acheson Academy, which is *extra* private," says Charles. "And everything is about Greek classics. The Blackest we get is *To Kill a Mockingbird* in seventh grade, and you know that's painful."

I never read it. After Luke tried to flush his copy down the toilet; he just told me enough to pass the stupid tests. DuBois is preparing me for something more than bubble tests, more than I'd even thought it would.

"You know how the Isle is like an oasis in the middle of camp?" continues Charles. When I give him side eye, he grimaces. "Oops, sorry. You'll pass the test and get out there, I know you will! Er, anyway, I just mean that DuBois is like my life oasis. I can be me without worrying about it."

"That sounds like fun," I say.

"You don't seem to worry about that stuff," says Charles.

Really? I struggle for a minute; it might be nice to keep up the illusion of cool. But... Charles is always honest with me, so...

"Yeah, well," I say. "It's not easy coming here and being around all these superstars. It feels like me might not be enough." I lean back against the tree. "But one thing I realized, with all these presentations we do around here, I feel like I can go back to my school and flex. I'll be talking like every month is Black History Month!"

Charles looks at me, and then we both say, "Because it *is*!" at the same time, and laugh.

We sit in silence for a minute. A group of boys run by with a soccer ball, singing the DuBois song in fake opera singer voices.

"You know, you just made me think of something," says Charles. "Tell me if this sounds stupid. The library in my neighborhood has programs for little kids. I could do bassoon presentations, teach about music. You never know where you'll find the next Joshua Elmore."

"I thought *you* were going to be the next Joshua Elmore," I say, glad I remember Charles's favorite Black bassoonist.

"There's room for us all," he says.

"Charles," I say, "I think it's a fantastic idea. I can help you plan if you want. You're a genius *and* a good guy. "

"As are you, my good man, as are you!" He gives me a fist bump.

I bump him back, and we both stand and bow without even checking to see if anyone can see us. Then we get up and start walking with a new bop in our step.

Chapter Twenty-Six

Even though Michelle and I are sure that nobody made anything better than our Morning Glory mini muffins, we still come in second place in today's Great DuBois Baking Show competition. With a little more than a week to go, we're running out of time to take the top spot.

"That's our second second this week!" says Michelle, throwing down her oven mitt. "I don't do second."

"I'm sorry," I say. "I went a little overboard with the cinnamon." Not only am I not winning anymore, I'm bringing my friends down too.

"No, I'm the one that suggested banana mash instead of banana chunks," she says sadly. "We gotta up our game for the next one. I think it's a veggie theme. Pumpkin Peppermint Brownie Swirls?"

"How about it's just a stupid bogus camp competition?" says Hannah, who apparently got to switch into this class even though camp's half over. "Y'all are acting like this is going to keep you out of college or something." She takes a muffin. "Tastes good to me," she says, and grabs two more as she walks out. Michelle and I look at her, then each other, then we just laugh and start a muffin swap with the rest of the class until it's time to go.

***

We have a really awesome Black to the Future conversation about "power, privilege, and utilizing available resources." Ade, who usually hangs with Derek, is in my group and for once he doesn't brag about his dad's Tesla. He even told us that it makes him uncomfortable when his dad complains that people in America don't have "Naija hustle," but he gives his dad a pass because he knows his dad got called an African booty scratcher for months when he first came from Nigeria. "People at my school were even calling me that for a while," says Ade. "Then I came in with my new phone and they got real quiet."

Lamar, who hasn't talked to me since registration day, gives Ade a nod.

Class is over before I realize that I didn't get the usual lump in the pit of my stomach when Ade talked about his dad. Progress?

At the end of class, I go over to Luke, who's giving Derek some instructions. They look over at me like I'm a mistake.

"What's up, E?" asks Luke.

"Uh, do you have a minute?" I say. I look at Derek. "In *private.*" Derek just smirks and doesn't move. Luke gets a concerned look immediately, so I add, "It's nothing bad, just wanted to uh, catch up."

"Sorry, E, we're leading a found objects diorama workshop right now. I gotta get over to the studio."

"Oh . . . maybe I can come to your class—"

"It's full," says Derek. "People signed up days ago. You missed the boat. Boat—haha! Guess anything on the water is not your style, right?" He snickers, and Luke raises his eyebrows, then tells Derek to go on ahead.

"You two got beef?" he asks, after Derek leaves. "Derek is all right."

"I'm your brother, though," I say. "And he's far from all right. He might be worse than Mac. You should have heard—"

Luke raises his hand. "E, I'll see you later, okay? This class was my idea, I had to talk Dr. Triphammer into it, so I need to go."

"Yeah, whatever," I say, flopping down into a chair. "So what I'm being bullied. Who cares."

Luke checks the time again, then sits down next to me. "Bro," he starts, "Don't make such a big deal out of this stuff. I'm sure Derek was just joking. He's not bad, he's just ... sarcastic sometimes. Maybe if you get to know him, he'll tell you his story."

"I'll pass on Derek's *story*," I say. "Is this your pep talk? Because it's gone downhill. Wayyy downhill."

"Sorry, Emmett. I just meant that Derek—"

"I don't get why it's so hard to call me E. I get that Derek is like your favorite word now, but is it that hard to call me E?"

"Sorry." He sighs. He looks at the time again.

"If you have to go, just go," I mutter. "Maybe if Derek has news, you'll make time to listen to him."

"Emmett, E—"

"Mr. Charles, don't you have somewhere to be?" booms a voice. We both jump; it's Dr. Triphammer.

"Sorry, Dr. Triphhammer," says Luke at the same time that I say, "Free period, sir."

"I was talking to the *junior counselor* Mr. Charles, not *camper* Mr. Charles," says Dr. Triphammer, pointing at

Luke. "Who apparently wasted thirty minutes of my time asking to lead an art workshop that he doesn't plan to show up for."

Luke stands. "I'm really sorry, sir, I'm heading to the studio now. My brother just . . . I had to . . ." He trails off.

"As you learned in training, we're all family here, and we have a responsibility to each other, not just to some people." He glances over at me. "If you're not ready for that responsibility . . ."

"I'm very sorry, sir, it won't happen again." Luke runs out without looking at me. A tiny part of me feels glad that he got taken down a little, even though it's the usual Dr. Triphammer extra bark, no bite.

Dr. Triphammer folds his arms and glares at me. "Didn't I see you lounging under a tree earlier today? You seem to have a lot free time."

"I wasn't exactly lounging, I . . ."

"Here, I have a job for you. Just because you have a free period doesn't mean you should fritter it away," he says, and I know better than to laugh at the fact that he said *fritter*. "I'm checking for trash left behind. Since you seem to have nothing better to do, you can look under these seats . . ." The man is obsessed.

So I spend ten minutes hanging with Dr. *Trashhammer* and picking up chip bags from the floor. He mellows out a little by the end, and I tell him that DuBois has inspired me to do good work when I get home. It feels like I'm laying it on a little thick, like the time I told Pastor Booth that the Bible was straight fire ("And brimstone, young man! And brimstone!" he answered), but Dr. Triphammer seems pleased. "You have good ideas," he grumbles. "Do the work to refine them." He peers a little more closely at me. "Aren't you the boy who's a Novice zero swimmer? You should use

195

this time to practice your strokes! When I took over DuBois, I pledged that every camper from the Bear Cubs on up would know how to swim by the end of three weeks. What are you?"

"Huh? A . . . a boy, sir."

"I mean what unit. Don't be smart."

I wasn't, and furthermore, aren't we all supposed to be smart here? I just say. "Oh. I'm in the Young Lions."

"So what's your plan, then?" he asks. "Have you been preparing to retake the test?"

I mumble some "Yes sir, okay, sir, and thank you sirs," and get out of there.

**

I'm not sure what to do next. As I head to my dorm, I've still got some free period left. I should be working on a solo street style routine for the competition, but I have ideas for Michelle's choreography, so I work on that instead. Charles is probably making puppy eyes at Michelle, or he's in the lounge having a bassoon battle with some of his music friends. It's . . . a unique sound.

"Everyone's in the game center," says Marcus as I walk into the building. "Do you want me to walk you over?"

"Uh, no," I say, and I'm not surprised when he looks relieved. Seriously, how did he get this job?

Maybe the same way you got into this camp, says a voice in my head. *Faking it till you make it. Have you made it yet?*

I'm here, and I belong here, my other voice says. *It's all good. I'm a star too.*

Marcus is still looking at me, and for a second I wonder if *he* heard the voices in my head too, or if I actually said all that stuff out loud. "Uh, but thanks, Marcus," I say quickly. "Thanks for making me feel, uh, welcome, and everything."

He smiles and claps my back so hard I almost fall over. "Really?! Thanks, little guy! I'm still trying to figure out this counseling thing. Uncle Trip has been on my back, and it's been tough."

Uncle Trip? "Trip—Dr. Triphammer's your uncle?" That explains a lot.

He nods and pats me on the back, only slightly softer this time. "You made my day, little E."

"It's just E."

"Thanks, little E." He waves to one of the kitchen staff, who rolls her eyes. "Gina! Let me holler at you for a second!"

***

I see Luke and the Gnat heading out of the art shack, as I'm walking toward the game center, and I swear he sees me too, but he keeps talking to that parasite intern of his. Whatever. I go over to them and start talking to Luke, ignoring Derek.

"Luke, I haven't had a chance to tell you about how I'm working on this play—"

He frowns and puts up his hand, looking around. "E," says Luke, "that's great. I heard you're dancing up a storm too. Do you. The whole point of you coming here was—"

"To hang out with you," I blurt out.

"Do you guys need a moment?" asks Derek in a fake voice that the old Luke would have caught in a second.

"No," says Luke right away. "D, I'm sorry for the interruption."

Wait, Luke's *apologizing* to *him*?

"I—" I start.

"Emmett, I'm trying to tell you and you don't want to hear me. I came here to work. You came here to . . . whatever, but I'm not going to let you ruin my experience." He takes a deep breath. "More than you already have, at least."

Derek whistles under his breath.

"What's that supposed to mean? How have I ruined—"

"E!" Charles runs over. "We were going to come get you—I'm so glad you're here!" He gently pulls me into the game center as I try to pick my jaw up from the ground. "That didn't look like it was going well," he says to me in a low voice. Out of the corner of my eye, I see Dr. Triphammer walk over to Luke and the Parasite. I hope he's telling them both off.

"You good?" asks Charles as he leads me over to Michelle and Natasha.

I nod. The speakers are blasting Normani, and my head hurts. I can't believe Luke. I guess getting into that school has really changed him already. Forget him! "Yeah, my mom wanted me to remind my brother . . . that she can't send him anymore Spider-Man underpants."

Charles gives me a ???? look, but I stay stone-faced.

"Uh," he says, "Well, if you need to talk . . . Anyway, we really were going to come find you. Michelle said you've been working hard on her show and probably need a break."

Nice to know *someone* cares. "Yeah, I wanted to spend a few minutes with the play, working on some ideas for *The Two Amys* in my head."

"Thanks for encouraging me with my library workshop idea," he says. "I told Michelle, and she loved it. She's going to suggest a Black theater class at her school. And you know Michelle. By 'suggest,' she means present them with a hundred-page plan." He laughs, and I try to join him, but it gets stuck in my throat.

"Yeah," I say slowly. "It really is a good idea, isn't it? The kind of thing that people will get behind." It's funny, that's the kind of thing that could have won me a camp award or something. I forgot that I'm trying to score points here. Maybe I should have played that differently.

"It's great!" says Charles. "I'm going to call my parents tonight and tell them. They'll love it, it's the kind of thing they'll be talking about putting on my college application, and I can do what I love. It's a win-win. Michelle was giving you lots of props."

"Why me?" I ask. "It was your idea. "She should be giving you the props. Girls like an ideas man."

"I told her you inspired it," he says, "I wouldn't have had the guts to even say it out loud if you hadn't started that conversation." We dap it up and laugh when we mess up and have to start over. It's a regional thing, I guess. But even if we can't get a good handshake going, we're good. We're a crew of two, but we're still a crew. The air hockey table is free, and we play until I'm laughing for real. We don't keep score. I can feel Luke's presence nearby a couple of times, but I don't look at him.

"Thanks, Charles," I say. "For everything."

Chapter Twenty-Seven

"Five, six, seven, eight," I call out. I'm teaching a bunch of seventies dance moves for a possible Camp Showcase ensemble routine called Soul Memories. Since I didn't have much time to come up with something new, I'd thought back to my audition and figured starting from *Soul Train* might be perfect. Last week of camp starts tomorrow and I've got to have something—a trophy, a certificate—to show for my time here. And now that I'm not ruining my stupid brother's experience, I can focus on shining in Street Style. I'm getting that solo. After I reminded Mom that she'd officially ended my punishment and triple-checked that I really did need to use my phone for camp work, she gave me free(ish) rein, so I've been watching tons of online videos and documentaries. I've learned about how so many street dances got smoothed out and became popular because of *Soul Train*. I think I'm coming up with something that has both old school and next generation appeal for the group routine. And it seems like people in the class agree, because today they voted that it should be the one that we do in the showcase. Even though some of the moves are kind of . . .

acrobatic, so far, everyone's making an effort.

I clap like a real choreographer. "Okay, guys, I know the Hustle is kind of complicated, let's break it down for each count. Back, right, left, right, left. Forward right, left, right, left, lean right, one, turn two . . ."

After about three tries, they get it! And even better, they're liking my work. Jeimy, who taught us all a fire bachata routine yesterday, comes up afterward during independent work time and says she thinks that I might help us end up with of the best showcase routines ever.

"I gotta admit," she says, "when you came in here talking about oldies, I couldn't see it, but this is good. And you're a good teacher. " She glances over at Hannah. "Some people are all, 'Just do it!' and that's not helpful."

"Your routine was really good," I say. "I didn't know all that stuff about DR." Triple M makes us talk about the cultural origins of any dances we demonstrate or share; after Jeimy's presentation, I seriously want to go to the Dominican Republic. Talking to Jeimy gives me an idea. "I would love to incorporate some of what you showed us," I say. "Maybe . . . maybe I can adjust my idea a little."

"How do you mean?"

"We bring our own spin on Black culture to this class, and it blows my mind every day. My aunties are all about *Soul Train*, but your family knows merengue and stuff. And Trina is always twerking when she thinks Triple M isn't looking and saying it's 'a hundred percent Atlanta,' but remember Fatou called it Mapouka and she's from the Ivory Coast."

When Triple M heard I was Jamaican(ish), he had me do some research on Jamaican dance history. I watched videos of the Jonkonnu, Gerreh, and Gumbay dances, and it was a pretty interesting mix of African, European, and

Indigenous influences. "Maybe the showcase routine could be . . . like Memories of Our Heritage or something like that. I'll come up with a better name. Or we can all brainstorm." I hope it doesn't seem like I'm trying to rip everybody off. "I can spend some time coming up with a . . . remix of my original idea that includes a little of everybody else's, but not in a stealing way." I add quickly, "More like . . ."

"You want it to be more *collaborative*," Triple M says from behind me, making me jump. "That's definitely one of the principles we like to promote here at DuBois." He gives me what could almost be a smile. "Oh! Have I given you all *The Collaborative Habit* to read yet? Twyla Tharp. I should make it required reading . . ." He goes over to his notebook on the bench and starts scribbling. Uh-oh. I hope I didn't just create more assignments for Street Style. Natasha gave me her outline to read to get ready for shooting, and I still have to choreograph a grand finale for Michelle. Normally I'd ask Luke to help me out. Normally I wouldn't have to ask. He'd know.

"I mean, that could be really good," says Jeimy. "Like, *really* good." We start fooling around with some moves right then and there. Marcus jumps in with the Harlem Shake— even though he's from Virginia Beach, his New York cousins would visit every summer and tell him it was the only dance people did in the city. By the time he learned that wasn't true, he was a pro. Then Triple M shows us the Chicken Noodle Soup, "a Harlem Shake evolutionary dance," whatever that means. Other people jump in, and family stories are mixed in with dancing, and we can't stop laughing. Suddenly Triple M is telling us that class ended five minutes ago, and I haven't even worked on my own routine. We all do a quick "Show Up! Show OUT!" huddle, then I grab my stuff and run to shower and change; I'm hoping to maneuver myself into the seat next to Natasha in Black to the Future.

The discussion has already started; Natasha's sitting between Michelle and someone else who is not me. Charles waves me over to the seat next to him.

"So would you guys agree that we've got something special here?" Charisse is asking.

Almost everyone mumbles yes or nods in answer. I hear Derek mutter something again about how DuBois is not what it used to be, but when he raises his voice all he says is "We definitely got hooked up with the staff this year," and points to Luke like they're connected in some way, which they're not.

"And it's something that a lot of our brothers and sisters don't have access to, right?" says Gordon. "Real talk, when I was a camper, I knew I was waayyyy out of my league with some of the other people who were here. People having horses at home . . ." I laugh along with everyone else; I know exactly how that feels.

"So we're gonna share the wealth, right? Redistribute resources?" asks Charisse.

A few less yesses, a lot of *ums*, and Bernard, who tells anyone who will listen (which is no one) that he started the first Black Republicans club at his school, says, "Aww, no, my parents are really gonna freak if this turns into some socialist thing."

We're just kind of looking at Charisse now, even Gordon has that I-don't-know-where-you're-going-with-this look. He glances at Dr. Triphammer, who is in the back of the room, probably making sure that we don't have a secret Styrofoam party or something.

"I'm asking, what are we going to do with what we got? What we all get by being here?" she asks, looking around the room.

"I'm gonna keep getting mines!" yells out a voice, and we laugh.

"Get *ours*," says Natasha. "Help our communities."

"So," says Charisse, walking over to where Natasha is sitting, which is too far away from me, "you think you have a lot to offer? You think you can do a lot to help?"

"Well . . ." Natasha frowns. "I mean, yeah, I do."

"What about you? What help do you need?"

"I . . ." Natasha looks around.

"My girl needs no help, she's the epitome of Black girl magic, she's flawless," yells out Michelle.

"Don't throw around words meant only for Beyoncé," says Hannah. "You don't know who's in the Beyhive. Act up, get snatched up!"

A few people start some low buzzing, but Gordon shushes them.

"I mean, shouldn't we try to do whatever we can to help our brothers and sisters who have . . . who are . . . disadvantaged?" says Natasha carefully. "Isn't that why we're here?"

"Doing, like, actual work instead of having fun?" adds Hannah. "I'm about to see if I can get community service credits for this summer for real."

Charisse smiles a little before she goes in. "The problem is . . . thinking of your own people as a problem, or a burden. Thinking that because you have more, you *are* more—"

Natasha starts to interrupt, but Charisse holds up a hand. "I'm not saying this to any one person here, or trying to make anyone feel guilty"—Gordon turns a snort into a very fake cough—"I just want you to think about these things. It can be very easy to think hierarchically, even when"— she looks at Dr. Triphammer—"there's no hierarchy, just community."

Gordon nods. "Let that marinate before you start talking," he says as a whole bunch of hands shoot up. We sit in silence for a minute.

Hannah is the first to talk. "I got you," she says. "It's like when the older kids at my school take those trips to help the *needy* in the third world"—she makes a face—"and they think poor people just need to be filled up with their free time and wack good intentions." Her eyes widen. "Ooh, have y'all ever seen that old movie *Cruel Intentions*? Talk about sick . . ."

Charisse claps. "Focus, Hannah, because you're making an important point. Thank you! You keep asking why we're doing this, but then you demonstrate exactly how important and good this is!"

Hannah crosses her hands behind her head and leans back.

"I get that," Natasha says slowly. "Like, if we think we're always rescuing people in need . . ."

"Then it's another form of enslavement," says Michelle. "Of the *mind*."

"Isn't it good to help people, though?" I ask. "I mean, you learn that from the minute you're born."

Charisse turns and writes a quote on the board:

"If you have come here to help me, you are wasting your time. But if you have come because your liberation is bound up with mine, then let us work together."

"Y'all know how much I love quotes," she says. "That's one that's usually attributed to the artist and educator Lilla Watson—look her up. Google is your friend," she says to Hannah's raised hand. "But she herself says they're the words of many Indigenous activists who came before her. So I want you guys to talk about that and some of the phrases that I'll write on the board. As usual, counselors will mingle and join in, ask questions . . ."

"But you all take the lead," finishes Gordon. Even though we're supposed to mix it up, we've all kind of made little permanent groups by now. Charles, Michelle, Troy, and Natasha are in mine. Derek and his buddy Ade look like they're going to hang with us for some reason, but after a bunch of kids make a beeline for Luke's group, Luke calls Derek over. It makes me glad when I see Derek look over at Natasha before he leaves, but I still get a twinge because Luke is turning to the enemy for help. I'm looking for a win, but it seems like I have to be satisfied with a draw.

Chapter Twenty-Eight

Triple M choreographed this eighties breakdancing routine for us to do at the Camp Showcase, and I have one of three solos! I've never danced so hard in my life. Soloists have to stay after class, so I'm a little late to my first meeting with Natasha's group. I'd planned to read those notes she gave me during lunch, but I had to meet with *The Two Amys* cast instead. I want to impress her so bad, and it looks like I'll be winging it.

There are ten people on her crew, and she goes around and shakes everyone's hand, like a politician or something. It makes me nervous, and when she gets to me, I salute as a joke and she rolls her eyes. I'm off my game, and I feel like it shows.

"Please stop with the salutes. I'm really not here for that," she says. She moves to the front of the small multipurpose room that she'd reserved for our meeting. "Okay, so everyone is assigned a specific role . . . we're going to go over that now, then I'll tell you guys what I was thinking for the film. I changed the name, I'm calling it *Representing and Responsibility*."

A few kids nod, but most people look as blank as I feel, which makes me glad.

A girl with round glasses and curly hair raises her hand. "What's the relevance of that title?"

"Hey, Vanessa, good question," answers Natasha. "I got inspired by Black to the Future. Remember that time when Gordon said W. E. B. DuBois believed in a whole 'talented tenth' of Black people?"

"You mean the cream of the crop high achievers like us . . . well, *most* of us," answers Vanessa, looking around like she's trying to catch someone out of the Black excellence zone.

"Uh . . . anyway," continues Natasha, "At first I thought that was cool, and, like, we're all part of it." She waves around the room, and Derek nods like she's only talking to him. Jerk. "But there's also a lot of pressure. Like how everything we do has to be heavy, or how it's like we're representing all Black people at every moment in our lives."

"That's deep," says Derek. "Like how when people say Black excellence, it feels good, but . . ."

"But it's also scary," says Vanessa, nodding. "I like this idea. Also a good strategy for college apps." She makes some notes.

"Aren't you in ninth grade?" asks another girl.

"Yep," Vanessa says. "Your question is?"

Natasha goes on. "So anyway, I kept thinking about it and started wondering if that talented tenth idea is kind of elitist, like only some people are important enough to contribute to the community. Ten percent? I mean, come on." More people are nodding. "And I think it would be interesting to explore the idea that we all have something to give, but we also have to think about giving too much."

She is so smart. Like not just regular-debate-team-honor-roll smart, but the kind of smart that makes me feel like I should be doing better.

"Yo, you sound like you've been talking to Charisse," I say, smiling.

"I have," she says, not smiling back. "She helped me put my plan together. I'm trying to win on Camp Showcase night, and I hope y'all are with me."

I hold up my hands. "Excuse me, Queen Bee," I say, trying to lighten the mood a bit. I'm also realizing that I'm going to have to step it up if *I* want to win.

Natasha steps forward. "We need to get going. Any questions?"

A few people in the group clap, and Natasha waves them off. I could hug her right now. Okay, I could hug her any time.

"Let's do this!" I say loudly, pumping my fist and trying to add bass to my voice. "Who's in?"

Everyone looks at me.

"Why are you trying to take over?" asks Derek. "Tasha's got it under control, so you can chill."

"Um, thanks, E," says Natasha, looking down at her iPad.

"Skylan." She points to a tall kid with glasses on. "You're going to be DP—director of photography. Vanessa, you're an assistant producer. " She goes down the list until she gets to me. "Emmett, you're boom operator."

Ooh, she moved me up from sound assistant! Is that special effects, like explosions and stuff? "That sounds cool," I say, adding some swag to the bass. "Better than sound assistant, no disrespect to the sound assistant, of course. What exactly does that mean?"

A few people giggle.

"Sound assistant," she says drily, and I don't know

why she bothers to hold back her smile, because the whole group busts out laughing. "You'll have the mic, record audio, and make sure our sound is on point."

Well, that sounds tedious. "Are you sure you don't mean assistant director?" I ask.

"That would be me," says a girl, smirking.

Vanessa laughs really loudly.

Great. I look like a complete clown in front of the girl I want to impress. What else can go wrong?

Chapter Twenty-Nine

Yo, this boom mic is GINORMOUS. If anyone is completely not right for the part of GIANT MICROPHONE CARRIER, it's me. I try to look taller and stronger.

"Whoa, looks like you need a hand," says a boy who's a production assistant, which seems to be a euphemism for "do all the things." "I don't think you'll be able to stand on your tippy toes like that all day."

"I got it," I say, trying to look as though I do. "But thanks." Chill with the "tippy toes," though.

The first person Natasha wants to interview is the camp nurse. In Black to The Future, a lot of people talked about how their parents say they have to "be twice as good to get half as much" as white people, so Natasha is hitting up the nurse's office to talk pressure and stress in the Black community. Vanessa adds that we should at least do a special spotlight on Black girls and women and the whole idea of Black girl magic, and the other girls agree. Natasha says that's a good idea and Vanessa acts like she just won camp. We trek over to the medical center, where it takes forever for Natasha to explain everything to the nurse, then for the nurse to decide her hair's right, then it takes forever to set up the shot. Then there is a lot of walking around and talking and shushing. I guess I'd imagined filmmaking to be . . . more like movies themselves? Exciting, artsy . . . interesting. This is kind of . . . boring.

Finally it's my turn to get in position with the boom. I get up on a chair a few feet away from Nurse Denene and hold the fishing pole thing that's holding the mic as high above my head as possible. Which isn't high enough, apparently, because everyone keeps shouting at me to MOVE BACK, MOVE BACK, and the director of photography, who seemed a little extra if you ask me, kept huffing and muttering about "remedial workshops for newbies" in one of those loud whispers that everyone can hear, and Natasha is telling everyone to be quiet. I can see Derek smirking out of the corner of my eye. I lean as far back as possible and—

"Well," says a voice. "It's a good thing we were already in the nurse's office."

"Very funny," says Natasha. "Emmett, are you okay?"

"Yeah, I'm fine," I say, trying to stand up. "I'm sorry, I guess I . . . dropped the mic."

More than a couple of people snicker. I didn't even mean it like that, but I play it off and take a bow. What else can I do after falling off a chair like I'm practicing to be a clown?

"Very funny. Listen, I'm sorry, I should have considered your size when I gave you that job," says Natasha.

You think? And also, do we have to talk about that now? I rub my head, and Nurse Denene frowns.

"I'll help you from now on," says Production Assistant Kid (whose name is Fred—even though he's annoying, we're brothers in the old timey name department) in an extra helpful way that is not helpful at all. He makes a big show of picking up the mic. "Maybe I should be solely assigned to Emmett, Natasha? I can be assistant to the sound assistant. Or I can be on mic duty alone. Emmett can have my job. It's demanding, of course, and takes some physical, er, prowess." He jogs and boxes in place, which is totally unnecessary, especially considering the fact that he's also six inches taller than me, so yeah, I get it. Ready Freddy looks up to the job.

"I'm fine, I got this," I say, standing up for real this time. "I'm just not used to it, but I'm a quick study." Everyone stands around looking skeptical, and I grab the equipment from Production Assistant Kid. "Thanks again." I look around. "So are we interviewing the nurse or what? Let's get this show on the road!"

So Natasha explains the project AGAIN while Nurse Denene makes me sit and rest and drink water, which makes an even bigger deal out of a minor accident than is necessary. Then Nurse Denene checks and rechecks about seven hundred times to make sure I'm okay—at one point I seriously expect her to give me a lollipop or something, she's being so extra—but this girl Fatou whispers that her mom is a lawyer and can lawsuit my fall into college tuition if I want her to, so maybe that's why the nurse is doing way too much right now.

We finally get everything set up . . . aaand about thirty seconds after Natasha says, "Roll sound!" the end-of-period bell starts clanging. And it so happens that the medical center is right next to the bell tower, so even Natasha's thirty seconds of intro is messed up. Perfect. Every time I think I've created an opportunity to shine, I . . . splat instead. As we walk out, there's grumbling about already being behind; I hear one person mutter something about "wasting time because that little—" and I hustle out the door so that I won't have to hear the rest.

"I heard you're a street style king," says Vanessa, pulling up to next to me. "Maybe you should stick to that. I'm here to be on a winning team. Usually that's Natasha's team. You're not just new, you act *brand-new*, and ain't nobody got time for that."

Chapter Thirty

"Hi, hi, honeybee," says Mom. She's standing way too close to the screen, so I can't see her whole face. "I can't believe I'll be hugging you in person in a week!"

"Mom, move back," I say. "I can't talk long, I gotta get to my next class."

"Oh, excuuuuse me," she says. "I guess things are going well, then?"

I shrug. "Whatever. It's cool." I should tell her about Street Style and ceramics, and Charles and Michelle, but I don't. I'm still embarrassed—Derek is stealing my brother and now my girl. There's a little mean ball in the pit of my stomach, and I want it to stay. I want to be angry. I don't know how I could have been smiling a few minutes ago. What was I thinking? Natasha's film is going to be amazing. Charles has been composing his heart out, and I'm sure his concert will be great. Michelle will probably end up taking *The Two Amys* to Broadway or something. And then there's me. My brother's a star, my friends are all stars, and I've flamed out before I've even gotten started. I don't have my dance together. Everybody knows where they're going, what they're doing. I'm not even sure who I am anymore.

"Come on, it's got to be more than just—" She imitates my shrug. "'It's cool. ' It's such a great opportunity for you! What have you been eating? How's your roommate?"

"How's studying?" I ask. "It must be nice, all that quiet, no worrying about us."

"Oh, you're in a mood," she says. "What's up? Isn't all that sunshine and green making you happy? That amazing food? The fact that you're on an extended vacation that you arranged for yourself behind my back?" She laughs, but I don't.

"Talk to me, buddy," she says.

"Why do you guys always think I don't have problems? I'm not some little kid just playing all day!" I yell, surprising myself. After a few seconds of silence, Marcus knocks. I still don't understand what he does all day between knocks.

"You okay in there, Emmett?" he asks.

"Yeah, sorry," I call out. "Just talking to my mom. I'm getting ready for swimming, I'll be out soon."

"Cool, cool," he says, and I hear him leave, probably to try to mack on another counselor.

Mom is just looking at me, waiting.

"Sorry for yelling," I say. "I think I'm just . . . tired."

"Have you talked to Luke about how you're feeling?" she asks. "I know he's got a lot going on with his job and all, but maybe he can give you some advice."

Yeah, right. "Mmmmm," I say. "I don't think he has time."

"He's your brother," Mom says. "If you need him, he'll be there for you."

"Mom, what happened when Dad got depressed?"

She gets close to the screen again. "What do you mean? Why would you ask that? Are you depressed?"

"Mom! Calm down! I just . . . was wondering." I grab my towel. "I gotta go to swimming. I'm actually doing pretty good in that area," I say.

"Emmett—"

"Mom, I gotta go," I lower my voice. "I love you." And I do a quick kissy face and hang up before she can say anything else. I'm tired of talking, and opportunities, and questions without answers. Maybe now she'll worry about me a little bit.

Chapter Thirty-One

"Guys, we're moving to the big pool," announces Brant.

"YAY!!!" cheers my group. Well, except Lance and me. I can't shake off that conversation with Mom. I don't know what Lance's deal is, but I'm thinking that the only thing worse than flailing around with floaties in the baby pool is flailing around with floaties in the big pool where everyone can see me.

I raise my hand.

"No, your stomach doesn't hurt," says Brant. "Neither does your head or anything. You're fine."

I don't have the nerve to fight him on that, especially since he was there when I was having a great time playing badminton a little while ago. I stomp to the end of our line and stay a little behind as we walk over to the big pool.

"I'm scared," says Lance. I've mostly stayed away from him since his accident that first week. No need to remind people about pee pants. Guilt by association is a terrible thing.

"Why?" I shrug. "Brant will be there."

"Will you hold my hand?" asks Lance. I feel bad, but

. . . no.

"Um . . . Brant!" I call out. "Lance wants you." I zip up to the front of the line while Brant goes to check on Lance.

When we get to the pool, Brant makes us walk around the whole thing, and I stare at the "9FT" markings on one end. Lance tries to stand next to me and I slide away. Does he think I'm a kindred spirit or something? I hope not. We start at the shallow end, where I can still stand. When Brant tells us to work on our strokes with a buddy, I walk as far from Lance as possible and link up with a kid who must be part polar bear or something because keeps complaining that the water's too warm. Lance looks pretty scared, though, and I feel bad. I also feel like if he pees in this pool, we might not notice right away, which is not a good thing.

"Nice work, E," says Brant. I'm doing pretty good, if I do say so myself. I can float on my back really well now. If I just think about the water, and close my eyes—

"Eyes open at all times!" shouts Brant. Oops. I practice the stroke for the front crawl with my feet firmly on the pool floor. I even tread water in the middle of the pool for a minute. Three is what you need to pass the Isle test.

"Deep end, everyone," says Brant. We cling to the edge and kick for a while, then one by one, Brant helps us "swim" by kinda, sorta holding us while we get from the middle of the pool to the edge. I do get a couple of real crawl strokes in between dog paddling.

"You gotta relax, E," says Brant. "You got this. Don't worry about how you look."

Easy for him to say. I've been trying to pretend that I don't see the other kids my age pretending not to see me. But Derek's not around (probably sucking up *to my* brother), so I don't hear any straight up ridicule.

"I think you're ready to try the test again," says Brant. "You've got the skills, you just need to believe in yourself."

"You sound like Shiny Suit Man," I say without thinking.

"Who?"

"Uh, never mind."

It's hard not to notice that Lance is really having trouble, he's crying and everything. At one point his snot gets out of control—and into the pool. Gross.

"Ewwwwwww!" says a kid. We've only got five more minutes, so Brant just dismisses us early. I'm trying to hustle out of there when he calls me over to where he's standing with Lance.

"Uh, do you want me to get a towel?" I say, not looking at Lance, who seems to be trying to blow the rest of the snot out onto the ground. I feel bad for him, but . . . ewwwww is right.

"I was wondering if you could hang out with Lance and me here for a couple of minutes, to help him get used to the deep end. You did so well today, I want Lance to see that he can too."

I don't know how I can help Lance. If anything, I'm probably a cautionary tale, like, *If you're not careful, kids, you'll end up left behind in the baby pool.* I focus on drying myself off. "Uh, well, I was going to shower and change . . ."

Charles, Michelle, and Natasha are coming toward us.

"E!" shouts Michelle. "Epic UNO game about to happen! You in?"

I look back and Brant and Lance, who's shivering now. "Sorry, Brant, maybe next time." I don't meet Brant's eyes. "You'll be fine, Lance. See you tomorrow!" I run toward my friends before either of them can answer.

After UNO, I find Luke showing a group of little kids a book about the artist Romare Bearden when I walk into his classroom. "Remember, Romare Bearden's style—" He stops when he sees me. "Hey!" he says, jumping up. "What are you doing here? Don't you have a class or something?"

"It's my free," I say, "and I need to talk to you. In case you haven't noticed, I've been leaving you alone lately. But Brant says I'm ready to take the swim test again. I'm freaking out."

"That's great, bro," he says, squeezing my shoulder but looking over at the kids, who are staring at me. "I'm sure you'll have fun whatever you do. I'm teaching right now, can we talk about this later?" He starts walking back to the kids. One of them points to me and asks, "Who's that?"

"My little brother," says Luke. "He's leaving now. Okay, now . . . who wants to work in the style of Romare Bearden? Do you remember the word that I used?"

"Collage!" yells out a girl.

"That's French," says another kid.

"I have a brother," says a girl with swirls of cornrows.

Luke claps three times. "Right now, it's my turn to talk, and your turn to listen."

All the little kids put their hands to their ears like they're working really, really hard to use them.

"Luke," I say, but he was ushering his group to a round table. "Luke!" I call out a little louder. He looks over at a woman at the other end of the room, then comes over to me.

"Come on, E, my boss is right there," he says, sounding annoyed.

"Sorry . . . I just really need to talk to you."

"Listen, Mom is blowing up my phone," he says,

taking his phone out of his pocket. "Do you know what that's about?"

Oops. "Uh, I don't know, I talked to her a little while ago . . . I'll call her back. But seriously, I'm nervous about the swim test. I've got less than a week. Can you take a break? Want me to ask?" I start walking toward his boss.

"No!" Luke's voice is sharp, and it startles me and the little kids. He sighs. "Emmett, I have to focus. I have a break later, during period seven, you can look for me then. Or—"

"I have an idea," I said. "I could be like your helper or assistant! I'm free now, and—"

"Seriously, Emmett, listen to me. Go. Now. Whatever it is, you'll work it out. Or talk to you counselor, that's what he's there for! Anyway, I have D, remember? He's been great."

"Yeah, right," I mutter.

Luke pats me on the shoulder. "Stop wasting your free. And good news about the swim test, right?"

"Well, can you at least come to my test?" I ask. "Show of support?" *If you even know what that means anymore.*

"Yep, sure, text me the time, I'll be there." He moves away quickly, chanting "Coll-age! Coll-age!" to the kids until they join in. It does make me feel good to see how much they love him. It reminds me of me when I was little.

Okay, E, you got this. Luke will be there. You know what you're doing. Mom will be so proud, and Dad is going to be fist bumping his angel-friends up in heaven. I take a deep breath, and as I head to Street Style, I start to smile. Maybe this is a turning point. Maybe my superhero moment is on its way.

Chapter Thirty-Two

Someone is banging on the door, hard, and I almost fall over as I'm trying to change my shirt. I spilled syrup on it at breakfast; I hope no one (and by no one, I mean Natasha) noticed. More banging. Gleam Dream Clean Machine doing a surprise check?

"What the—" I jump up and open it, and Luke bogarts his way in.

"Why would you start asking Mom about Dad like that?" he says. "And about being *depressed*? Are you crazy???"

Finally! Luke is visiting me! Better late than never, I guess. But it's way too early in the day for dragon-level aggression. But it's not exactly working out the way I expected.

"'Crazy'? That language is kind of ableist," says Charles, who sits up in his bed and moves one of his accordion folders full of sheet music to the floor. He said it helps him digest. He keeps talking. "I have a thesaurus that . . ."

Luke turns to him, and it doesn't look good.

"Uh, Charles?" I start.

He looks up and gives me a thumbs-up. "Say no more," he says. "I'm gonna go . . . brush my teeth. Again." He leaves. "These choppers don't gleam all on their own." He glances at Luke, then grabs his bassoon case. "And uh, maybe I'll practice in the lounge too."

As soon as the door closes, Luke sits down and runs his hands through his hair. "What were you thinking, E?"

"I was just . . . asking a question," I say. "I was just in a bad mood or something."

"What kind of mood do you think you put Mom in, huh?" he asks. "The one thing I asked of you, you couldn't even do that."

"What are you talking about?" I ask.

"We're supposed to be making life easier for her," he says. "She's finally doing this doctor thing, the last thing she needs to worry about is . . . you talking about Dad."

"*Nobody* talks to me about Dad!" I say. "I ask questions because I want to know. You guys got to have him longer. Did you ever think about how I feel?"

"You do that enough for all of us," he mutters. That stops me cold. Luke's been mad at me before, but he's never talked like this. Either I've really messed up, or he's really changed. He didn't even ask me if I *am* depressed.

"Ever since you got into that school," I say, "you've changed."

"People are supposed to change, Emmett," he says. "That's growing up."

We sit for a while. I don't get why he's so mad at me, but at least he's here. I'm not trying to take Mom's opportunities away. But I remember when being the little brother meant that Mom and Luke were looking out for me. Now I feel like an obstacle.

Luke stands up. "Whatever. I told Mom that you were just having a bad day. Can you call her back, please?"

"Yeah," I answer, not looking at him. I didn't mean to upset Mom. Or maybe I did a little, at the time, but I feel bad about it now. "Yeah, I'll call her. And I'm . . . sorry."

He hugs me, and it takes a lot for me not to burst into tears like a baby. "Don't worry about it," he says. "Just call her. Listen, I gotta—"

"I know," I say. "You've got to work. See you later. I'll text you about the swim test, okay?"

Charles pops his head back in. "E, we have Black to the Future in five minutes."

"You know you're good with that swim test, bro," Luke says. "Brant says you can pass in your sleep."

"Not a good idea," says Charles. "I suspect most would advise staying wide awake in the water. Safety first!" Luke just looks at him, shakes his head, and leaves. "I guess my sense of humor didn't translate," says Charles.

"I get you, C-money," I say. "Don't worry about him."

"Charles."

"C-money is so good, though!" I say, and we joke-argue all the way to class.

***

I call Mom that night and apologize and she gets all mushy when I ask her if it's okay if we talk about Dad when I get back.

"Yes, honey, I'm sorry, I thought it would make you sad."

"And it makes you sad," I say. "Maybe we can comfort each other?"

Then she gets all mushy again, so I'm glad when Charles comes back into the room to get his English horn.

He says hi and offers to play for her and she says yes so then they spend time bonding while I just sit there.

"Your mom is cool," says Charles.

"My mom?"

"I mean, going to med school and stuff, that must be hard at her age."

"Yeah, she is mad old," I say. "I guess she's cool in a mom kind of way."

I don't take out Mr. Elefancy and Boo Boo after Charles falls asleep. It's enough for me to know they're there.

Chapter Thirty-Three

"Aw, man!" I say a few other words under my breath as my clay collapses into itself for the fourth time. I'd gotten all pumped up after we watched a movie about Dave the potter, an enslaved man who made all kinds of pottery and signed it because he could read and write. He even wrote poetry but had to keep it low key on account of racism and the fact that literacy could legit get him killed. I want to make something in honor of Dave. I've got less than a week left at DuBois, and at this rate, I'm gonna come out of the ceramics class with a pair of preschool-looking pinch pots.

"Yo, that looks like a demonstration in astronomy," says Troy. "Like the galaxy in motion or stars orbiting a planet."

"Are you a science major here or something?" I grumble, trying to gather up soggy bits of clay. "I thought this place was just about the arts."

"No, I'm ceramics, remember?" he says. Oh yeah. I look over; he's finishing up a tajine, which Ms. Clay told us was a Moroccan cooking pot. He's been making a set of cookware from around the world as a wedding gift for his aunt.

"That's . . . really good," I say.

"Yeah," he says. "I get three periods a day to work on this stuff, so . . ." He smiles at me. "I'm sure your street style routines are fire."

It's weird to see how hard people work when they don't have to. Well, Charisse would say Black people always have to.

"I see you've been studying Georgia Henrietta Harris, the Catawba artist," says Ms. Clay, strolling by. "Nice work, E."

"Uh, yes?" I say, and she smiles.

"Take your time, connect with your clay. There's no rush," she says. "Remember, you can continue your work even when you're not at DuBois."

I do know that I used up a lot of time trying to hang out with Luke. I look at Troy's tajine again and wonder what kind of dance routine I could have come up with by now.

***

That afternoon, Triple M is wondering the same thing. "You must be planning on very productive independent periods," he says after I pass again on showing the class what I've been working on for my solo.

"I got you," I say. But I've also got Michelle, and Natasha, and . . .

"Since this is a whole class project, we will work on what you plan—in your independent periods, Sparky—during a portion of class time. You just have to come prepared."

"I got you," I said again. "And I got this."

Famous last words, I guess. It's not so easy to plan a film project; a choreography routine; and help Michelle, Natasha, and Charles during my one independent period a day. I am trying to get stuff done during regular free periods too, but that's not going so well either.

"We did this combination yesterday, we all got it down," says Jeimy. "Do you have any new stuff to teach us yet?"

"Let's go over it again," I say, stalling for time.

"He's stalling," says Hannah, "He doesn't have anything."

"I do!" I say. "It's just . . . it's not ready yet."

"And when exactly," starts Triple M, "do you expect to be ready? You've got a few periods left to teach, rehearse, polish." I just look at the shiny wooden floor. Triple M claps. "Can someone tell Mr. Charles when the Camp Showcase occurs?"

"On the last night of camp," chants the class. Sheesh. He said someone, not everyone.

"Perhaps Mr. Charles is not a math genius, let's help him out. When is the last night of camp?"

"In six days."

I look up. The mirrors in the studio make it hard not to see yourself, especially when you really don't want to. "I got it, I apologize."

We spend the rest of the period on a trap music tribute that Hannah's been working on instead. At the end of class, I go over to Jeimy.

"Nice work today," I say. "You are really good."

She's stone-faced as she wipes her face with a towel. "You know, it's a big deal for a new kid to have his ideas picked for the show," she says. "Seems like we took you more seriously than you take yourself. If you don't give us something to work with, we'll all look bad. And also? I know I'm good." And she leaves.

I slowly gather up my things. Triple M is sitting cross-legged on the floor, writing something in his notebook. I stand there for a minute, but anything I can think of to say gets stuck at the bottom of my throat. He never looks up, so I walk out.

***

It hasn't been a good shoot. Natasha had scheduled a bunch of interviews with the younger kids, but no one had realized how much background noise there would be in their classrooms. And by no one, I mean me.

"Sorry," I call out, lowering the mic. "But I can tell that I'm picking up everything. It's going to be annoying."

Vanessa throws up her hands. "How are we going to stay on schedule? And why didn't we figure this out earlier? We've had the schedule for days. Days!" She probably would have wrung her hands at that moment except she had gone to spa class the day before and gotten fake talons longer than a predator bird's and had been walking around holding her hands out in front of her like a self-important zombie.

Trixie, the DP, points a thumb over at me. "Emmett signed off on each of these locations two days ago," she says.

Natasha turns to me. "Did you cross-reference the location and the schedule? You know we always have to know what's going to be happening while we film interviews."

"Um," I say. I do remember getting a sheet of paper during class the other day and just checking things off. I'd kind of thought it was just an exercise for learning's sake. "I checked it off on the sheet . . ."

"Okay," says Natasha slowly, "But did you know what you were checking off? I mean, I'm not sure why you didn't tell the rest of us that circus class would be going on ten feet away from our location." Right on cue, a bunch of little clowns started honking red horns and giggling.

When Vanessa glares at them, their TA glares back. "We're in circus," she says. "What were you expecting? We'll be miming tomorrow if you want to come back when it's quiet."

"I'm sorry," I say. "I messed up."

No one speaks as we pack up. Derek comes running across the grass and puts an arm around Natasha's slumped shoulders. He speaks to her in a low voice for a minute, then Natasha looks up, smiling.

"Hey everyone, D to the rescue! He's the producer for his team and he says they were going to shoot here tomorrow, but we can use their time instead. It'll be a lot easier to work during mime class." Her eyes slide over me. "I take full responsibility for today's issues. We'll make it up tomorrow. And I thank all of you for the support. We're going to make a great film, I promise. Huddle up!" Everyone runs over to her and gets into a huddle. I kind of hover on the outside until it breaks up. I try to say something to Natasha as everyone is leaving and not looking at me, but she follows their lead and walks right past me as though I'm invisible. And right about now, I am wishing I was.

Chapter Thirty-Four

The next day it really hits me that three weeks really is no time at all. I'm behind on my Street Style mini reports and forget about the choreography . . . I still haven't done my Black to the Future assignment, and even though I've graduated to coil pots, I've only managed one and it looks like it was made by my baby cousin Taden.

The swim test is hanging over my head like a perpetual storm cloud. It's become a mission for Dr. Triphammer, and I can tell he talked to my friends about it too. Every once in a while we'll be hanging in the room, and Charles will look up from his book and say something like, "When states were ordered to desegregate public pools, many chose to close them down instead." And somehow, when I was quizzing Natasha for the Blackity Bowl, we got to: "Legend has it that this person, the first Black woman nominated for an Oscar for Best Actress, dipped her toe into a hotel pool to protest segregation in the 1950s. So the hotel drained the pool." I looked at her hard when she answered, "Dorothy Dandridge," but she wasn't laughing.

"Do you always win?" I ask one day. We're sitting on

the stone benches near the main building. The sprinklers are on, and every once in a while a light spray of cool water hits my toes.

"Huh?" she asks, looking down at her notes. "Oh wait—that's not a Bowl question, that's a me question."

"Yeah, you," I say. "You've never gotten one of these wrong. You're the queen of everything around here, and everyone knows it. And they still *like* you! Do you ever slip up?"

"I mean . . ." She looks up. "This is kind of . . . deep. If you want to stop quizzing me, that's fine." She smiles. "What's going on with your plan? You haven't given me an assignment or anything. I'm worried that—"

"I don't have a plan," I say abruptly. I can't even play it off anymore. "I had an idea and I had no idea how to execute and I'm in this place where everyone else seems to know how to do stuff and for once I think I've gotten myself into something that I can't get myself out of."

"Oh no!" she says. "Come on, don't give up, we can fix this!" She picks up her notebook and pen, but then she sighs and puts it back down. "That's not what I meant."

"You mean I should give up, and we can't fix this?" I say. "Yeah, thanks for confirming." She really does think I'm a loser.

"No, I mean . . ." She takes a deep breath. "You can't tell anybody this, okay?" I nod. "I went back to Nurse Denene after we interviewed her."

I wait. Is Natasha sick?

She takes a deep breath. "I'm scared."

Huh? "What do you mean?"

"I mean that I'm scared. And I'm not supposed to be, ever. I've been so focused on achieving for so long, I feel like I have to keep going, no matter what. I know Michelle thinks she's hyping me up, but every time she says all that stuff about how great I am, I feel sick."

"But . . . you, you are always so calm and confident," I say. "*All* the time!"

What I'm saying is, it takes a lot to make it look easy. Like it's literally making me sick.
My head starts pounding . . ."

"And your stomach clenches up," I finish. I look at her and nod. "Been there."

"Nurse Denene says that the road from Black girl magic to strong Black woman can be harder than it seems. I don't want to disappoint my parents, I like having people think I've got it all together, but . . . it's hard to play that role twenty-four seven."

I take a deep breath. "Back home, it was easy for me to do stuff. I'm a debate star, I'm on the honor roll, teachers love me, I'm funny, I'm a great dancer"—I sneak a sideways glance—"people think I'm cute."

"They do?" she asks. "What people?" Then she laughs.

"I just thought I'd throw that in," I say. "But then there was this debate championship at the end of the year . . . and I didn't feel ready. Usually, I know I have it on lock, but . . . this time I wasn't sure. See, usually Luke helps me prep and stuff, but this time . . . he didn't. He was getting his portfolio ready for Rowell."

"Oh yeah! That's so cool. So, how did it go?"

"It didn't. I withdrew. I pretended that I wanted to give other people a chance to win, but I didn't want to risk losing."

"That's deep," she says.

"I don't know if I can do anything without my brother there to help me," I say, almost in a whisper. "And that's really scary."

She laughs. "Okay, this is depressing. We're quite a team."

I smile, mostly about the part about us being a team, because that's almost the same as being a couple. Maybe I didn't ruin things by confessing that I'm basically my own kryptonite.

We sit in silence for a while. A couple of geese stroll nearby. One of them looks straight at me and honks like, "Make a move, fool!" There's a little gap between me and Natasha; if I do a fake stretch, I can probably close it but . . .

"Well, this is good timing," she says, standing up. "We're having this conversation, and now we need to head to the last Superhero Secrets session."

I am the king of missed opportunities. I stand too. "Yeah, too bad we won't get any real tips there." I think back to that conversation with Reggie. "But maybe we can help ourselves? Shiny Suit Man is just going to look at his phone anyway. We can pretend to be doing the workbook but actually talk some real talk. I mean you, me, Charles, and Michelle." I not trying to have a heart to heart with the whole camp.

She nods slowly. "And maybe get some work done?" she says. "I'm scared of failing, but I'm not trying to. I still want to win on Camp Showcase night."

"Blackity Bowl or the film?"

She gives me a look. "Both, of course!"

Dr. Triphammer is walking toward us, yelling about who left the sprinkler on, so we get going fast.

"Are you going to talk to your brother?" Natasha asks as we run.

"Maybe," I say. "He'll probably get all choked up and feel guilty for leaving me hanging for most of the summer, but I'll tell him it's okay and maybe he'll make it up to me by dumping a bucket of horse poop from the stables on his intern's head." A boy can dream.

She laughs again, and says, "You're cute."

Yep. A boy can dream.

Chapter Thirty-Five

The next day, I spend most of my free time working with Michelle's cast on three routines that I've made up for *The Two Amys*. At first, I just worked in the room when Charles wasn't there, but it turns out that my friends really take this "creative community building" stuff seriously. Natasha had some clips of people like the Nicholas Brothers and Gregory Hines, and we watch them one evening during rec time. Without saying anything, I pretend we were on a date until she says, "And please don't get all weird on me like we're on some kind of date." And Charles is good at being a kind of crash test dummy—despite my best efforts, he hasn't gotten past his jerky specialty move, so I test out my teaching on him. If he can come close to the move I want, then I know I that the *Two Amys* performers will get it. I've just finished teaching him the big "Africa for Africans, At Home and Abroad" number when there's a knock on the door. I open it, it's my assistant Fred.

"Hey, Fred, what's up," I say as Charles does something almost like what I showed up.

"We have a meeting with Natasha," he says. "Actually,

it was supposed to start ten minutes ago. She's wondering where you are."

Oops. I leave with Fred and run over to the multipurpose room that Natasha had booked for our meeting. She's standing in the doorway with her arms folded.

Even though we had that whole conversation, Natasha is still . . . Natasha as far as I can tell. I wouldn't be surprised if she tried to win the Street Style competition too at this point. She keeps scheduling these extra "conferences" with her film crew and when I joked that "ain't nobody got time for that," she didn't even crack a smile. It's not even like she wants to have a one-on-one; she keeps pulling Ready Freddy and me aside to talk sound like I don't know what I'm doing. Which I don't, but still. It's humiliating.

"Did you forget again?" she asks as soon as I sit down.

Yes. "No," I say. "I was just . . ."

"It's not like we don't need to go over how to handle the equipment or anything, not like we haven't had accidents already," she says. "And by *we*, I mean *you*."

"I had one mishap, Natasha, and you're acting like I can't turn on a microphone," I say. Fred chuckles.

"You didn't, when we shot Triple M, remember?"

Fred laughs louder this time, then he looks at me and clears his throat.

Natasha sighs and goes on. "You're going to have to ask him when we can schedule a reshoot, by the way. It's not gonna be *me* up in his face."

Triple M had been giving me the stink eye the whole time and I know why. Everyone who wants to do a solo dance was supposed to show it to him already. I want a showstopper, but I'm . . . stuck. Everything I come up with,

I give to Michelle for *The Two Amys* or to the class for the group routine. That's actually coming together nicely; she's so good at telling me about the story she's trying to tell, I can really see it.

"Fred, can you give us a minute?" I ask. He moves like six inches away. I keep looking at him; finally he walks over to a tree. Then he comes back.

"We've got some great ambient noise happening right now—the birds, the swimming races in the background," he says. "I'm going to record some before lunch, if that's okay. I'll have it ready for our meeting."

"We're not meeting," I say.

"We're definitely meeting," says Natasha. "And thanks, Fred. Way to step up." He salutes, but she rolls her eyes and he puts his hand down fast. This time I laugh, and Fred finally leaves.

"Really not a good look for me," I grumble. "Can you chill a little on the whole way-to-step-up-Fred attitude?"

"Can you do some stepping up?" she asks, folding her arms. Immediately I go into some steps—I've finally learned the routine everyone was doing on the first night. She does not look amused or impressed. "And less clowning. I thought you wanted to help me win this thing."

We've been filming kids in all the classes; usually I let Fred do the recording while I "supervise" (which is really just me scheming on ways to hang out with Luke). I mean, I'm also trying to give Fred a chance to live his dream, so the way I see it, I'm doing a double good thing. That's what I keep telling myself.

"Natasha, you know you're going to win. You win every year. This project is great already, you can relax a little. You don't have to be all about the trophy for once. I thought you said—" I stop when she glares at me.

"No, I can't relax!" she says, and I raise my eyebrows. "I told you, I'm a legacy. People think I just get the film award because of my mom. It's up to me to prove them wrong."

"Nobody thinks that."

"Yeah, right," she says. "I know they're wrong, but still. I want them to know it too."

"Isn't the important thing that you know it?" I ask. "That you're being the best *you* you can be?"

She gives me some side eye for a minute, then we both laugh.

"Nice," she says. "Guess you've been hitting up that workbook."

"I've been perusing it as Charles would say." I shrug. "It stays terrible."

"Okay, what about you?" she asks. "You said you wanted to help me with this, and I'm sorry, but you haven't done that much.

Busted. "Okay, I do love movies—especially watching them. I told you how my brother and I were going to do that summer film festival at home . . ."

"Yeah, like a million times," she says drily.

"I've just been distracted. And overwhelmed. And I don't even know if film is a thing for me," I trail off. "Not like choreography. I love that for real. But I'm messing that up too."

"I'm not trying to say I told you so," she says. The bell for lunch rings, and kids start running toward the dining hall. "But I totally told you so!"

"Okay, okay," I say. "You were right. And so was I—remember I said I was a secretly a failure? I think that means I win!" She doesn't laugh. "The truth is," I continue, "I'm really behind on my dance for Street Style, and they're depending on me . . . and Triple M is about to annihilate me . . ."

"It's fine," she says. "Let's just be honest with each other, okay? I thought we were friends—and no shade—but it's pretty obvious that Fred has been doing most of the work."

"Ouch," I say.

"Not because you're a failure, Emmet. In fact, a lot of your problem is because you've been a good friend. Both Michelle and Charles have talked about how much you're helping them. And . . . well, even if you haven't been a big help on this film, you've listened to me, and I appreciate that. So, what about you? What's up with your solo?"

"It's great, just putting on the finishing touches," I say quickly. I may not be a complete failure yet, but I still need to win something. And I might have a shot with Natasha if I show up and show out big time at the Camp Showcase. "It's gonna be fire." I smile. You'll feel good about losing to me."

She smiles back and starts to walk away, then turns back to look at me. "Good luck. But make no mistake, I want to win," she says. "And since, as you say, I'm amazing, I should!" She pauses. "I'm gonna go meet with Fred, make him the official sound guy. I'll talk to you later."

I wave goodbye, glad that she didn't get all twisted up about what I said. Natasha's cool. And she's smart—I should probably talk to her more about my film festival, she might have some good ideas. I know I'm not doing a great job of showing her my best self, but there's still time. Then I see Derek catch up to her. He puts his arm on her shoulder, and instead of shrugging him off, she leans in. Guess she's not that smart after all.

Chapter Thirty-Six

In Black to the Future, Charisse and Gordon ask a kid named Chris to come up and read something.

"'We don't have to be what you want us to be,'" Chris reads slowly, and then sits down and high-fives all the people around him like he did some real work.

"That's a quote attributed to Bill Russell," says Charisse. "A man who many consider to be one of the greatest professional basketball players of all time."

Someone coughs out, "LeBron," and this girl Eloisa yells, "Jorrrrdannnnn!"

"Bill Russell led the Celtics to eleven championships and was an outspoken social activist," says Charisse, looking unbothered. "LeBron James follows a similar path in many ways. Anyway, Russell often refused to 'play the game' to get ahead in the business of pro ball, which may be why many of you don't know his name."

"Our topic today is Great Expectations and Blaxploitation" says Gordon. "And yes, I came up with that myself." He smiles. "Pretty good, right?"

Charisse rolls her eyes. "We want to talk about how

we may sometimes feel that we have to be a certain way in order to succeed as Black people, whether or not we feel like we can just "be."

I raise my hand. "I thought Blaxploitation films were all about stereotypes of Black people. Why would we talk about that?"

"Sometimes those films had political messages," chimes in Natasha.

"And they're part of our culture," adds another kid.

"My mom says we don't need to be showing out in front of white people," says a boy. "We're already trying to fight negative images of our community."

"Um, hello? Who created those images in the first place? And why are we even worrying about what white people think?" asks Michelle. "We already know that it's not going to be good, when it comes to us. We need to just do our own things, like Marcus Garvey said."

I know all about Marcus Garvey now! Yardies unite!

"But we have to 'do our own thing' in a white world," says Troy. "So we gotta be realistic."

And we're off. We've gotten so comfortable that Gordon and Charisse mostly sit back and let us talk, but I can tell they're really listening. After a while, Charisse asks us about our favorite YouTubers.

"Oh wait, don't try and take away my videos," says a kid. "You're ruining all the fun!"

Everybody laughs, but I'm seriously a little nervous that they'll tell me that some of my faves are problematic. Everything's so complicated when you know more about how complicated everything is.

Luke speaks up. "What I don't get is why people like that guy Brett in the Hood can act all hard core and call himself a thug and have six million subscribers, but an actual Black person doing the same thing can't get anything except maybe wrongly arrested." He gets many snaps after that comment.

"Performing Blackness," says Charisse. "Let's dig in. How do you feel about it?"

"I mean, I take it as a compliment," says a kid who goes by N. T. "Everybody wants to be cool like us."

"Yeah," says Luke, "but no one wants to be us, right?" This time he gets applause. I join in too, keeping my hands low because I'm still mad.

"Or even be around us," adds Troy. "Like, I live in New York City—"

"WE KNOW!" yell a bunch of people. He does bring it up a lot.

"And anyway," he continues, "all the schools in my neighborhood are like a hundred and ten percent Black people, with a few Dominicans in the mix. But there are a lot of white kids who live in the neighborhood now, except they all go to other schools. I'm cool with some of them, but there's still this line. It's like we live in an invisible, separate world or something."

"So, does anyone get a pass?" asks Charisse. "Do we all have that non-Black friend who's 'down' or 'cool'? Is there a series of tests that has to be passed?"

"Knowledge of Hip-Hop one oh one!" someone yells out.

"Being able to clap on the two and four!"

"Not crying when you get called out!"

"Knowing there's no such thing as reverse racism," says Luke. "Being anti-racist instead of just not-racist." Standing O for my brother.

"But for why," yells out Hannah, "Why do we have to talk about being Black? Why can't we just *be Black*?"

"Why not both?" I say without thinking, and to my surprise, I get some claps. I clear my throat. "I mean, maybe you guys are more used to this, but it's been . . . interesting in a good way, having these discussions. I'm thinking about myself more than I ever have before."

"That doesn't seem possible," says Luke, and the laughs are a little louder than I'd like.

"I mean," I say, "about my . . . Blackness. And how much I can just love it. How all of us can. Maybe some of us don't realize that yet, or . . . just need reminders."

"On that note," says Gordon," we'll stop there. Now I know this is camp, so you're not really trying to do a whole lot of homework but . . ."

Loud groans.

"Too late," calls out Hannah. "All y'all had us doing presentations and reports like it's summer school, not summer camp."

The boy who always asks if there's going to be a test raises his hand. I think his name is Malcolm. "Maybe we should get grades," he starts, but he's drowned out by boos.

Gordon shushes us. "This is optional. We want you to write a letter to yourself at . . . ten years old. A point before you realized how complex issues of race are."

"What would you tell yourself to help you get through now?" adds Charisse. "What advice would you give? How would you want you to be, to walk in the world?"

"Does it have to be written?" asks Natasha. "What about other forms of media and expression?"

"Oooooh!" says Charisse, jumping up. "That gives me an idea!" She gets in a quick huddle with Gordon, then she announces, "Pending a conversation with Dr. Triphammer, we will have a Black to the Future group presentation on showcase night! We know it's only a couple of days from now, so don't worry about doing anything elaborate, and you can use any media or creative form of expression for this project. It's really about just sharing what's been important to you." There's an excited buzz, and I see Derek run up to Luke; he looks like he's asking him a question.

Maybe-Malcolm raises his hand again. "Since it's not school, I know we can't get grades. Are there going to be prizes or anything?"

Gordon and Charisse just look at him, and then they both say "Boy, bye," at the same time, and we all laugh.

Chapter Thirty-Seven

Sometimes, it's hard to figure out what we would like to do. Try to write down all the things you like to do for fun. Do you like to write stories? Draw? Do you like to talk? Make things? Read? Make a list. Now think about the things that you DON'T like to do. Maybe you don't like them because they seem hard, or "everybody else" doesn't like them either. Maybe you just need a little help, or you need to find someone who likes doing those things, too. Remember, it's okay to like things other people may not like. It doesn't make you weird or strange, it just means that you are a special individual.

I toss Shiny Suit Man's workbook to the floor, and finish getting ready to meet Charles for breakfast. I don't even know why I'm reading it; only a few days of camp left and I'm not any different than I was when I got here. Hmmm . . . .DuBois *has* given me choreographer goals that I never knew I had. And friends like Charles and Michelle that I've never actually had. I love hanging out and joking around with WeeDee and Billy, but this . . . is different. More. Yes,

I'm a special individual, Shiny Suit Man, but it feels good not to be the One, the Black One, and something even more special happens when we're together.

I like to dance.

I like to make up dances

I like teaching people the dances I make up

Despite our inauspicious start, I like Charles (and I'm using words like "inauspicious" so I guess he's rubbing off on me).

I like movies.

I like Michelle.

I like Natasha. A lot.

I like Flamin' Peppa Cheese Puffies on top of vanilla ice cream a lot too.

Even though I didn't mean to get Mom and Luke all upset, I like being reminded that my brother is there for me because deep down I still know I'm on kind of shaky ground when he's not.

I guess it's a start.

Chapter Thirty-Eight

Dr. Triphammer stops me as I'm bussing my breakfast tray. "Your name again, young man? A member of the Young Lions, right?"

He remembers. "Uh, I'm Emmett . . . Emmett Charles."

"Right," he says. "You're taking another swim test today, I hear."

I swallow and nod. I've been trying not to think about it all morning, which means I've been thinking about it all morning.

"Good luck." I'm pretty sure that by *good luck* he means "don't mess it up," and I can also tell that instead of *mess* he's really thinking a different word, one that Mom would freak if she heard me say.

"Thanks, sir. I need it."

"You know"—he pats my on the shoulder—"you've already had good luck when it comes to DuBois. That's how you got here!"

"Huh?"

"I remembered your name . . . Emmett Charles. You

were one of the people who applied right before the summer program started."

"That's right, I was . . . so excited to hear about my brother Luke's opportunity, I, um . . . threw myself into applying. Thanks so much for your consideration."

"Oh, it was actually no trouble at all. That's what I mean," he says. "We had so many applications for that last-minute opening that we decided to do a lottery, and your name was picked out of a hat. And then you turned out to be the younger brother of one of my most promising hires! I call that some good fortune all around!" He laughs.

Wait, so I didn't really get in? All this time I've been thinking that my insecurities were all in my head, but . . . maybe I really don't belong? "I . . . um . . ." I can't get anything out. I pick up a stray orange that's been left on a tray.

"So," he says, "take advantage of the opportunity." He leans down and puts his face pretty close to mine. I think he had a spinach omelet for breakfast. "At DuBois we swim. Show UP! Show OUT!" He stands up straight and smiles again. "Good luck with that test!" He walks away, and it's a full minute before a thin trickle of wetness in my palm makes me realize that I'm still holding the orange, and I've squeezed it open like a burst, soggy, balloon.

***

"You know you got this, right?" says Brant as Charles and I walk up to the pool. "You've got the skills, you just gotta get outside of your own head, get over the anxiety."

I'd sent Luke a text this morning and a reminder a little while ago.

"It's not that," I say quickly. "It's . . . complicated."

Brant looks at his watch. "We gotta get going. I have a group coming in ten minutes. Trianna and Robert are re-testing too. Hit the shower."

Charles walks over to the locker room with me, trying to make me laugh with some dance moves. "Are you okay?" he asks. "You look a little sick. What did you have for breakfast?"

Shattered illusions. "I'm fine," I say. "Just want to get this over with."

I see Michelle, Natasha, Troy, and Hannah standing by the pool now. They all wave, and I lift a quick hand in return. I have an audience, but not the one I need. "Luke is supposed to be here," I say, looking around. "Can you keep a lookout for him?"

Charles nods. "Should I keep dancing? You know, for the ladies?" We both laugh.

"Yeah, I think we're all good," I say. "And . . . thanks. My, um, dad was going to teach me to swim . . . and then he died."

"I'm sorry," Charles says. I know that's about all he can say, but still.

I'm angry all of a sudden. "Yeah, me too." I fake a smile. "So, Luke has always been like, dadly in a way . . . he's always there for me. He was gonna teach me this summer, but now . . ." I shrug.

"Now, you got this! You can beat your brother in a swim race during the next free period!" Charles says. After a pause, he adds. "I bet your dad would be proud of you."

"I guess," I say. "I haven't passed yet." I go in and take the mandatory quick freezing cold shower. When I get back outside, Charles shakes his head.

"Haven't seen him." he says. Since I left my phone in the locker room, I use Charles's to text Luke again. "Do you want me to stay?" Charles asks. "I have chamber ensemble, but I can cut. We've been working on the same four measures for the last five days."

I give him a fist bump. "Nah, it's fine. You go ahead. I'll ask Brant if I can go last. Luke should be here by the time I get in the water." Charles gives me another fist bump, then jogs off.

I walk slowly over to Brant, who gives me a funny look. "You okay, Emmett? You were gone for a while."

"Have you seen Luke?" I ask.

"Your brother? He's probably with his group," says Brant. "Why? Something wrong? You want me to get Marcus?"

"No, it's just that Luke was supposed to meet me here. For my test. Not that it's a big deal, it's just like . . . a tradition. Not that I've taken a lot of swim tests before, because I haven't, but . . ." I trail off.

Brant shrugs. "We need to get started. He looks at his waterproof watch, which had looked so cool to me on the first day, like something Aquaman would wear. But right now, even though it's digital, I think I can hear it ticking, and it's like: COUNTDOWN TO YOUR DOOM, EMMETT. Do I even hear an echo? I look over to where Natasha and the others are standing. Charles is back! I can't believe he's cutting his class for this.

"Can I go last?" I ask, pointing to Trianna and Robert. They're both in the youngest camper group and not even novices. Just re-testing so that they can move up a level and flex on people like me. Like those people who do the extra credit so they can have a score over a hundred. I know that move. I've been those people.

Brant sighs. "Sure, Emmett. But it's only going to be a few minutes. So be ready."

It's like I literally blink, and then it's my turn. Luke is not here. The Isle looks a million miles away. I walk to the edge of the big pool, take a deep breath, and then lower myself in.

***

The bell rings as I'm climbing out of the pool. Brant squats down. "It's in your head, bro. I'm sorry. You can sign up for the test all the way up until it's time to go home, okay? Four more days . . . " He pats me on the shoulder and lifts me the rest of the way out of the water.

I don't say anything, I don't even grab my towel. I just run toward the art shack. I can't believe it. This is all Luke's fault. My brother let me down for real.

***

Luke isn't at the art shack, so I try his dorm. I'm out of breath and still dripping wet when I bang on his door.

"Bro, chill," says a counselor named Tommy. He frowns. "Can I help you with something?"

"Have you seen Luke Charles?"

"Not since this morning when he took his group on a mini hike," says Tommy. "He's a busy guy. You want to leave him a message?"

"Yeah," I say. "Tell him his brother needed him. If that matters at all."

***

When I get to dinner, Marcus asks "How did it—" and my face must tell the whole story, because none of my friends bring up the test after that.

"Hey!" says Luke, walking up to my table with a smile. "You would not believe how great today went! This morning I took some kids on a field trip to find natural ephemera for their three-D collages and—"

"Whatever, Luke," I say, not looking up at him. There's a pause, and he says. "I couldn't text you back, bro, I'm sorry. Brant told me you were more than ready to pass, though. How was it? You going to race me?"

I keep eating and not looking at him. Michelle clears her throat.

"Oh, wait, no," Luke says, "Wait . . . really?"

"Yeah, you really didn't show up," I snap. "Thanks a lot, you ruined it for me."

"Emmett, it's not easy, I can't always just take time off to babysit you—"

"I thought you realized how important this was," I say. "It's not like I was just asking you to hang out with me. You're the one who's been saying what a big deal this stupid swim test was. I don't even want to learn to swim." It's like my brain and my mouth are moving in two different directions. I know I'm being stupid, but I can't stop.

"I knew you *didn't* need me," he says. "And other people did. But I—"

"Well, I guess you were wrong, because I failed. Again. Thanks, bro." I stand and collect my dinner trash. Derek runs over and taps Luke on the shoulder.

"Hey, Dr. Triphammer says we can use the multipurpose room," he says. Derek looks at Charles, Michelle, and me and nods quickly.

Luke gives me a quick shoulder hug and leans in to whisper. "I'm sorry, okay? But I talked to Brant yesterday and he said you were golden. You must have just gotten afraid."

I stare straight ahead. Michelle clears her throat again, and Charles starts humming some marching band kind of tune. After a minute, Luke leaves with Derek, who glances back a couple of times with a puzzled look on his face.

Chapter Thirty-Nine

We've got four days left, and I'm not checking for Luke anymore, I'm not even thinking about him. I don't even notice Derek and him together all the time. And Derek is always following him around with a camera, probably distracting my brother from his job so he can help on some stupid project. I bet he kept Luke from showing up for my swim test. Whatever, I'm not doing it again. Maybe I'll try when I get home and none of these people are around, maybe not. I was doing fine. Just when I thought I was settling in, that jerk had to ruin it for me.

During badminton, I low key try to impress Natasha with my form.

"You look like Arthur Ashe!" she says.

"Who's he?" I ask.

"Never mind, and you actually don't," she answers, laughing. "I was just trying to be encouraging."

I like the easy way we can joke with each other. Normally I'd ask Luke for some tips on how to take it to the next level. As we put away the rackets and birdies, I remember how he tried to help me talk to Tonya when we were home. My brother wouldn't have left me hanging unless it was for a very good reason. I bet Derek made up some stupid story and my stupid brother fell for it because all he cares about these days is looking like a super mentor junior counselor or whatever, and not being my brother. But whatever, I don't even care about that anymore. I wasted too much time on that stupid film idea. Not anymore. If I really got here on a fluke, I'm going to prove that I should have been here all along.

Charles has given me one of his backup planners, and I carry it everywhere, just like him. It's actually helping me schedule time to work on Michelle's play, take my turns at quizzing Natasha, work on my choreography for the Street Style team dance and my letter to myself for Black to the Future. The one thing I haven't worked on is my solo. Triple M stopped asking me about it. I know it's the thing that will help me leave this place with a good impression, but I just don't have time.

Charles has been around Michelle's rehearsals as much as he can, so I end up spending a lot of time with my friends anyway. Every once in a while, I work with Charles on some moves so he can impress Michelle on the last night, but he doesn't get far beyond the two step; he's so happy about having even a little rhythm that it seems like he'll be cool with uncle-at-the-wedding dancing for the rest of his life.

I've been seeing Natasha and a few of her team members huddle up at lunch or after dinner, and I think about joining them, but it seems like she has it covered. I've been trying to do better after our little talk, but also look like I'm not trying too hard, the way Derek does, always in her face (when he's not in Luke's.) But then I miss out on opportunities to talk to her, and that's frustrating. Charles says it's a self-fulfilling prophecy, and then he says a lot more things that he's read in his *Encyclopedia of Prophecy and Prediction*. It doesn't help.

***

Ms. Clay makes me take all my finished pinch pots out of the studio; I know I won't have room for thirty-seven bowlish-shaped objects in my room, but maybe Mom will appreciate my "sustained artistic effort," which is what Ms. Clay calls it as she gives me a box to carry them back to my room. I can feel the end of camp getting closer, and I'm not sure what I'll have to show for it. Yesterday, Michelle and I came in third on the gingerbread house challenge; our Leaning Tower of Pisa just fell over. But it was delicious.

***

I'm late for Street Style, but I promised Michelle I'd record some choreography for the *Two Amys* cast to practice with. I need a tripod for my phone, so I run over to the media center to borrow one. Of *course* it's locked, and it takes me twenty minutes before I can find someone on the maintenance team to open it. Mr. Bookman has a huge key ring with about 762 keys on it; it seems like he tries each one before getting to the one that opens the room.

"Um, thanks very much, sir," I say, hoping good manners will prevent questions. Technically I'm not supposed to be able to borrow anything without a counselor present to sign it out. But he just waves me inside and walks away, key ring jangling. I wait in the doorway until he's out of sight.

The media center is empty and the AC is blasting, which means it's the perfect spot for me right now, because I feel like I could spontaneously combust.

I take some deep breaths. I'm now twenty-five minutes late for Street Style, and I can feel the wrath already. Just hoping that the fact that I've finished my routine will make up for it. But I got so caught up in my impromptu film idea, I forgot to change for rehearsal, which means I'm going to have to go back to the dorm before I go to Street Style and make Triple M even madder than he's already going to be. I sigh and look around for a place to put the camera.

There's an empty shelf above the row of computer stations, where a bunch of cameras and equipment are connected to the desktops. As I maneuver past, I can see that a lot of film students are in the process of transferring footage from their cameras. I see Natasha's name on a screen that says "transfer complete." Of course she's done. I keep walking, and it's a minute before I realize that I'm standing in front of Derek's project. A camera is connected, and it says "transfer in progress" on the screen. There's also a flash drive connected to the computer, probably full of photos. There's a folder up on the screen called "Reaching Up and Out," which is stupid because Derek is stupid. Without thinking, I click on it and the first thing that comes up is a big close-up of Luke and Derek. I keep going, and there's Luke teaching a group of kids of how to build something out of toothpicks, Luke tying some kids' shoes, Luke leading an outdoor art walk, Luke showing little kids how to mix paints, Luke talking about Augusta Savage in Black to the Future . . . Derek really made a whole film about *my* brother. And it looks way better than anything I could have done.

Before my mind can connect with my hand, I press delete.

Are you sure you want to delete?

I click the mouse hard on yes. I pull the camera out of the computer, then I pull out the flash drive too. I pry open the drive, drop the pieces on the floor, and kick them under the table. The bell starts ringing—or is that in my ears? What did I just do? I shake myself and rush to the door. As I'm closing it, I take another look back at the computer; there's a sad face on the screen now. I back out, starting to pull the door shut—and crash into someone. We both almost fall.

It's Derek.

"Watch it, Emmett!" he growls, shoving me lightly as he gets up. He pushes past me and continues into the media center. It hits me, what I just did.

Are you sure you want to delete?

I sigh and follow Derek inside, walking right to my destruction.

He's sitting in front of the computer where his project had been transferring, staring. I stand a little away, keeping my eyes on him, just in case he tries to take me down. For a second, I picture him doing back flips toward me and nunchucking my brains out like some kind of martial arts superhero, but he just sits there, staring. The air conditioner's humming feels like it's gotten louder, and I shiver. Now I'm cold. I clear my throat.

He doesn't look at me. "Where's the flash drive?" he asks in a flat voice.

"I—It's . . ." I croak. I point under the table, where the pieces are. "Under there."

He looks down, picks up the pieces, and starts trying to put them back together. He still doesn't look at me, and after a minute, I move closer.

"It was me," I say. I sit down in the seat next to him.

"I did it. I deleted your folder too."

He still doesn't look at me or say anything. As though I'm not there, he starts muttering to himself. "I still have the footage I just shot . . . maybe Reggie can figure out how to retrieve—"

"Did you hear me?" I say louder. "I did that. Just now. So . . . come at me, bro." I really wish my voice didn't crack at the worst possible times. Still, I stand up and try to look tough.

Finally he turns to me . . . and shrugs. "Whatever." He goes back to the pieces and muttering to himself.

I raise my voice. "I—I just. You've been monopolizing my brother since we got here, and it makes me sick, like he things you're some kind of good guy—you don't deserve to hang out with Luke!"

"Okay, whatever."

Now I'm mad again, and I push my face closer to his. "See what I mean? You don't even care! You just do stuff to be a jerk. You probably knew I wanted to make a movie with my brother and you just did this to get to me. Like, why are you all up in his face all the time anyway? It's kind of *creepy*, actually. He's not your brother, he's mine! Are you jealous?" I stop, breathing hard.

He stands too and leans toward me. I want to step back so badly, but I don't.

"Yeah. I am jealous. Your brother has been real cool to me. I didn't even want to come back this year, but my parents made me. My brother died last Halloween. Hit and run. He was a senior. He was about to be homecoming king. He used to make me sandwiches and we'd have middle of the night *Star Wars* marathons."

I sit back down.

"My parents made me come because they didn't

want me sitting around being depressed. Like, what else am I supposed to be? They think playing basketball and running around outside is supposed to make me forget that Duane is dead? I'd hear them whispering about him, but if they saw me, they stopped. They never talk about him in front of me. It's like they want me to forget, as if that's possible."

"I'm . . . I'm sorry," I say in a very small voice. I don't think he hears me, and I know that doesn't matter.

"Luke showed me these collages he made, about . . . about your dad. He lets me talk about my brother and how mad I get sometimes, even at him—and he never makes me feel guilty. Or like I'm a punk. So yeah, I guess I am all up in his face all the time."

"I'm sorry," I say, louder.

"I just thought the film would be a cool project, and . . . a way to say thank you . . . Oh well. Stupid idea."

"I didn't know—"

But it doesn't matter, does it?

Derek shrugs. "Whatever. It probably sucked. You did me a favor, I bet. So, sorry if you thought you were going to make me cry or something. You lose, again."

"I . . . saw some of it. It looked good," I say. "I . . . Was that really all the footage you had?" Derek doesn't answer. I clear my throat. "Luke talked to you about our dad?"

Derek nods and looks away. "Yeah, a little."

"He never talks about him to me, neither does Mom. Nobody does. And I was so little . . . I'm scared I'm forgetting. Luke doesn't get that."

Why am I telling Derek all this?

"It hurts for me to remember. Your brother got that. He let it be hard, didn't try to cheer me up all the time."

All of a sudden I remember this time that Dad took me and Luke to this sorry little amusement park a couple of hours away. I was too little to go on the good rides, and I cried until he got me this cardboard kaleidoscope. I thought it was amazing, and while Dad and Luke went on this wild loop-the-loop roller coaster, I waited with the attendant, looking through my kaleidoscope and loving how I could turn it and it would go from the confusing mishmash into a picture, clear and true. Sometimes, in an instant, my brain does that, like now. I see Luke in my mind, all of him—the artist, the counselor tying shoes, the brother who saved me from being Pee Pants, Mom's chef . . . I hadn't thought about how much Luke might be hurting. He wasn't supposed to hurt, he was just supposed to be my big brother.

Derek sits down. "I shot some footage right now. I can probably make something out of it." He looks over at me. "If you don't mind, I'd like to work alone."

"Maybe . . . maybe I can help. As a way of making it up to you?" I say. "I'm just . . . sorry."

Derek shakes his head. "No, thanks. But if you're worried I'm going to tell, don't. I'm not a snitch."

"I wouldn't blame you. But that's not why I want to help. *I* did this. It's my fault, I should help. It's the right thing to do."

Derek shakes his head again. "I said no. And to be honest, I take back the thanks. Just leave me alone, please? Why don't you go swimming or something? Oh, right—you can't swim."

I sit there for a while, waiting. But he stares straight ahead. I guess the best I can do at this point is . . . what he's asking me to do.

"I'm sorry," I say again. But I don't feel better for saying it. And I guess sometimes, that's how it goes.

Chapter Forty

I make the video for Michelle and her cast, going through the motions without even thinking. By the time I get to the studio, Triple M is there alone; the rest of the class is long gone. He's standing and looking at his clipboard; he has all our placements laid out on sheets of paper on the floor.

"You missed class," he says, without turning around.

"I'm sorry, Mr. Micah McDowell," I say quickly. "I truly apologize. There's no excuse." I think of all the things he says to us in class. "I hold myself accountable for my actions. I let my team down, and I'm sorry. I'll get any changes from Trixie or Kelly. I can practice with the others during dinner, or after dinner, or whenever they're available. I'll make myself available. I have the whole routine worked out, and I can teach it to each person individually, whenever they want. And . . . the truth is, I'm officially withdrawing from trying out for a solo." I take a deep breath. "I haven't worked on it enough, and I don't want to embarrass myself . . . or you."

He looks up at me. "Okay. Apology accepted. And your official withdrawal too." He goes back to his clipboard.

"Goodbye."

"Um, sir, I'm really, really sorry. I—"

"I heard you," he asks. "As you clearly know, class is over. I'm going to go work on some routines with the advanced ballet students, I have another class to prepare for. You are dismissed."

"But—"

"Thank you for coming to apologize. Now, go." He starts picking up his papers.

"I've really been working hard!" I burst out. "And I've been trying to help everybody else with stuff . . . you know I'm the first one here every time—except this time—and I—" My voice breaks, and I have to stop for a second, because I am NOT going to cry. "I love this class. It's my favorite. Can I just show *you* the solo? I know you'll love it. Please, Mr. Micah McDowell." I want him to at least know what I could have done.

He walks over to his gym bag. "I said what I said. I am busy right now."

"You haven't even said anything about all the work I've been doing!" I say. "You know how good I am, it's why you let me in the class! I've been working so hard, doing all this stuff to—"

"To what?" His voice is dangerously low. "I'm assuming that the next words out of your mouth are going to be 'to help your team, your community.' Right? Not for your own personal glory, yes? Because now, you won't be dancing in the group number either. Now, please—"

"But I made the whole thing up! That's not fair!"

"It wasn't fair to your teammates for you to miss the final rehearsal."

I don't look him in the eye. Not only am I not a good guy, I messed up my own chance to be great. I'll be leaving this place the same way I came in—not able to shine on my own.

"Feel free to cheer your teammates on at the Camp Showcase, even though you won't have the spotlight you seem to think is so essential. Now I'm late for my appointment. So, since you haven't left, I'll go instead." And he swoops up his bag, marches past me, and leaves.

I stand in the studio alone. After a few seconds I start doing my solo routine without even thinking. I watch myself in the mirror—it's fire, just like I knew it would be. I run through it a few more times. Then I lie on the floor and stay in the studio until the bell rings for dinner.

***

"Where've you been?" asks Charles. Tonight is make your own pasta and he's trying to decide between the cauliflower gnocchi and the sweet spaghetti.

I shrug. "Just . . . nowhere. I had to talk to Triple M."

"Oh yeah, did you show him your solo? What did he say? Remember, a Triple M blink is like a hug. And if he said okay, then you're gold." The server gives him two plates so he can get both the gnocchi and the spaghetti. "Thanks!" he says, like he just won a million dollars. I get bowties but forget to get a topping, so I have a heaping bowl of plain bowties and a milk carton. When we get to the table, my plate looks like a toddler's.

"Super appetizing," says Michelle, looking at me. Troy is asking her about her next project, and she's telling him that she's already started researching someone named Funmilayo Kuti.

He acts all proud when he says, "Oh yeah, Fela's mom?" And Michelle chews him out about saying "Fela's mom" instead of her actual name, which makes Charles happy. I just sit and poke at my bowties.

"I am so ready for this night hike," Charles loud-whispers to me. "I'm going to do *the thing* there. I even got permission from Dr. Triphammer. The rest of the ensemble is primed and ready. They didn't even laugh at me that much. Thanks, E. I owe this all to you."

"Huh?" I ask. He gives me a look and elbows me so hard I almost fall off the bench. "Oh—yeah." His Michelle concert. I forgot all about that. "Wait, why'd you talk to Dr. Triphammer?"

"I'm going to play for everyone around the campfire," he says. "You gave me the confidence to talk to some of the other kids in wind ensemble, and we put together a whole mini-show. A few other people have their own compositions to perform too. Gabby is going to do a saxophone piece, and Brianna is bringing out her tuba! A bunch of us are going to have to help carry it."

"Oh, that's . . . great," I say. "But I thought this was supposed to be a thing for you and" —I lean my head toward Michelle—"you know who."

Charles shrugs and scoops up a spoonful of each of his pastas. "Yeah, well, camp's almost over, and it's kind of fun to do it as a group thing. And the strings always do concerts—this is our chance to really blow, and shine, so to speak. Blow, get it?" He lowers his voice to a real whisper. "And the truth is, I don't know if my nerves could take it. This way, she'll still hear it. And she'll still be my friend. I can live with that for now." He smiles. "And by the time I'm ready, I'll have this smooth Jeffrey Osborne piece all worked out on the keytar, so watch out, Michelle."

"Who?" I ask. "Never mind, actually. You and your keytar know, that's enough."

"Ha, you'll come around. And you know, Jeffrey

Osborne, "On the Wings of Love'? It's a classic! Timeless!" He starts singing it,

"Got it, got it," I cover my ears. "That's an uncle and auntie staple," I say. "Great-uncle and auntie! You can stop now." We both laugh.

"Thanks for helping me work that out, E. You really had my back. We make a good team."

"Uh, yeah, okay, you're welcome, I guess," I say.

Natasha comes over, with her food in a to-go container. "Hey, guys, I just wanted to say hi. My film group is going to eat over at the studio, we're finishing up a few things."

"I thought you were done," I blurt out. Oops. I probably wasn't supposed to know that.
She gives me a funny look. "We had time to do a documentary about our process, what we learned about each other, from working together."

"That's a great idea," I say.

Natasha nods. "Cool, cool. Okay, I gotta go, we don't have much time."

"Should I come too?" I ask weakly. "Maybe I can help Fred?"

She shrugs. "Nah, he's good." She doesn't even sound mad, and somehow that makes me feel worse.

"I'm sorry," I say again.

"You've been under a lot of pressure," says Natasha. "You're new, you've been helping all of us, you're like the star of Street Style . . ." I open my mouth, but she goes on. "I've learned a lot about pressure and expectations this summer."

"Y'all are so bougie, talking about *lessons learned*—" starts Troy from across the table, but Natasha stops him with a look.

"Okay, I *really* have to go," she says. "I'll see you at the hike!" She smiles a small smile and leaves.

Charles and Michelle look from me to Natasha and back again. Natasha catches up to a few other people in the film group, including Derek.

"That was . . ." says Charles. "I feel like there were parts of that conversation that I missed, even though I heard every word."

"Emmett messed up somehow, and Natasha was stressed about it but trying to act unbothered," says Michelle. "Not that difficult." She looks at me. "Don't worry, she doesn't hold grudges. She probably won't even be thinking about you in ten minutes."

"I'm no expert on this stuff," says Charles, "but I don't think that made my boy E feel any better."

I eat some of my bowties while Charles pats me on the back.

Chapter Forty-One

Charles is very talky as we get our stuff together for the night hike. He's got this huge backpack, and his bassoon in his case, and another bag with bug spray, granola bars, flashlight, Chapstick, sunscreen, a poncho, a mini pillow, and water bottles.

"This hike is just tonight right?" I ask. "And it's not all night?"

"Yep!" he says. "I used to overpack, but I've learned my lesson."

I look at him. "Sunscreen? I mean, it's a *night* hike. And you're Black, anyway."

"UV rays never sleep," he answers, but he takes it out of the bag. Then he puts a bottle of lotion in. "You're not gonna let me be ashy," he says.

I shrug and pick up my one backpack with a flashlight and the bag of raisins from Mom's last care package.

"No stuffed animals?" he asks, wiggling his eyebrows. Wait, he *knew*? I scowl at him for a minute, but then I have to laugh. We both do, and that feels good.

"You got jokes. No, bruh, they're staying here," I say.

"They're Black too, which means they're smart enough to know that a night hike in the woods probably means killers in hockey masks lurking around every corner. Or mosquitos at least, which I now believe are just as bad."

When we get to the meetup spot, everyone is buzzing. A few people from Street Style come up and say they heard I wasn't going to be in the routine that I choreographed, but I just apologize for missing rehearsal.

"I thought I had to take care of something," I say, "but I was wrong." I work hard to keep my face fixed when I realize that the girl who's doing the solo, Kelly, is the one who's always talking about how she goes to dance classes at Alvin Ailey. She's good. They're not going to miss me.

"What happened?" asks Charles. "You missed rehearsal?!"

I'm saved from answering when Michelle, Natasha, and Troy walk over. Natasha says hey in my general direction. I'll take it. The counselors yell at us to get together, Dr. Triphammer blah-blah-blahs the rules, and Marcus claps (which is his outside version of knocking). Finally the night hike begins.

"Wow, the moon is bright tonight," says Michelle as we walk. "I almost didn't need to bring this flashlight."

Charles gives me a significant look. "*Some* people told me to leave my sunscreen at home. I mean, do we really *know* that the moon doesn't damage our skin?"

"Yeah, actually we do," says Natasha. "Speaking of moon, can you guys quiz me as we walk? Did you know Ed Dwight might have been the first Black astronaut in space but ended up becoming a sculptor instead?"

"Anyway, our melanin protects us," says Troy. "Black people can't get sunburned."

"That's what *I* said!" I say.

"Are you serious?" asks Michelle. "That's another stereotype. A dangerous one. Black people need to protect their skin from the sun too." A couple of counselors shush us. I guess we're supposed to be enjoying the beauteous mysteries of night nature or whatever, but it's clearly all the same stuff we see during the day, so it's not that magical. In fact, I have to ask Charles if I can borrow his bug spray because the mosquitoes seem to be the ones enjoying the hike the most.

"And you're real light-skinned, Troy, talking like that about how you got vibranium-level melanin," whispers Natasha. We all laugh, but we cover our mouths fast after Marcus claps at us. "A mind is a terrible thing to waste," she adds, shaking her head, but she nudges Troy in a jokey way. I try to catch her eye, but then she and Michelle walk ahead of us and start going over the Black scientist category.

"Why did you miss rehearsal?" Charles asks again. "And when do you think I should give the signal for the serenade?"

"It was just a mix-up," I say. "I don't really feel like talking about it." I'm too embarrassed to tell Charles what I did. Every time I see Derek talking to someone my stomach tightens up, but it looks like he means it when he says he doesn't snitch. Dr. Triphammer hasn't come and dragged me away, Mom hasn't whirled up here like an angry parental tornado, and Triple M just looks through me every time I'm in his line of vision, which is worse than yelling. It's like I've disappeared. "I think you should do the concert when we stop for s'mores by the big lake," I say. "We'll all be sitting and ready to focus." *And too tired to make fun of a night hike wind ensemble concert.* "How many miles is the hike again?"

"I keep forgetting this is your first year," says Charles.

"It's about five miles total. Didn't you read the orientation packet?"

Five miles!

"Uh, can I get one of those granola bars?" He smiles and hands me two. Charles is a good guy. He goes over to talk to Marcus and Dr. Triphammer about his wind ensemble takeover plans. Luke is up ahead, so even though I'm thinking I need to conserve energy, I know there's something else I need to do even more. I fast-walk closer to him and his group.

"Hey," I say, ignoring the looks of the little kids around him. Two are holding his hands, one on each side, so I have to speak louder than I really want to. "How's it going?"

Luke raises his eyebrows. "Fine," he says. A little boy runs up.

"I heard there's a tiger in the woods!" The other kids scream, and Luke reminds them that we're in the same New York woods that we're in every day, and tigers are not a part of it. Then he leads them in singing the DuBois song, and he looks at me until I join in.

After a while, his senior counselor takes the group ahead for some kind of scavenger hunt.

"Whew." Luke takes a long drink from his water bottle. I guess he read the orientation packet. "Those kids can be a lot."

"Yeah," I start eagerly. "You must be tired. You've got a lot of responsibility here, and . . ." I trail off under the look of skepticism on his face.

"What do you need now, Emmett?" he says. "You've been icing me out ever since your swim test. What's up?"

"Um, yeah . . . about that . . ." I clear my throat. "I'm sorry. I was just frustrated and I took it out on you. But you did promise," I can't help but add.

"Yeah. I shouldn't have. I know that my time isn't my own here. I've been telling you that since we got here. Since before we got here. You don't listen."

"I know, I'm sorry. But why did you promise, then?"

"Because you were making me feel bad! It's hard enough, trying to get you to be more independent when I'm worried about how you're going to manage at Heart High next year. Mac is a punk, but he's an annoying punk. And who's going to cook and shop and help Mom?"

I'm just staring at him and end up tripping over a rock as we walk. Luke grabs my arm and sighs. "I was mad at first about you going behind my back to come here," he says. "But then I thought, 'Okay, it's a way to help him see how great he already is, how much he can do himself, how he doesn't need me jumping in all the time.' I'm trying to let you do you, but you don't want to let me do me!"

"I didn't realize that I was such a burden," I say. "I guess it's good that you're going to that school, with all those rich kids. Rich people care about one thing—getting theirs. You'll probably fit right in. And no wonder you and Derek—" I stop. After what I did, I feel like I lost the right to talk about Derek. Especially since it's clear he really didn't tell anyone.

"E, I didn't mean that I don't care—"

"Forget it," I say. "Clearly I'm a big baby. I need to grow up; I get it." We walk in silence for a minute.

Then a little kid named Nathaniel comes up. "I have to pee," he says to Luke. Luke looks around. "Uh, maybe over there?" he says, pointing to a clump of bushes.

"That's the poison ivy pee patch," I mutter. I learned that from hanging out with Lance. I take Nathaniel's hand and bring him over to a safe spot, far away from Dr.

Triphammer's eagle eyes. "Make it quick," I say.

When we get back, Luke gives Nathaniel some hand sanitizer, and Nathaniel runs away to catch up with his friends. He doesn't say thank you or look back at me.

"Little kids, man," says Luke. "They're a lot."

"Yeah, I get it," I say. "You don't have to keep rubbing it in."

"I'm not talking about you, Emmett, come on. I just . . . This job is hard. I'm not sure it's right for me. I've been trying hard to lock in a senior counselor position for next summer, but . . . I may not even want that."

I'm surprised. "But you always look so smooth and the kids all like you." I don't add that Derek lives to be his mini-me.

"I'm trying my best, but it's stressful," says Luke. "I don't even know if I'd ever want to work with kids again. I may not be cut out for it. But I got responsibilities, I got things I can still learn from this."

Just then, Derek walks up next to Luke on his other side. "Hey, Luke . . ." He glances at me. "Are we still going to sketch at the campfire? I brought the little pencils for the group."

"Thanks, Derek," he says. "You are an intern supreme." As they start talking, I move away and look around for my friends. There's a tap at my back. I turn; it's Lance.

"I'm afraid," he says. "Can I hold your hand?" He sniffles and wipes a little snot from under his nose. "And I need a tissue."

I'm afraid to even think of what kind of nasty germs are partying on Lance's hands right now. I start to tell him to wait until I can find Nathaniel and the hand sanitizer, or tell him to get some wipes from his counselor, but then I look at him and stop. Lance has been a mess since day one. I know how that goes. And how good it feels to have friends in spite of that.

"Okay, let's go find some tissues together," I say, taking his hand.

Chapter Forty-Two

If you make a mistake, it's okay! Some people act like a mistake is the end of the world. If that were true, none of us would be here, because everybody makes mistakes. Just try to find out what the mistake was, let it go, and try not to do it again. Just because you make a mistake, there is nothing wrong with you. It just means that, like everybody else, you still have more to learn. Sometimes, people make the same mistake over and over again. That's okay. Just make sure you always try to do the right thing and try to do your best at whatever you do.

There are two days of camp left and even though it's our last real day of classes, I hang around the Street Style studio until I can chat with Triple M. He glances up when I walk in, but by the way he keeps packing up fast, he's not welcoming a heart-to-heart with me today. I take a deep breath.

"Mr. Micah McDowell?" I wait until he looks at me. "I wanted to . . . apologize. Again."

"Accepted," he says, going back to his packing. I still stand there, and he looks up again. "Can I help you with anything else?"

"It may not seem like it, but I've grown a lot here . . ." The look he gives me reminds me of how short I am. "I mean, not literally, maybe, but . . . I've learned a lot. About dance, and history, and now, and . . . me. So, I want to say that I'm sorry and thank you."

He nods. "I've heard good things about the work you've been doing with that play . . ."

"*The Two Amys*?"

He nods again. "And contrary to what you may believe, I did see you helping out your classmates—you have the makings of a choreographer, Emmett."

"Really, sir?" I can't believe he's saying something nice to me. "Like you?"

"Not at all like me," he says, laughing a short laugh. "But like you."

"I don't even know who I am anymore," I say, sitting on the bench and leaning against the mirror.

"Did you think you knew who you were before?" This time he laughs for real. "That's what life is, figuring and refiguring that out. But it's your identity, and no one can take that away from you," he says, then he pauses. "Or give it to you either."

There's no way that he can know how much I thought I needed Luke to survive, right? Sometimes Triple M seems like some kind of wizard. "This place. It's like some kind of Black Hogwarts," I mutter.

"Try Virginia Hamilton," he says.

"Who's Virginia Hamilton?"

He shakes his head. "A great writer. Stories about the best kind of Black magic. The true kind. Also Octavia Butler and Nnedi Okorafor."

"I don't get . . ." I start, but he puts up a hand.

"You might later," he says. "Or you might not. It's up to you." Then he leaves, not even waiting to make sure I leave first so he can lock up. So I stay for a while, looking at myself in the mirror. And then I start working on a new dance.

***

I'm sure Triphammer thought it would be a good idea to end the camp session with a Superhero Secrets class, but we all wish we could have had a double period of Black to the Future instead.

"Well, it's our last time together," says Shiny Suit Man, who's actually wearing jeans today. They're super sharply creased down the front, like they've been ironed by the Hulk, and he's wearing a light blue button-down shirt and these weird platformy shoes that look like they have woven straw at the bottom. No one even pays attention to him clearing his throat up in front anymore; this has been such a waste. Finally Marcus does some of his signature hand claps, and we settle down.

Vanessa raises her hand. "Are you wearing espadrilles?" she asks. "Because that's corny."

A few people laugh, but most of us just sit there.

"Yes, they are espadrilles, and they may be corny to *you*, but I've liked them ever since I went to Italy for a language immersion program," says Shiny Suit Man. "They bring me good memories."

"Oh, so you're just bougie, then," yells out Troy, and more people laugh. Marcus threatens to clap us away or something, and we quiet down.

Shiny Suit Man shrugs. "I'm me," he says. "And I'm working every day to be the best me that I can be. I hope you are too. Those are the lessons that I've tried to share here. I'm going to give you this final period for reflection, written or otherwise." He looks at the staff and Triphammer, who are all huddled on the right side of the room. "Feel free to send me any feedback." They look surprised, probably because they expected him to do a little more for the last class. I'm not, though; Shiny Suit Man is nothing if not consistent. Well, and also corny. He starts packing up his stuff and walking toward the door, ignoring the murmurs of the campers who are already taking out phones, making paper airplanes out of his workbook pages, and practicing for the Camp Showcase. At the door, he turns around. "And while y'all are worrying about my shoes and how corny I am? I'll be fine, living my best life as usual. Ciao." He shuts the door. And we all spontaneously burst into applause. Because, well, that was a pretty great exit. Respect.

***

I sit on the aisle for Black to the Future, because I'm hoping to catch Kelly before class starts. She comes in with Triple M, showing him a few moves as they enter the auditorium. I wait until he leaves, then I go up to her. "You look ready for your solo," I say.

"Yeah," she says. "I've been working." She smiles an uncomfortable smile, and I can tell she doesn't know what to say.

"I'll be cheering," I say. "If you want me to help you warm up before the show, I can."

She smiles a real smile. "Thanks, I appreciate that. And, I'm sorry, you know, that you . . . that you're not doing this. The stuff you were showing us was fire. You're really good."

I shrug. "Next summer," I say. "So watch your back." She laughs, and I go back to my seat.

Triphammer is standing up front with Charisse and Gordon, and since nobody is trying to get in trouble right before our parents come to pick us up, we settle down as soon as he blows his whistle. "I've been reading over your written reflections about this class," he begins.

I never finished mine! Another thing I didn't do. Camp went by so fast.

"And I'm impressed. Every year, DuBois campers show me that they're made of greatness. That they truly are the descendants of kings and queens—"

"And plumbers," calls out Troy.

"Navy SEALS!" yells another kid.

"Visiting nurses!" says Hannah. "Three generations!"

Suddenly everyone is yelling out their parents' and grandparents' and great-grandparents' jobs. "Filmmakers and chefs!" says Natasha, who's sitting in the row behind me. I could have been going to her for Mom surprise meal tips all this time.

"Orchestra musicians," says Charles.

"Both of your parents?" I ask.

"Three generations," he replies. "You can't be surprised."

It keeps going, and for once Triphammer doesn't make us stop; he just stays up there smiling.

"Nurse-turned-doctor and . . ." I whisper, then I stop. My dad never even finished becoming who he was. I don't know, maybe he would have done something different like Mom is now. Or maybe he was an artist, like Luke, and I don't remember. I feel the tears, but it's okay. "And someone who loved hard," I say. Michelle pats me on my shoulder from one side, Charles from the other. I feel a hand on my back. I look up; it's Luke.

"I see all the best parts of him and Mom in you, you

know. We should talk about it on the way home. But most of all, I see all the best parts of you. I always will, even when the . . . not so great traits rear their ugly heads."

I nod and smile as Lance leans over and hands me a possibly not-new tissue. "Ugly?" I say to Luke. "You wish you looked like me." He leans down and gives me a quick hug, then he heads back to the section where his group is.

"So our final question was going to be 'When did you first realize you were Black?'" starts Gordon. "But we figure if you're here, you know it now, and that's what counts."

"'And if you don't know, now you know,'" chimes in Charisse, quoting Biggie Smalls. It's never corny when *she* does that stuff. "The new question is 'What does it mean for you to be Black?'"

Triphammer raises his eyebrows, then shrugs and nods.

"Talk among yourselves," says Gordon. And we really do, except Hannah, who starts taking selfies.

"What is being Black anyway?" asks Michelle. "The Amys would probably say it's having a connection to our African roots."

"It's feeling music deep in your soul," says a girl. "Always having rhythm, not even having to try."

"That's a stereotype," says another girl. "All Black people are not dancing all the time. White people try to portray us that way, we shouldn't do it ourselves."

"Who cares about what white people do?" asks Natasha. "The whole point of this, of being here, is being . . . free within ourselves, like that Langston Hughes thing Charisse said. We can dance if we feel like dancing."

"Yeah, my brother came home from college and he went *in* on my parents after they told him he had to watch his step around white people," says a boy. "He said that kind of talk is respectability politics and he's not here for any of it."

"I get that they'd be worried, though," says a quiet girl whose name I don't know. "Old people have seen some things . . ."

"Also, I know that I'm very Black, and I can't dance at all," says Charles after a pause, looking over at me. "And I've tried. I've really, really tried."

Everyone laughs.

I grin. "That's okay," I say. "But we know he can play a mean bassoon concerto!" I turn to him and clap.

"Blerds united will never be defeated!" someone yells out.

I jump up and get a standing ovation going for Charles. Then he stands and invites the rest of the wind ensemble to stand with him, which is a very Charles thing to do. That night hike concert had been a hit with just about everyone.

"Being Black is about revolution, liberation," says one of the counselors I can't see. It might have been Reggie.

"If you're talking economic freedom, I'm down," says another. "Because the only color that really matters in this world is green."

"Money's not necessarily green in most of the world," starts Charles, but then he stops himself. "But that's not the point, is it?"

I high-five him.

"All y'all are fake," calls out Hannah. "Trying to talk serious and joking at the same time. It's like when people post something on Photogram after a tragedy, like, 'Oh police brutality got me in my feelings,' and then five minutes later they're posting a cat meme."

"But isn't that life?" asks Charisse gently. "Comedy and tragedy can and do coexist. That's real."

That starts a whole new wave of conversation. We talk and talk, and people bring up all types of stuff, but when Marcus claps us quiet, no one volunteers an answer.

"Anyone?" asks Charisse. There's a long pause. "I promise there's not going to be a grade or anything," she says.

"Then what's the point?" calls out a kid. More laughter.

Then Natasha stands up. "The answer is that there is no answer. We have a lot of common experiences and things that can bond us because of the color of our skin and what that means in this world," she says, sounding like Charisse 2.0. "And we are diverse, we are . . . *multitudes*. There's no one way to be Black. We don't need to put ourselves into boxes. One thing I love about being here is that I can just be. I'm going to try to do that when I'm not here too." She sits, and after a minute, there's a roar of applause.

I turn around. "See, I was right? You really are amazing," I say.

"I know," she says, smiling. "I've been knowing. But thanks for recognizing."

"Excuuuuse you," I say.

"I'm kidding," she says. "We all have growing to do, right?" She smiles at me, a big, real one. "But if you want to work your way up to my level, you've got a lot of work to do."

And it's funny because it's true.

"I work fast" is all I answer. "We'll see who's checking for who next summer." And we both laugh, and it's easy, not awkward.

I decide that I'm still going to write that letter to my younger self, maybe on the train ride home. Maybe I can bring it back with me next year to help the new Lance—

or the old one, since he seems like he has a little ways to go. Like me. I look back to where Luke is, and he's already looking at me. He raises a fist, and I raise it back. Then I turn and talk to my friends.

Chapter Forty-Three

"You're a hard man to find," says Luke, tapping my shoulder. One day left, we're at the last BBQ Blast, and if they want us to leave with good food memories, they're on the right track. I've just finished doing the "Jerusalema" dance with some people; we didn't miss a beat or drop a crumb. My plate is piled high with chicken, yellow rice and beans, even salad. And Charles says there's banana pudding for dessert.

"Hey!" I say to my brother. And I'm happy to see him, and happy that finally, I didn't need to.

"I've got something for you," he says. "Walk over to the art shack with me."

He's quiet as we walk, and I notice once again how he commands respect; even the mosquito vampires seem to be deferring to Luke (and attacking me in droves). As we head to the art shack, I see Derek watching us out of the corner of my eye. He starts to get up, but then Luke waves at him and he just nods and sits back down.

"Ta-da!" Luke says, flinging open the art shack door. On the opposite wall are hanging a series of collages, or maybe they're collage and paint. I get closer to see. And each one has photos of Dad and Luke and Mom and me—at the fair, at home, there's even a picture of Dad holding me in the pool. And there are fragments of newspaper clippings and some graffiti lettering, and I almost stop breathing, it's so beautiful and so amazing and my brother made this. About my dad. For me.

"Wow," I breathe. "Just . . . wow. Luke, this is amazing."

"I was going for a Bearden-Basquiat effect," he says. "What do you think?"

"Once I know what that means, I'll tell you," I say, and he laughs.

"I'll show you some more of their work when we get home."

"Sounds good," I say. "I do know that it's amazing. Are these really for me?"

"Yeah," he says. "You're going to have some extra wall space in the room next year, so I thought this might cover it nicely."

I keep staring. There are bits of photos from Dad's childhood, his wedding photo, pictures of me in diapers. "I never realized how much I look like him," I say. "Do you think so?"

Luke nods. "Mom and I both think so." He sighs. "E, I know you want to ask questions and talk about him and know more, and I'm sorry I haven't been ready or able to do that. I guess I'm still not. But I can give you this. I want you to know always . . . I love Dad. And I love you. And this is the best, realest way that I can show how much."

"This is . . . How did you get those pictures?"

"Mom's been helping me out," he says. "We've been talking. And we want you to know that we see you."

I see you too, I want to say. *I wasn't looking hard*

enough before, but I see you too.

I hug him like I'm five again and we're both crying and I'm not sure who's supposed to be comforting who. I want to say that I'm sorry and that I know he's always had my back and so many other things.

"I'd like to know more about this Bearden-Basquiat thing" is what I end up saying. "And how you did this."

"Really?" he asks.

"Yeah, really," I say. "One thing I've learned, coming to DuBois, is that I have a lot to learn."

So he tells me about cutting and pasting techniques, and how Basquiat was this eighties artist who did street art and fancy gallery shows and how Bearden did collage but also designed costumes for dance companies. It all gives me a lot of ideas for next summer, but I don't say anything. I'll remember to write them all down later in the planner Charles gave me. Right now, it's Luke's turn to talk. And mine to listen.

Chapter Forty-Four

Final night. Dr. Triphammer really went all out on the decorations in the main building for the Camp Showcase. Charles and I decided on jeans and polo shirts (Luke smirked when he saw the alligator on mine), and I'm not sure if all the body spray we used will be enough; it's already hot in here, and no one's started dancing.

The DJ is pretty hype; the rumor is that he used to be Hip Hop Harry on TV, which seems plausible because he keeps shouting, "When I say dance, you say circle!" Hip Hop Harry did that every episode. But we just kind of mill around and wait for the show.

"It's like this every year," says Marcus. "After the show, we're going to have to drag all y'all off the dance floor."

"Well, the prizes are pretty sweet," says Michelle. "I know I'm trying to win that Broadway pass, it's good for three shows of your choice! Speaking of that, E, can I have a word?" She asks me to go over a couple of combinations with the girl playing Amy Ashwood, who says she can't remember anything, including which Amy she is. I start with deep breathing.

A few minutes later, I see Charles, Michelle, Natasha, and Jeimy talking to Triple M, which is weird. Then he looks straight at me, which is scary. Charles starts doing something—I guess it's dancing, and Michelle and Natasha are really animated. Jeimy points right at me, and I wonder if she's asking him to give me more consequences for not doing my job. I'm about to swallow my fear of Triple M and go over there, when he starts walking toward me. Unfortunately about ten mimes are practicing on one side of me, and a jazz ensemble is on the other. No escape. As he gets closer, the Amy next to me gulps. "I'm good," she says, and disappears.

Triple M seems taller. "Did you send your friends to talk to me?"

"About what?" I ask. "But no! No, I didn't ask them to talk to you. They wouldn't anyway, you're too—"

"Too what?" His voice gets dangerously low.

"Too . . . too busy," I say. "We all know how busy you are. Street Style opens and closes the show, right? I'm sure you've got a lot to do. Um, don't let me keep you."

He looks at me for a long moment. "I do have a lot to do, so I'll keep this short. I hope you return next year. You are a good dancer, and perhaps an even better choreographer. Keep working. And then work harder."

"I . . . I will."

"And you did come up with a fire routine." he says.

"Thanks!" I wish I'd been recording this!

"And you've made some good friends. Some would say that's even more important." He frowns. "I don't really understand those people, but there it is. Well. Enjoy the show." He leaves, and I lean against the wall for a minute. My friends rush over.

"What did he say?" asks Charles. "Did he give you back your solo?"

"Are you doing the grand finale?" asks Natasha.

"Huh?" I ask. "Are you kidding? No! Why would he do that?"

Michelle groans. "Aw, I told you guys. Triple M doesn't have changes of heart. He barely has a heart." Charles laughs way too loud and long, and Michelle rolls her eyes.

"That's my Charles, always awkward," she says.

"Uh—*your* Charles?" he asks. "Do you mean *your* like the guy you know very well in a strictly platonic sense, or *your*, like, you know, your man?"

"Did you just use the word *like*, like in a colloquial sense?" I say. "I didn't know you could talk regular like that!"

Michelle rolls her eyes again. "Seriously, Charles? You want to have this conversation now?"

He gulps. "Uh, forget it."

"What did you mean, change of heart?" I ask Michelle.

"We asked Triple M if he'd let you do your solo," says Natasha.

I look at Charles. "You told them?"

"I didn't have to," he says. "Everybody knows. And Jeimy was saying she feels really bad for you, you're not even in the big finale. Why didn't you tell us?"

I sigh. "I was embarrassed. You're all . . . superstars, and I feel like I blew every chance I got to shine. I wanted to . . . show you what a big time genius I was, and I flopped." I think about swimming. "Like, belly flopped."

"You're right," says Charles. He looks at Michelle. "Why have we been wasting time with this guy?"

"I have no idea," she says. "Since all we care about is . . . being superstars or whatever."

"You know what I—"

"No, you know," says Natasha. "I told you, you've been a friend. That means a lot."

"Group hug!" says Michelle.

"I'm touched, you guys! Thanks," I say. "Thanks a lot."

"Well, our pleas to Triple M didn't work," says Natasha.

"It means a lot that you tried," I say, looking directly at her. "And there's always next year."

She looks back at me, then smiles. "Second chances. We all need them. Fred turned out to be great, by the way. He said you gave him a lot of opportunities to take the lead." I can't even look her in the eye, but then she adds, "Even if you did it for . . . reasons." I look up and she's smiling. "Anyway, you're lucky," she says. "It doesn't take a genius to be a friend."

"Okay, but do you know my IQ, though," I say, "because even if I didn't show it, I've got skills!" We laugh, and then we all stand around not looking at each other.

Charles clears his throat. "You know, E. B. White once declined an invitation 'for secret reasons,'" he says.

"Who's E. B. White?" I ask. "And you are the king of non-sequiturs for real."

"He wrote *Charlotte's Web*, Ernest," says a voice behind me.

"Oh, come on, Derek, you know his name is Emmett," says Natasha. "Can you just relax and hang out? Stop trying to flex for no reason."

He scowls and stands next to her. "We're setting up the screening room," he mumbles. We don't look at or acknowledge each other. He won't be screening anything, and it's my fault. I still can't believe he hasn't told anyone.

I want to say thank you, but my gratitude is mixed up with some other complicated feelings. I'm not there yet.

"Okay, see you guys later," Natasha says. "Wish me luck in the Blackity Bowl!"

As she leaves, I get another hug, which takes the sting out of the fact that she walks away with Derek. After a few minutes, Charles goes to warm up with his band, and Michelle rushes off to her actors. I stand near the wall and spend a few minutes slowly eating pretzels. The big feast will happen after the award announcement, and from what everyone says, all the chefs throw down on the last night. That way the last DuBois meal we remember is a phenomenal one. I see the Street Style team rehearsing, and I offer to help them go over some of the showstopper moves. Kelly comes over to me.

"Thanks for helping," she says. "Can you give me your honest opinion on my solo?"

"You got this," I say. "But sure." She goes through her routine and it's perfect. Maybe better than mine, and I tell her so.

Triphammer lumbers up on stage and picks up the mic. "DuBois fam, I have an important announcement about the Camp Showcase competitions," he booms, and everyone quiets. "That Reggie, Gordon, and Charisse are going to make," he finishes.

Charisse makes her way to the stage first. "To address our dear contrarian friend Hannah's frequent concerns," says Charisse, "we know that the summer is supposed to be about fun, and we do know you guys work hard. We're proud of how much you stretched yourselves in Black to the Future. Dr. Triphammer has agreed that it will become a formal part of the summer program from now on." She pauses while we all clap and cheer. "And we hope it has been fun." She stops, a little choked up.

"You got this, Reese!" a counselor calls out, and she smiles.

Charisse takes a deep breath. "Toni Morrison said that the function of racism was distraction, keeping you focused on explaining your reason for being. That's not what Black to the Future has been about. It's about knowing that you matter, that you are more than worthy, that you are loved."

The crowd literally goes wild, lots of people are hugging and crying. I high-five a bunch of people around me that I don't even know, then Jeimy and some of the Street Style crew come over for a group hug.

Charisse goes on. "You all had so many ideas about what it means to be Black," she shouts out. "And it all boiled down to being a community. A diverse, powerful, and beautiful community made up of individuals with different opinions, priorities, and gifts, but a community nonetheless."

"We see how you look out for each other," adds Gordon, "How you know that in the face of all kinds of nonsense, you know that you're even stronger when you big each other up. We are proud of each of you for speaking your truth, in your own way."

"We know that our silence will not protect us," yells out Hannah, and we turn to look at her. "Audre Lorde. And as Martin Luther King said, 'No one is free until we are all free,' which is also attributed to writer Emma Lazarus."

Everyone is staring at her now, and a lot of mouths are open. "What?" she asks. "I still listened. And Google is my friend."

"Anyway," says Reggie, "the announcement is that as of this moment, the Camp Showcase will no longer include competitions. It's a chance to share and celebrate one another's gifts!" A few people clap, most of just look at each other, confused.

"So no more gift cards," says the boy who said the only color that mattered was green.

Gordon shakes his head. "Correct. DuBois will donate the ones that we bought for this year to purchases much-needed items for young people in a nearby juvenile detention center."

"So bougie," mutters Troy, but he's drowned out by cheers and applause.

"What about the Black to the Future presentations?" asks Vanessa. "I spent a lot of time on mine."

Gordon grimaces. "Yeah, so, we didn't actually clear that before we assigned it, and it turns out there isn't time to share tonight."

I'm not mad, since I didn't have anything to share, and it seems like a lot of people are in the same boat, but Vanessa looks like she's about to dog walk somebody.

"I'd be happy to check it out, though, Vanessa," says Charisse, and I think that calms Vanessa down a little. "You can even have the box of award ribbons we bought. But of course, I'm sure that you'll agree that there is enough value in just learning, without external rewards."

"I'll take that box of ribbons," says Vanessa. "They'll come in handy."

Charisse shakes her head, and Reggie say that the show will begin in five minutes. Those of us who are going to be in the audience grab seats. All my friends are in the show, so I'm alone.

I catch Reggie's eye, and he slides into the seat next to me. "Yo, Emmett, how'd it go with the workbook?" he asks.

"It was actually kind of helpful," I say. "Once I figured out how to use it."

"I knew you were a smart guy." Reggie hands me a piece of paper. "Here's my email, let's stay in touch. Who's picking you up tomorrow? Please introduce me."

"My mom," I say, realizing that I really can't wait to hug her. "I thought I'd have a whole new Emmett to show her . . . I had a lot of plans that didn't quite work out."

He pats my shoulder. "But I bet the not working out helped you make new plans," he says. "Sometimes the lessons we learn from our mistakes make for more success than we could have ever dreamed of."

"What does that even mean? Are you sure you're not Shiny Suit Man's son?" I ask, and he laughs.

Some people are grumbling about the Camp Showcase competition getting snatched, but most of us are just sitting back and enjoying the show. Street Style comes out and kills it. I think about how much I wanted to be in that class, and how hard I worked. Then I think about how hard everyone up there is working. Kelly's solo is flawless, and I try to clap the loudest when she's done. Even Marcus the Clapmaster can't compete.

Charles' ensemble gets cheers before they even start, and I can tell that he loves it. After they're done, he stands up and does the robot and at first I wish I had a hook to yank him offstage but the crowd loves it, and the truth is, so do I. Michelle's play is a little bit of a downer, but then she has the two Amys do a reprise of my big finale routine and everyone cheers. Even though I'm not actually up there, it's like I am, and it feels good.

Brant comes over with Lance. "Hey, Emmett, this guy's been looking for you," he says.

"Hi, Emmett," says Lance. "I'm going to take my

swim test again in the morning. Will you come and cheer for me?"

I don't hesitate. "Absolutely. We're swim buddies, right? Oh wait, no we're not—" His eyes get wide. "We're *buddy* buddies!" I finish, I give him a high-five. Thank goodness his hands are dry and look relatively clean.

Brant smiles. "Lance, if you promise to listen to Emmett, you can sit with him for the Blackity Bowl, okay? I'll tell your counselor where you are."

"I'll look out for Lance," I say. "We got this."

The Blackity Bowl is silly and fun, and even though Natasha worked so hard this whole time, she seems to have the most fun now that everybody wins. All the competitors get giant crowns shaped like Sphinxes when it's over.

***

Marcus was right, after the showcase and everything are over, everyone gets on the dance floor, even Triphammer and Mrs. Triphammer, who we haven't seen this whole time. The rumor was that she was a ghost that he talked to when he was alone. But she's flesh and blood and really loves the Wobble.

"Camp DuBois makes me happy!" I'm singing all the words now, and I got the dance down like everyone else.

Charles gets all tongue-tied asking Michelle to dance, and she just takes his hand and starts dancing.

"Want to dance?" asks Natasha. I look around for a group.

"Just me?" I ask.

"For now," she says. "I've got lots of options and I intend to exercise them." She smiles, and we hit the floor.

"Oh, you think you got moves," I say, and start going all out. I bump into someone; it's Derek. "Oh—my bad," I say.

He nods. "No worries," he says, not smiling. "Natasha, you know you would have won." He dances over to the other side of her like we invited him to our personal dance party.

She shrugs. "I like this better. Less pressure, more purpose." Derek and I both shrug back and say, "Okay, whatever," at the same time. There's an awkward pause.

"Uh, you guys keep um, cutting a rug, I'm going to get something to drink," I say and walk away quickly. *Cutting a rug?* What if Charles has transferred some weird superpower to me, and I start talking like him every time I'm nervous? I guess worse things could happen to me. I drink down a cup of soda and talk with a few people from Street Style. Charles and Michelle now have everyone doing a move that I can only describe as Hot Coals Meets Poison Ivy dance because they're jumping around and twisting and turning like nothing I've ever seen before. I know Michelle can do better than that, but she's laughing, and so is Charles, and so is everyone.

I start walking over to join in, then I see Luke across the room. Brant's also a few feet away, and I wave. I drop my plastic cup in the recyclable bin under the watchful eyes of a crunchy granola looking girl with locs and thick leather sandals that look like monster feet. I give her a nod and the peace sign. Then I head toward my brother.

Epilogue

"No stalling this time," says Brant. "You didn't sign up in advance, and Dr. Triphammer will be furious if he finds out. So move it, I need to get over to the Main Hall for pickup."

"I'm ready," I say. I stick a toe into the pool. "Wow, y'all turned off the heat already, huh." I look out across the water. The pool seems huge.

"The water is the same temperature it's always been," says Brant. "And if you want to take this test, you have to get going now. *I* know you can do this, but *you* gotta know you can do this."

I take a deep breath.

"And I'm here, remember," he says gently. "If anything happens, you get nervous, I'll jump right in and get you. Nobody has to know. You were already brave to ask to try this again."

I nod and take another breath. Then I jump in and start swimming.

***

It feels like it's been forever. My arms are tired, my legs

are tired, and I'm not breathing right. I slow down and pull myself together. *I can swim.* Brant said it's okay to stop and tread water for a couple of minutes, so I stop swimming and pop my head out of the water. The other side still looks far. I turn back to look at Brant and—

"YESSSSSS, EMMMETTTTT!" My friends are there on the grass, next to Brant, jumping up and down and cheering and screaming. I keep treading water and give them a little wave. Oh well. So much for my secret test. I guess if I fail, I fail in front of my friends. Brant is smiling and gives me a thumbs-up. More people hear the cheering and come over to the lake.

I see Lance, who's jumping in a way that means he's either really excited for me, or that he has to pee. I see kids I don't even know, they're cheering too. Triple M is smiling and actually pumping his fist, and Marcus is clapping harder than ever. I guess if I fail, I fail in front of everyone.

I put my head back in the water and keep going.

Acknowledgments

An abundance of gratitude to Kikelomo Amusa-Shonubi, Adedayo Rhuday Perkovich, DJ Johnson, and Batman, who entertained my endless "thinking out loud"s and "what do you think of . . . ?"s and read, and read, and read. (Well, Batman didn't read, because he's a cat. But sometimes I caught him at the computer, so . . .)

I'm abundantly grateful for brilliant storyteller friends like Dhonielle Clayton, Lamar Giles, Kelly Starling Lyons, Laura Pegram, Julia Torres, and Renée Watson; Tracey Baptiste, Kelly Barnhill, Martha Brockenbrough, Kate Messner, Laura Ruby, Laurel Snyder, Linda Urban, and Anne Ursu; Mike Jung, Ellen Oh, and Audrey Vernick. You are bright lights in my life and precious treasures in this world.

I say a round of thank yous every day for Marietta Zacker, who is so much more than an agent. Thank you for your incredibly generous spirit, wisdom, and humour; for believing that I can take on a challenge, and then helping me figure out just how to do it. You are someone in whom I have infinite trust and am honoured to call my friend.

Much gratitude to Coert Voorhees, Vicky Wight and the Six Foot team for giving me wide open spaces to write in, and to Miles Brown and Skylan Brooks for the charming and nuanced performances that told inspiring stories of Black boy joy. An abundance of thanks to Arianne Lewin for her good humour, great questions, and total support all the way through, and Jody Corbett for her thoughtful and meticulous copyediting.

Thank you, thank you, Gordon C. James, for the extraordinary cover art – it brought tears to my eyes.

Thank you to all of the educators in classrooms, libraries, community centers, and in homes, who know the power of story and work so incredibly hard to help us hold onto that power and use it for growth, for change, for good. Most of all, thank you to the readers of all ages who open their hearts to my characters and their lives. Your stories are precious – let them shine.

About the Author

Olugbemisola Rhuday-Perkovich is the author of *8th Grade Superzero*, which was named a Notable Book for a Global Society, *Alice's Adventures in Wonderland*, an adaptation for Sesame Workshop's *Ghostwriter*, and *Operation Sisterhood*. She is the coauthor of NAACP Image Award nominee *Two Naomis*, a Junior Library Guild selection, and its sequel, *Naomis Too*. She also writes nonfiction, including *Above and Beyond: NASA's Journey to Tomorrow, Someday is Now: Clara Luper and the 1958 Oklahoma City Sit-Ins*, and *Saving Earth: Climate Change and the Fight for Our Future*.

Olugbemisola is a member of the Brown Bookshelf, editor of the We Need Diverse Books anthology *The Hero Next Door*, and teaches at the Solstice MFA Program in Creative Writing. She holds an MA in education, and has written frequently on parenting and literacy-related topics for PBS Parents, Brightly, American Baby, Healthy Kids, and other outlets.

Visit Olugbemisola online at:
olugbemisolabooks.com
and on Instagram:
@olugbemisolarhudayperkovich